THE IMMACULATE HEART

ANDREW RAYMOND DRENNAN

Cargo Publishing (UK) Ltd
Reg. No. SC376700
www.cargopublishing.com

"The Immaculate Heart"
Drennan, Andrew Raymond
ISBN-13 978-0-9563083-1-3
BIC Code-
FA Modern and contemporary fiction (post c. 1945)

CIP Record is available from the British Library

First Published in the UK 2011
Published By Cargo Publishing
Printed and bound by the CPI Anthony Rowe, England

www.cargopublishing.com

For
Ava Mairi Swan
(when she's old enough to read)

In memoriam
Uncle Duncan and Auntie Jean

'This is not love.'
'This (sentence) is not love.'
'This (image of love) is not love.'
'This (love story) is not love.'

1
Funeral

The coffin was pulled out the back of the rickety hearse – a poorly converted J-reg Cortina estate – to whoops and cheers from the congregation leaving the church. They thrust their arms up into the late-morning sunlight, releasing greedy fistfuls of confetti about their heads, which blew towards a smattering of black-clad mourners in C&A suits and Debenhams sale hats, waiting in the courtyard, looking at their watches. The wedding party fell quiet, their warm faces cooling to solemnity when they noticed the hearse in the foreground, the confetti taken by the breeze, fluttering down on the toes of the mourners' black shoes.

Bill and Jean, father and mother of the young and suddenly deceased, stood by the hearse boot door pointed at the church, awaiting instructions: they had never buried a daughter before; protocol was unclear, roles were undefined. Maggie, their remaining daughter, stood at the other end of the hearse, next to Bertrand, now, and as long as she could remember, her only friend. He looked up at the sky – leaning on his cane – with a confused expression, which he often wore during the day, or at night, or at home, or in public places with Maggie, as if the idea of someone's heart no longer beating was too overwhelming for him.

'I want to sit at the back with you, Bertrand,' Maggie whispered.

Bertrand kept looking up.

'Bill doesn't even look upset.'

Bertrand turned his body as he followed a rushing cloud, masking his face from the sun with his free hand. 'So what does grief look like?'

'I don't know, crying or something.'

'Does it.'

'I mean, he looks sad. I don't know what he feels though.'

'So how can you tell?'

'You can't, I suppose.'

'And what about love. What does love look like? What does love feel like?'

Maggie walked forward to stand next to Bill and Jean; neither of them acknowledged her.

As the wedding party bid a hasty exit for the reception,

the bride and groom offered consoling nods to the deceased's parents on their way past: regret their first act together as man and wife. A porcelain pavement under their feet.

'Right,' Bill puffed, turning to face the Cortina boot door, casting a shadow over Jean and Maggie, 'we should probably get moving,' and beckoned the other pall bearers to take over from the undertakers. Once the coffin was half out Uncle Tommy wiped his hands down the fronts of his trousers from the white paint flaking off the shell. It looked used, recoated in cheap white emulsion to cover up cracks in the wood and the poor fitting around the dull-brass handles. 'Hold on, Bill, here comes the chaplain.'

Bill sighed at being delayed.

The priest strode towards them, one hand out in attrition, the other adjusting his newly changed wedding shawl around his neck. 'I'm so sorry about the wedding overrunning. We nearly didn't have a bride. Her Daimler broke down on the motorway.'

Bill extended a hand to Jean. 'See - didn't I tell you? Doesn't matter what you pay for car hire.'

The priest hesitated. 'Indeed ... Shall we go inside?'

Jean, still to look Maggie in the eyes since they left the house, led her into the church by the upper arm, as if she were being told off, ahead of the coffin carried by Bill and his three brothers. Their arms intertwined behind each other's backs, tied up in knots of grief.

The organist started playing as Bill led them inside, down the aisle, walking a little too fast at the front, the others struggling to keep up as he paced towards the altar, noting from his peripheral vision the seats at the front row: Christ, Jean's crying already. It's like that post-natal ... all over again. DEPRESSION? Don't talk to me about depression ... Right. Let's get this over with.

Maggie rested her head on Jean's shoulder, feeling little vibrations of sorrow travelling through her body, every little tremble a reminder of how much more Trish was loved than her. If for some reason she didn't make her fifteenth birthday that October, Maggie couldn't imagine making Jean vibrate quite so harshly; the aftershocks of Trish's childbirth now a death rattle. After all, Jean hadn't sheltered and fed Maggie in her swollen belly for nine months: she was delivered – with appropriate paperwork - on a prearranged date.

Bill and his brothers untangled their arms as they let the coffin down, dispersing their tide of grief-energy.

On the benches across the hall sat Jenny Spanner and

some of her crew from Trish's year at school, along with a teacher, dismally wearing the same grey suit as he did every other day. The girls next to him had been given permission to come along, to 'grieve' with the Burns family, but what they were really after was morning off classes, and they all sat there, quietly chewing gum and swinging their crossed legs with the surety, the armoured hearts, that come with the knowledge of being the most attractive girls in school. Jenny had at least managed to write a card for some flowers the girls left by the side of the road where the car had hit Trish:

"i wont 4get wen we usd 2 go shoplftn 2gthr n gt well drnk n park n get nabbd by the fckn pigs. c u l8r Trsh av a gud 1 upstairs yeh :)"

Maggie lifted her head from Jean's shoulder, not wanting to look quite so young and weak in front of Jenny's crew. The bench groaned with Bill's weight as he dumped himself down between Jean and Maggie, pushing them away by splaying his legs wide open, taking up as much room as he could fill, like water. His hands slapped down on his thighs like oars. Maggie couldn't understand why he was wearing aftershave for such an occasion. Surely attractiveness was not an issue today?

The economy coffin sat on its stand by the altar, as if run in by rickshaw, paling in comparison to the opulent marble and lush, high contrast red and purple altar dressings that surrounded it, almost incidental to the funeral itself. It wasn't about a dead body – it was about words now; expressions of love, not objects.

Maggie couldn't look up, knowing the reality that her dead sister was lying in a box a few feet away, that Trish's heart was no longer beating, that it had expressed everything that body would ever feel; all those feelings of love locked inside a body without a key. Maggie couldn't help but feel it was her that had locked it, chasing after Trish down the street like that. All Maggie wanted was her piece of paper back, but Trish wouldn't let up with her taunts of, 'Maggie's got a boyfriend, Maggie's got a boyfriend!' 'I haven't.' 'Yes you haaave.' 'I don't have anything.' Trish turned into the traffic without looking, she was so busy shouting out what was written down. The paper vanished from the scene afterwards.

She dipped the crown of her head towards the coffin, her face soaking from the eyes down.

The sum total of the Burn's family and friends could only fill another three rows back, where the exiled relatives sat: Uncle Joe, who Trish said snuck into her bedroom two Christmases ago and felt up her tiny tits while she pretended to sleep; Aunt Joan, whose breath smelled of cat food; and cousin Dee-dee, who had flunked out of university – the first one in the family to make it there – only to end up in the mental ward at County after smoking too much grass and became party to "delusions" and "hallucinations". Now she sat in a plastic-covered armchair, compulsively rereading the same old newspaper day after day.

Every reading was a revelation to Dee-dee, full of imagined proclamations of love from the boy that had broken her heart in what she still thought of as her Grass Days. The doctors had to find ways around not diagnosing her with a broken heart. They had no pills for that; and they couldn't talk her out of it. It was almost fair: you shouldn't be able to recover from a broken heart.

Dee-dee sat near the back with Uncle Tommy, the newspaper open in her lap. 'He says he loves me. He says he'll tell me in here,' she whispered, hands resting on the pages.

Bertrand sat in a row by himself, his cane planted between his feet, hands resting on top of its arc, his elbows hanging down, weary from all the death in the room.

When it was time for Bill's reading he stood up, straightening his black tie with thick, rigid fingers, and made his way reluctantly to the altar, clasping some prepared words written on pages ripped from Maggie's English jotter. She had listened to him practicing the speech in the bathroom the night before. He had stood in front of the mirror, straightening an imaginary tie, raising then dropping his chin, watching the ring of chubby flesh tighten then loosen. 'What I want to say is...' he started, then repeated it, quieter to himself. The more he repeated it the more it sounded like he was asking himself a question. 'What I want to say is? What I want to say is?'

Bill coughed to clear his throat, accidentally directing it straight into the microphone. He spoke like a man of his build: thickly, barely tidied up from his work-talk at the mechanics; the casual way he missed his Ts and dropped his Gs, how the Scottish endeavour to lose as many syllables from words as possible. 'This shouldn't be an emotional day. What I mean is, I know it's a tough day, for Jean, for me. I remember my father's ... you know, whathaveyou. He told my mum before he died, "anywan who cries disnae get a penny."'

A few titters among the mourners which segued into light coughing as they realised it was no joke.

Jean squirmed in her seat as Bill shuffled through the pieces of paper at the lectern, the silence growing. Bill looked

down at what he had written: every sentence incomplete.
If Trish could be here now, I hope she'd say I was a
I'd like to think I've been a
When I think about what I love most

He couldn't even get in some standard greeting card message sentiments about love, and how much love he felt, just to keep some FUCKING DISTANCE from the actual events taking hold of his life. And there certainly weren't any witty anecdotes about how much Trish loved life, and how every morning when she got up she would race to the door for her first glimpse of sunshine. Trish was only happy when she was with Jenny Spanner and her crew, shoplifting or getting well drunk in the park and getting nabbed by the fucking pigs. Always mumbling things under her breath (she was sixteen after all).

Trish told Maggie that when she was brought home from the Home, Trish ran to her room and locked the door, refusing to come out for hours. Only the promise of sweets changed her mind. Maggie knew it must have been hard for Trish, though, not having a real sister. Maggie had entirely different blood in her body and nothing was going to change that. Family makes us all geneticists, so intrigued by the makeup of our blood.

Bertrand often quoted the opening line from Anna Karenina, his favourite book, that "Happy families are all alike; each unhappy family is unhappy in its own way." But Maggie didn't agree: 'What if a family's been unhappy for as long as they can remember, so they don't know what real happiness looks like?'

Bill ended with, 'I'm a...' then shook his head and departed the altar, leaving his papers sitting on the lectern.

Maggie had always found solace in churches since she was a little girl. When she and her friend Susy J (youth detention had since gotten hold of her) were barred from all the shopping centres in town, they got stuck in the rain one day with nowhere to go, the day before Suzy's day at court. The girls both knew she was going down this time, and now their last hurrah was turning into a last wet whimper. Neither of them wanted to go home. Susy J's mum had died a year before, and understood why Maggie didn't want to go home either. They were wandering back through the town centre and found St Mary's of the Immaculate Heart with its door wide open for lunchtime service. The wooden sign outside said "Jesus saves" and Suzy J carved "me and Maggie from the rain" with her butterfly knife underneath.

Outside, a preacher cowering under a golf umbrella was bellowing prophecy and apocalyptic verse through a megaphone. It was hard to discern if he was trying to lead people in or flush people out. Suzy J ended up smoking a rollie with the preacher's helper.

Inside the church were mostly old people, sensing their life-fatigue, their death-drive speeding up, locked on an escalator for the top floor, or a lift for the bottom. The rain pounded down on the skylight above them, sounding like galloping hooves. The harder it rained, the harder they prayed.

Maggie watched the old folks, all sitting alone, a respectful distance apart, faces tense with love and fear and prayer, thinking about all the good they had done in this life, and why it had led them to such a cold, dire house, where so much thought had been put into convincing you that someone was in there – in your head – listening to your concerns and demands and hostilities and broken dreams and holy Mary Mother of God what I would do with my life if I could have it all over again! Please Lord!

Maggie shut her eyes and said the closest thing to a prayer she would ever make. Only, she didn't know she wasn't meant to say it aloud.

'I thought the world was meant to be a beautiful place. Why are you such a prick, God?' A few of the oldies eyeballed her. That was when she first saw Bertrand.

When Maggie opened her eyes he was coming in from the rain, taking a seat in the back row next to her. An organ started playing the loudest, most dramatic music she had ever heard. It was like in a Dracula film she had been watching, but shouldn't have, because it was an 18. Sometimes she was allowed to watch 18s if they didn't use the four letter 'C' word (no not that one, the other one) and 15s were usually alright. It hardly mattered. She heard a lot worse in the playground at school, and even worse still from Suzy J's filthy fucking mouth, but especially from Trish:

'Maggie, you're a fucking bitch. I heard MY Mum say she was going to drown you when you were wee cos I asked her to. No one loves you, you skinny cunt.' (that was the first time she heard that 'C' word, though she didn't know what it meant).

Maggie looked at the pictures that lined the wall, showing Jesus' suffering and ultimate crucifixion. Every church had their own design, but it just so happened that St Mary's of the Immaculate Heart was the kind with friendly, wood-carved figures with angular, Cubist faces, their chins sharpened to points, their arms constantly raised to Heaven in benevolence.

It made dying look quite selfless; that it could make so many people happy.

Bertrand edged down, pointing at one of the stations. That looks like Ben-hur, that one.
Maggie agreed. That's funny: I watched Ben-hur in my room last Christmas. It was nice ... watching it alone.

Yes, I have to watch things alone too.

I wish I was the daughter of God and the kids on the estate could crucify me. That way I could die for everyone's sins and people would love me. Except I'd be dead.

There are worse things than dying.

Oh yeah. Like what?

Bertrand didn't answer.

It turned out he lived on the same estate as Maggie.

Whereabouts? Maggie asked.

Top of Hunterhill.

I live at the bottom.

Maggie and Bertrand left the church and found the preacher still hurling invective into the street, the people faceless, made of brollies from the shoulders up.

Bertrand whispered, That man is being terribly rude, don't you think? Maggie went straight up to him, taking the megaphone down from his mouth and, right on her tiptoes, screamed an inch away from his face, GOD DOESN'T HAVE TO SHOUT!

Suzy J bombed her rollie at the preacher's feet, dragging her into a forest of legs, away from Bertrand.

The family were lucky to get a church nearly as grand as St Mary's for Trish's funeral. The priest wasn't convinced they were regularly practicing Catholics (they weren't). It had the nice long aisle Jean thought her little girl deserved as a send off, seeing as she would never walk down one for her wedding day. But it was really because Jean never got to make that walk herself, making do with a dingy registry office heated by an electric radiator, the smell of lager oozing over from Bill in the dry heat. Throughout the funeral Jean's gaze went upwards at the amazing height of the ceiling, at everything she could have had.

Once the service was over, Maggie sat on a railing at the top of the car park, far back from the real family, watching the coffin being loaded back in the hearse for the crematorium. Just behind her, on the street, some girls from the estate were passing. One of them pushed a pram, a decadent model of pink and white frill and trill, her boyfriend's arm dangling over her shoulder. She jeered her, 'Skanky Maggie!'

Only one of the girls voiced tentative opposition, but with a laugh that ruled out any sense of sincerity, 'Here's that's pure shite, by the way.'

Maggie turned round quickly to look at the boy, but she never caught his face. Even still, how badly she wanted his arm around her, to pine for his attention when he was texting, to gel his hair in the morning. Bertrand walked wearily towards her. She felt Bertrand put his arm around her as she started to cry. 'There are things worse than dying,' he assured her, mistaking the source of her tears.

'I know,' she croaked.

Down by their car, Bill and Jean were having the same argument they'd been having for the past week about the crematorium.

Jean had made many pleas on the subject. 'I don't want her body burned. That means I have nothing to stand by except a bloody marble jar. I won't stare endlessly at my daughter in a jar.'

'There's no point having her in a cemetery. You're only going to end up standing out there all day crying your eyes out. It's not worth it, Jean. I'm telling you.'

Now, as they watched the boot door close on the hearse, Jean pulled Bill's arm around her. It unsettled him; he didn't know what to do with her grief except try to be the strong one, the one who people would say in years to come, admiringly even, that Bill had really kept himself together at his daughter's funeral, and how impressive he was for having managed so strongly. He imagined them using the word 'strongly' a lot.

Bill sat in the driver's seat, hands on his thighs. 'You're doing fine, Bill,' he told himself. 'It's nearly over.'

Jean was crying harder than ever when she got in the passenger seat.

Bill wondered what he could do about it. What if she never stopped? What then? 'It's alright,' he said as if this were self-evident. 'The worst of it's pretty much over.' He started the car engine. 'Put your belt on, Maggie.'

Jean continued to cry. 'Can we just wait a second. Christ, what's the rush?'

'It's no me!' Bill snapped, 'The hearse is waiting for us.'

Jean dipped her head between her knees like she was going to be sick.

'Look, my dad told me once - and you know he never said fuck all – you can't let your emotions,' he found the word embarrassing to say, a word only posh folk used, 'get the better of you. It only makes you do stupid...' he gesticulated to help find a word, 'things.'

Bill's dad never believed in love – only in common sense. He had reared as many children as he could. He told Bill on his seventh birthday, leaning in close enough for Bill to smell the sixth whisky of the afternoon on his breath, 'Being a father isnae about lovin yer weans. It's about throwing seeds. Some make it intae great big trees that everycunt takes photees uv, an some are fir the dugs to piss against. Guess whit kind ye are HAHA!...'

This didn't stop his father attempt to change Bill, trying to beat the life into him, beat the greatness, the strength, into him. His mind operated on an antithetical basis: beatings meant vitality; silence meant love; lack of touch meant warmth; he wanted sex but was disgusted in any women who would provide it. As he grew up Bill found himself screaming every word like his father, no matter how inconsequential: 'I NEED THE TOILET!' 'WHAT'S SANTA BRINGING ME THIS YEAR?'

A heart requires a sturdy defence. Bill realised this as a young man, that a heart needs to be a fortress, with battlements, and a moat made of booze; he had numerous contingents in case of attack. Nothing could climb his walls. Bill – chin up, remembering his father's mantra – would say, 'I'm the man of this family!'

The family had been welcomed into the crematorium with derisory politeness. A man at the front desk flicked quickly through a tan leather binder, squinting at the page he was inspecting, there was a problem. His suit smelled of recently-smoked cigarettes. 'I've only got seats laid out for nine. And we did say upon booking-' Some odd, unmatching chairs were dragged in from a cellar to make up the shortfall, with people sitting either much higher or lower than the person next to them.

Jean took her seat at the front, wondering where the coffin was. She didn't know the men behind the curtain were shaking their heads at the state of it. 'Has this been used?' one of them smirked.

The curtains parted, and the coffin appeared like some afternoon variety act, as a generic CD titled 'Organ Music' played overhead. The priest – who at this point just wanted to get home and get his shoes off – rhymed off some words he had said a thousand times before at a thousand different funerals, something about life going on after death, which everyone sighed inwardly at, then turned and blessed the coffin, his crucifix motion lazy and uncaring, closer to an 'X'. The volume was up far too high for the tiny hi-fi speakers attached to the walls, making the music come out muffled and indistinct, meaning the lyrics to Robbie Williams' Angels – that quantum of generic, unspecific grief (or was it about love?) – couldn't be made out. Jean found herself mouthing along to the vocals, waiting, her tears reserved just for the climactic guitar solo that never came, because as the drum fill kicked in and Jean's eyes were watering in anticipation for those bended high notes on the guitar, the CD stuttered from a scratch mark before clicking over on a loop. The coffin slowly lowered: the final insult. The foreman whispered something and the hi-fi was shut off; the coffin disappeared in silence.

Jean looked outside at the black clouds reforming, thinking to herself, There is no cloud. There is no cloud.

Bill stopped in the middle of the car park. 'Where's the urn?'

Jean stopped too. 'I thought you had it?'

'I was with my brothers.'

Bill did the/that stumbling half-jog men do when trying to look in a rush without actually caring, back to the main door where a man came out with the urn which was covered by a purple silk cloth. Bill did the same half-jog back to the car, immediately passing the urn to Jean. It reminded Maggie of when they went to McDonald's and had to wait for their burger, so they brought it out to your car when it was done.

Here's your daughter. Sorry about the wait.

2
Jean Sleeps

Bill had done some repair work on the hotel manager's Mercedes and managed to haggle down the price of a function room, which was far too big for the Burns family. At one end of the room – a hard kick of a football away – stood a long buffet table, half-filled with Farmfoods cocktail sausages, clearance quiches and sweating cheeses on polystyrene trays. Small circles of family clung to each other, talking towards the floor, no one wanting to be the first person who laughed post-cremation. Most of the men stood by the bar waiting for the shutter to raise so they could get the bloody drinks in! Uncle Tommy had a small transistor radio with earphones so they could listen to the Old Firm match. Ha ha, stupid cops think they can stop us drinking and enjoying the game by putting it on at midday. Ha ha! That's what life was to people like Uncle Tommy: seeing what he could extract from life for his own benefit, the bored, soporific Fagin.

The women huddled round Jean, secretly swigging their gin from the flasks hidden in their 'Los Vitton' leather handbags (2 for £20, Barras market). The three of them sat at one of the large undressed circular tables with edges of exposed chipboard. Apparently there was a limit to the Burns' discount on the room.

Making little use of her day release, Dee-dee sat at a table alone, flicking urgently through the pages of her newspaper, only bothered by people brave enough to sample the buffet beside her. She reached the sports section at the back and paused for just a second. Then she flipped the paper over and started scanning through the pages from the front to the back again.

She didn't break concentration as Maggie tentatively dragged a seat next to her, not wanting to get too close, putting down a paper plate with cocktail sausages on the table. Maggie shook herself out her red coat and hung it on the back of her seat. 'I'm just going to sit here, Dee-dee. We don't have to talk or anything.' Maggie watched her go through the whole paper, then starting again, twice over.

Dee-dee looked up for a second. 'The sausages look like bath fingers.'

'I guess they do.' Maggie couldn't help but look at Dee-dee with the knowledge that she was mad, that madness must be all Dee-dee ever saw: madness was the colour of her eyes, the taste on her tongue, the size of her shoes, the feel of her newspaper, the beat of her heart. Yet it was all perfectly sane to Dee-dee. Her madness made perfect sense.

Maggie whispered, facing the centre of the table, 'It's me Maggie. We met that Christmas at ... I'm not really one of the family, remember-'

Dee-dee suddenly stopped turning pages and flung herself with open arms at Maggie, violently enough that the two of them flew back off their chairs, knocking the plate of food over onto the floor.

'Have you seen this day?' Dee-dee beamed, her and Maggie getting back on their chairs. 'I just want to show you. No one else understands, you see.' Dee-dee resumed her flicking of the pages, her fingers finding the same worn out spot at the bottom of each page.

'What is it you're looking for?'

'I don't know. I mean, I'll know it when I see it.'

'You don't know what you're looking for?' Maggie stared, hypnotized by the passing pages.

Her speech was punctuated with sporadic, nervous giggles, and she ran her fingers through her long black hair in long sweeping rhythms, like she were bowing a cello. 'Love, maybe, I don't know. He said he loved me. The boy, before I got taken to County. I was so sure of it. But you never know with love, do you. Do you ever think about it: how meaningless it all is if you're alone.'

'I'm not alone.'

'Sure you are. We all are,' Dee-dee said defiantly, running her blackened finger tips over her lips, as if she didn't believe she had actually been speaking. That she wasn't really there at all. Dee-dee's eyebrows slanted, suddenly confused as to where she was. 'This is actually happening,' she glowed. 'This is real. I mean, this right now is reality, and I'm alive-' She slid her chair back away from Maggie. 'Did you tell them I was here?'

'Who? What is it?' Maggie asked, rising in her seat. 'It's ok, Dee-dee.'

'Look at them,' Dee-dee nodded towards the men at the bar, their drinking arms rising and falling alternately. 'Look at them. They're going to get me this time. All those men.' Her voice rose above the murmur of the room, the pre-match banter getting louder, and then everyone was staring at Dee-dee. She shook Maggie by the shoulders, using her as a shield as Bill marched towards the girls. 'Get away from me. Tell them,

Maggie...'

Bill wrenched Maggie away while Uncle Tommy restrained Dee-dee. He waved Bill back who was trying to help him. 'It's ok. She's my daughter, Bill, I'll deal with it. I'm so sorry about this,' he explained to the room. 'I can't believe this is happening, here of all places. With the game about to start.'

Dee-dee's arms spazzed and flailed, finding nothing but fresh air. 'You can't be here! No, let go of me! Let go of me...' Uncle Tommy hoisted her out into the foyer where Dee-dee continued kicking the air. The hotel manager, Henry Spence, came across from behind reception.

'Is there a problem?' he asked, forcing a smile as Dee-dee screamed at all the well-dressed guests standing at reception.

'...and my newspaper! It's my day! You're all alone, because you've only got room in your hearts for yourselves! Make way, people, make way!'

The manager peeked in the function room door just as it slowly swung shut. Maggie suddenly burst through, almost smacking him in the face, waving the newspaper. 'I've got it Dee-dee.'

Dee-dee managed to grab it as Uncle Tommy wrestled her out through the revolving door - 'My heart isn't full up yet...!' she yelled - then threw her in his taxi and locked it. He'd take her back to the ward after the game. Maggie went back inside as Dee-dee resumed her reading in the backseat like nothing had happened.

Sitting, listening to the men's talk, their fag smoke drifting through the women's circles of silence, Maggie thought about the possibility of Dee-dee's heart being made of smoke: vulnerable to the capriciousness of breezes; never in control of it herself; she would always have to succumb to the whims of her environment. Nothing was hers. Except her paper. Her day that she could hold within her hands, something that could be described to her, made sense of by correspondents, its ending at the back page clear to her, unlike this life. This fucking life. Life is no object. It's just here, never giving you a moment's peace. It's tinnitus that you can see and feel. And it's so bloody painful to be alone. And it's so bloody beautiful to not be.

'What's the matter with you? Frightening her like that,' Bill snapped, jerking Maggie's arm like he was shaking creases out of a duvet. He made her retire to Jean's table. 'As if today isn't hard enough on your mum.'

She's not my mum, Maggie thought. And you're not my dad.

Bill and the guys got the fucking drinks in and settled down to the game now the fuss was over. Uncle Tommy muttered to himself on the way back in, 'See if I missed any goals...'

Jean – now legless - was being consoled by Mary who pushed her large tumbler of gin over to Jean.

'On you go, pet,' Mary said. 'It'll do you more good than me.'

Jean took a long swig.

'You've got to pick yourself up. I thought you did awright at the crematorium, didn't she Tina...' Mary looked to Tina for some support as she put down a tray-full of drinks down on the table.

'Oh aye, you did fine, hen,' Tina said.

Jean stared into her glass. 'Now I've got nowhere to go and see my daughter.'

'Aye, you can,' Tina insisted. 'She's sitting in the Belmont outside, ain't she?'

Mary stared at her with a grimace. 'She's no talking about the urn, Tina.'

Maggie stared at the wall opposite as Tina and Mary bickered on, and wished Bertrand was there. The women ignored Maggie as they always did. More gibberish. Always mumbling that one. She was nothing more than an ersatz Trish, anyway. Always had been.

Jean ran her finger around the rim of her glass. Her eyes were vacant and her speech slowing, languid.

'Why didn't Rick leave a note?' she asked.

Mary looked at Tina (ohmygod, she's caked on that bloody mascara), Tina looked at Mary (doesn't dye her hair, my arse).

'Who's Rick?' Mary asked, her buttocks climbing forward in her chair in anticipation.

'You know. Rick. He said he would meet me after, but why didn't he leave a note?'

As Jean rambled on, Tina gestured to Mary that she was going crazy.

'You don't know any Ricks,' Mary said.

'You don't know me.'

'So where did you meet him, this Rick?'

'Where do most people normally find love, Mary?'

Mary squinted at her glass then said, 'You went on a dating website?'

Tina offered, 'That new Wetherspoons down by the Spray Tan?'

'No. The Café Americain.'

'Cos there's nothing wrong with going on a dating website, mind I met that one fella-' She rooted around in her bag, sprinkled with multi-coloured LVs that were flaking off the cheap leather. 'I mean I've probably got some numbers in here that could sort you out...'

'It's ok, Mary. Rick's coming to see me tonight and-'

Mary urgently shushed her as Bill approached, in what some would say, 'not a straight line', but what Bill would definitely describe as THE STRAIGHTEST FUCKING LINE ANY CUNT'S EVER WALKED.

'Who's coming to see you tonight?' Bill boomed with three pints' worth.

Jean swirled about the wrinkled olive in her glass. 'No one, luv. Just one of the girls.'

He pulled her chair out with such speed she felt weightless for a moment. 'We've got to go. Come on, just get out that, you're plastered so you are.' At the function room doors Henry Spence stood, legs apart making his trousers ride up, showing white socks, and tapped his watch. Bill gestured that they were on their way out. 'We need to get home,' he told Jean. 'Second half's starting soon anyway.'

A half-assed crankshaft job on a Mercedes only buys so much time.

Jean and the other women collected the paper plates of leftover buffet food and wrapped them in cling film. Not wasting all that; paid good money for it! Jean gave the same drunken speech about the importance of family to each person in the car park, one at a time, much to Bill's annoyance who honked the car horn and flashed the headlights at them, turning the women into poltergeists for a few frames. A cigarette stuck to his bottom lip, as limp as his penis would be when he tried to corral Jean into having sex later.

Maggie stared at the back of Bill's cropped, sweating hairline, thrushed red where his shirt collar had been jutting in. She wondered what it was like being him, seeing his face looking back in the mirror every day. Masturbating about the female presenter from Sky Sports News. Maggie hated sitting in the living room with him, knowing he was looking at women with those eyes: the eyes of need and want, of undressing, of potent, constant masculinity. Every word, every gesture, every movement was about that to him. About conveying an idea of himself. It was why he told boorish anecdotes about the time Jean asked him to fetch her vanity case, 'like I know what a fucking vanity case is!'. He knew exactly what it was. He saw her with it and calling it a vanity case all the time, but then he wouldn't be able to portray himself as the Big Man, and how could a Big Man know what a vanity case was?

Maggie wondered if Bill thought life was what he hoped it would be. Would he even know?

'I know it would mean a lot to her, you coming to pay your respects,' Jean promised the women. Most of them gave the same reply, 'I'm sure she's looking down on us right now.' But Jean knew she wasn't. She was sitting on the dashboard of their cherry Belmont in a bargain basement urn, ready to be taken home.

There is no cloud. There is no cloud. Jean sat picking at the dinner on her lap, looking off to the mantelpiece, her gaze from the urn since the car park still unbroken, smoke from her cigarette rolling up and out the open window. She couldn't help but think of Rick, and how her wedding should have been all those years ago: everything would be so full of promise. He would be wearing his white dinner jacket and black bowtie, the kind of man who enjoyed making an effort, who wanted to look attractive for her. And they would go home and have all kinds of wonderful sex. They would have Soft-Romantic-Scented-Candle-By-The-Bed Sex, Firm-Rigorous-Fuck-Me-Till-I-Can-No-Longer-Move Sex, Lazy-Afternoon Sex, and – her favourite – Enter-Me-Gently-Telling-Me-You-Love-Me-Over-And-Over-And-Over-Again-And-That-My-Life-Is-Worth-Living-If-Only-For-You Sex. Instead she got Bill, because she was just skinny little Jean from Murray Street, and who else was going to marry her? The only man who refused to wear a kilt for their wedding, and insisted on sneaking a joke in to his speech about how Celtic had won the league that year. From then on she resigned herself to her least favourite kinds of sex: Fucking-You-Once-News-At-Ten-Is-Over Sex, and the absolute worst: I-Don't-Really-Love-You Sex; hands in their regulation position on his dowdy-haired shoulders, just to reassure him she was paying attention. Staring blankly at the ceiling, then down at the fork-in-the-road at her groin, then back at the ceiling, thinking, 'at least I've got somebody.' Bill, the only man that would have her; Jean, the only woman that would have him; him and his fire-poker fingers; her and her spongy stumps too weak to play piano, that cracked in the winter and swelled in the summer; him and his angry eyes that painted everything he saw red; her childish eyes that looked like they belonged on a fourteen-year-old, too small for her face, always seconds away from crying.

She bent forward on the sofa to refill yet another large gin, watching EastEnders on the television which was turned down so low to be almost inaudible. The moving images comforted her; reminding her of her own realness, or the seamless cutting from scene to scene instilling in her the concept that life is linear. Her own jump cut: from the urn in the car, to the urn on her mantle, didn't help this idea. And with each tip of the gin bottle getting steeper and steeper, her jaw hanging lower and lower, her head falling forward, came the realisation that life is not linear. Jean's TV enjoyed an endless battle of problem-resolution, with no rest, because as soon as one problem was resolved out popped another. It pounded her into submission: adverts constantly bellowing at her to buy things so she wouldn't be so bloody ugly, and all the programmes of beautiful karaoke contestants, and celebrities locked up in a house, fooling her that she had a 'vote', she HAD A VOICE! When really TV was laughing under its breath, 'You're all spectators here; we're running the show (texts cost 25p plus standard network rate).' Now Jean was experiencing life as a series of abrupt endings, with no resolutions, no meaning, no exposition - and it scared her to death. She turned the sound up on EastEnders, the remote shaking in her hand, her neck wavering from side to side like her head was a spinning plate, her insides arid and sexless with grief.

Soap operas' pretence of dysfunction used to comfort her: perhaps my loneliness isn't so silly. Perhaps I'm not the only one, like poor Tiffany and that stupid brute, Grant. She would watch like a tricoteuse – those hardy women of the French revolution who would gather at public executions for their gossip and tattle – as the characters rattled through death, love and life in their allotted thirty minutes with aching abandon.

Every time one of her favourite characters was hard done by it felt like a personal slander on herself. She found herself living through them, sometimes screaming at the TV, gesturing wildly at how unfair it was to kill off Tiffany. Sometimes Jean would cry about it when Bill was out in the garage, and Maggie was upstairs hiding under her blanket. All she wanted was someone to love her. Poor Tiff.

Bill slammed his knife and fork down on the kitchen table. 'Jean. Jean! Where's that bloody Maggie got to ... Don't tell me to calm down! Her fucking dinner's on the table and she's no eating it again! She's probb-ly off with that bloody old man again ... She's fourteen years old. She should be out messing around with boys in the park like all the other lassies-'

Block all this out, she thought. There is no cloud. There is no cloud. There is no cloud.

'-I'm fed up with it! It's no healthy.'

Grant Mitchell swaggered into frame and Jean – without realising - made a fist by her side. She suddenly felt nothing but contempt for the ridiculous lives on the TV in front of her, as the characters passed nonchalantly from death to childbirth to love to affairs to lesbian affairs to rape to homosexual rape then back to death again. It always ended up in the same place. And now they had killed off Tiffany, and just rolled right on to the next misery. What hope was there now? She winced as the overhead map of the Thames that accompanied the credits appeared. She didn't want to see that. It made her feel small and dispensable: seeing Earth from space. She didn't want a world that just simply forgot as soon as one misery was over then cartwheeled into the next. My Rick is coming, Jean thought, closing her eyes. She thought about switching on her Casablanca DVD again, the only one in the house (apart from Bill's porn, but only he knew about them). Rick will be here anytime soon and I won't have to worry anymore. Yes. Because Rick is the only thing that can make me feel real anymore. Not this. Not this! NOT THIS!

But there was really only one place Jean wanted to be that night. She got up quickly, taking the bottle of gin with her, ripping her jacket off the peg in the hall and slamming the door behind her.

Maggie took the tartan blanket off her head and looked down from the top stair. 'Where you going?' she asked but got no reply. She had been sitting in her room blessing everything in it by making a sign of the cross over it. This is easy, she thought. I can bless anything.

Bill paused over his steak and potatoes dinner, still drunk from after the match. 'Jean? I told you before, I don't want slammed doors in my house!'

Maggie came into the kitchen, not looking at Bill. 'Jean went out for a bit.'

'Where is she going?'

'I don't know. Can I go out for a bit?'

'To see that bloody old man again?'

Maggie said nothing.

'You've got some nerve going over there after what's happened. You know what I'm talking about. That bloody note on those flowers. Aye, I know it was him. Upset your mum so it did.'

'I don't think you can really blame Bertrand-'

'I don't blame him. I blame you. Chasing her across the road like that.'

'I didn't mean for her to-'

He mocked her: '"I didn't mean".' He waved his hand towards the door before stuffing another forkful of gristle down his gaping hatch. 'Go on then. Piss off out of it.'

Maggie put on her red coat, raising the hood over her head, and skipped down the driveway, slowing to a walk through the estate. As the rain started she put her hands in her pockets and felt something in her right hand. A piece of paper. She stopped in the middle of the pavement, leaning over it with her hood to shelter the ink. It had Maggie's name written on the front of a folded piece of A4 paper. She opened it up: '4th October. 1981. Read me.' She put it back in her pocket and ran as fast as she could to the top of Hunterhill. Bertrand would know what to do.

Jean got in the Belmont and sped away from the house, spinning the tyres as she went, blasting her horn, ploughing through some boys' game of football on the road, nosing their ball away with the front of the car. There is no cloud there is no cloud there is no cloud... She wiped the condensation from the windscreen as she drove, swerving wildly around the corner into Espedair Street, then out of town up towards Glennifer Braes, drinking as much gin and emptying her prescription bottle of Xanax as fast as possible between gear changes.

She pulled up in a lay-by and pushed the driver's seat back. It was totally secluded. Safe to be by herself. Safe to enjoy another drink. But she wasn't by herself. There was a tap on the window. He was looking off into the distance, smoking a cigarette, holding a bottle of Bourbon as the wind and rain blew the collar of his brilliant-white linen suit up. He was completely unmoved by the gale, still immaculate.

'Rick! You're here!' she cried and opened the door for him.

He kept looking off to the distance, at the dull streetlights of the cruddy town far below them. He flicked his cigarette away, ice cool, the flaming butt rocketing off into the darkness. 'Of all the Belmonts, in all the towns, in all the world...'

How she needed Rick right now, going seamlessly from sitting next to her, kissing her, to lying on top of her, the headlights of occasional passing cars casting shadows under his chiselled jawline. Jean opened the door, offering herself to him. As he eased his way inside her – never closing his eyes; why would he want to? – she gripped his miraculous arms and felt the slow rhythm of his toned, flat stomach grinding against her pelvic bone as he thrust deep inside her like a warm meal. He poured Bourbon in her mouth and she swallowed it all. Her stomach started to ring like the town bells. It had been so long since the townspeople had heard them ring, they downed their tools and ran out of their shanties, pointing to the clock tower and the two bells swinging back and forth, that were creating the most perfectly harmonious tune.

'She's coming!' they all cried. 'She's coming!' The townspeople ran and embraced each other, celebrating the end of the drought.

Jean cried in ecstasy, feeling tiny beads of sweat running down the crevice between Rick's shoulder blades. 'I love you, Rick!' she said breathlessly as she made one last lap of her fore and middle fingers over her clitoris, just enough to get her over the line, then she arched her fingers inside, imagining Rick scooping out her insides with the smoothest, gentlest shovel.

And then he was gone as soon as Jean came.

She awoke some hours later, her head still sparkling from orgasm and intoxication, and drove back down the Braes towards the town, constantly straying into the wrong lane, still drunk as hell. She rambled incoherently to herself, the thought of her girl's ashes back in her broken mind: 'This can't be what life is like. It can't just be here one day then gone the next. No, someone can't allow that. I have to make a stand. When will things just stay still?' She tried to compose herself as the darkness of the country roads gave way for the streetlights that lined the birch trees, marking the edge of town. She said aloud, 'There is no cloud.'

She pulled up outside the park and looked in at all the alcopop kids next to the fountain, flushing booze down their tiny waiflike bodies, ready for it all to reappear in an hour or so. She remembered the police calling her, to come and pick up Trish from the park. There had been a discussion about throwing glass bottles at cars. There she was, standing by the fountain, chucking up the dinner Jean made for her a few hours earlier. Some nights it would be a knock on the door, the hallway filled with the turning lights of the police van in the driveway, the hated silhouette through the frosted window of the door, the sound of the policeman's radio before she opened it: to find Trish steaming.

What's happened to you, love?

Fuck off! - then vomit.

Jean reached over to the passenger seat, realising the bottle of gin was finished, and started the car again, retracing the hearse route from earlier: the school (so many trips to see the headmaster), the Russell Institute (you get free condoms if you come with a parent - some 'parental responsibility' thing), the police station (so many D&Ds and assaults, they knew her by her first name).

She came screeching to a halt at Murray Street (skinny little Jean from...) back where she started on her mother's linoleum floor thirty-one years ago. The flow of vitriol she had been yelling at herself since leaving the park finally stopped. Why wasn't I stronger? I wasn't really going to go through with it! I could never hurt her. Still. I was very depressed at the time. No one would have understood. She collapsed in exhaustion against the horn on the steering wheel. 'Mah ... li-uhl ... gihl,' she slurred.

She ran out the car, leaving the driver's door flapping in the howling wind and rain as she scanned the teddy bears and flowers, each signed by a familiar name from the estate, or the pub, or the bingo: they expressed a surety about the existence of heaven, of God, of love, of how warm and loving a person Trish was: all so sure, with their words, and images of afterlife. She stood there, hugging herself from the chill, singing Angels to herself, guitar solo and all.

And of course that unsigned note next to the biggest bunch of flowers there. She wanted to throw them away as soon as she could, but Maggie insisted it stay there with the others on the railing next to the road.

"I know the pain is almost too much to contemplate right now - for you are dead - but you are the lucky one! Death can be the most beautiful thing. How lucky you are to move on so quickly to the next chapter. I wish dearly that I could follow you but now I can see. Your death has made me realise that there is so much love in the world. There must be because you make me dream the most wonderful dream. A dream where I am loved and the world isn't such a horrible place anymore. It's going to be magnificent. For that I am eternally grateful. I have decided that I am going to live in this beautiful world of mine forever."

The card was left unsigned. Only Maggie knew who it was from. It would be their secret.

Jean moved it away from the others, tying it to the pedestrian railing beside the road that five days earlier Trish had been knocked down on, with Maggie's piece of paper in her hand. How could words on a piece of paper mean so much to Maggie,

to cause all this? Only she knew what was on it.
Jean sat with her legs crossed, kissing the teddies one by one, as if she were kissing all her children goodnight. They should have written nursery rhymes about Jean from Murray Street. Taking the blanket from the boot, she snuggled in the backseat of the car, holding one of the bears. She ran her hand across the word 'Forever' stitched in black thread across the light brown circle of its belly.

...and with that she fell asleep.

She couldn't see it, but as she slept – kept warm by the tartan blanket she was wrapped up in, and further dreams of Rick annexing her - the coldness of her breath puffed out her nostrils in tiny burstings, evaporating almost as soon as they appeared. Perhaps if people could see themselves sleep they wouldn't hate themselves so much. Sleep was the great equaliser – everyone looked the same when they slept: no one looked evil or dangerous or happy or sad; they could be in love or they could have nothing. It was impossible to tell.

Bill glanced across at the digital clock next to the bed, trying to fool himself he wasn't bothered that it was long past one in the morning and Jean still hadn't come home. Thoughts tumbled through his head about every guy he had ever seen her speak to down the pub, every phone call she had made where he didn't know who was on the other end, every late run to the shops, every twitch from her when he touched her in bed, was now under the greatest scrutiny. He heard the name 'Rick.' He knew that much, but that was all he knew.

He wondered if Charlotte would still be up. Maybe she would bring her car back into the mechanic's. Christ, she was something. Maybe he could just give her a phone while Jean was out? Maybe he could get away with that.

He felt the picture of his father staring at him from across the room. 'LOOK AT YOU! ANY OTHER MAN RIGHT NOW WOULD BE MARCHIN THE BLOODY STREETS TO LOOK FER HER DRUNKEN ARSE. BUT YE CANNAE EVEN DAE THAT. SHE DOESN'T EVEN WANT TAE FUCK YOU ANYMAIR. SHE WANTS SOMEBODY CALL'D RICK. AND YE DINNAE EVEN KNOW WHO HE IS! HA! TAE HINK AH CALLED YE MA SON. YER A JOKE. THINK YER A MAN? I WIS A MAN. AND AWRIGHT, YOU SAW THE BACK OF MA HAND ON THE ODD OCCASION, AND ... AWRIGHT, MAYBE EVEN THE FRONT AN ALL, BUT A BAD DA? HA! AN ANAIR HING! WHEN YER STAMPING UP AND DOON THE HALL LIKE A FUCKIN ELEPHANT CAN YOU MEBBE TRY AN REMEMBER YER DA'S

BEEN WORKING NIGHTSHIFT? CAN YE DAE THAT? CAN YE? I SUPPOSE YER GAWN TO START CRYIN NOW? AYE. THERE GO THE FUCKING WATERWORKS. YE PATHETIC (backhanded slap across the cheek - punch on top of the head) ROTTEN LITTLE WEE SHITE. GO ON, GET OUT MA SIGHT BEFORE AH...

Bill rubbed his eyes and turned over. 1.21am. Too late to call Charlotte.

3
Letters That Remind Me Of Love

The estate was quiet for a Wednesday night: no screaming of laughter, no screaming of crying, no screaming of screaming. Some boys played football on the street, talking about some crazy woman almost knocking them down.

Maggie traipsed away from her semi-detached towards the derelict blocks where the bulldozers had moved in some months ago – the council were going to rebuild them, but it wasn't long before the money ran out, and the job remained unfinished. There wasn't any real need to start it up again because the papers had already carried the story on the front page about how much the council was doing to help regeneration of the aging, dying town. That was all that mattered. Johnny P from down the Swannie Road told Maggie, the Primed Minister is coming to check on the houses, but Maggie said he was too busy regenerating someplace else, far away out in the desert, thanks to him and his friend, George Bush (Johnny P, who was a stupid dickwad, laughed when Maggie told him the name, Bush, hehe ... that's what my dad calls a woman's fanny).

Bertrand's house was near the empty, half-destroyed houses, on the cusp of the dividing line between old and older, broke and broker. The curtains had been drawn since the first time Maggie had been there. Suzy J had just been sent down, and Maggie was walking round the estate, looking at all the groups of friends playing together, the teenage mums leaning over into their prams, their faces emerging bright and smiling when they rose, faces full of love, and all Maggie could think was how alone she was and how she wanted a baby as well. That was when she saw him again, walking round to the back of his house. She chased after him, running through to his garden covered in garbage. From then on she would go and see him there almost every day, and he would give her some writing of his from a vast archive stored in boxes all over his house, like Steptoe and Son had been made curators of Borges's Library of Babel.

She sat in his basement for hours, wondering why Bertrand still hadn't come down to read with her. While she waited she wrote by candlelight in her notepad that now swelled with statements like, 'If I was god I would be the nicest god in the world and everyone would love me because I would never let any bad things happen ever Ever EVER! instead of being a prick which I think this one might be'.

The neighbours had all packed up and fucked off long ago. Bertrand was the last person in those houses. Imagine being the only person in the world – something Maggie had thought about a lot. She couldn't watch the boys playing football in the park, then. And look at their lovely legs.

The front door had been boarded up for months, so Maggie nipped round the back where she made her way through an assault course of car tyres and junk that filled the insubstantial garden - then in through the open back door.

The cupboards in Bertrand's kitchen always seemed to be empty when she arrived, all the surfaces left with crumby remnants and flecks, like a hoover bag's contents had been spread widely around the house. Maggie was yet to pin down the smell there: it was solitude. The same thing that made him miss the same little patch of growth on his face when shaving. When there's no one around to inform you...

All down the hall was lined with stacks and stacks of boxes, all heaving and groaning under tremendous weight, their bottom corners buckling under the pressure of the history within them. One day Maggie discovered, hidden away underneath old newspapers, hand-drawn pictures of the same girl: A3-sized charcoal pictures of the girl's face made up of hundreds and hundreds of tiny love hearts; her standing at a pier as the sun set in the background of the island of South Uist in the north-west of Scotland; pictures of a silhouette you could still tell were of her; and in all different sizes, some in colour, others in black and white, of a burning ship in the sea at night-time. Underneath every single one of these ship pictures Bertrand had written, "Please don't let me forget the first time I fell in love!" The exclamation made the warning seem more real, the threat more dire.

It wasn't long before Maggie was finding long passages about a girl called Rose from South Uist. She would sprinkle the floor with the pages and walk between them, her palms angled to the floor, as if on a balance beam, physically travelling through the stories. She used to imagine that Rose was her real mother, modestly red-cheeked, and home to a gentle touch she had never felt before. Maggie could tell from Rose's face what her voice would have sounded like. How undramatically she would explain about the time of the month and not have to go and read books about it in the library; or explain how pointless boys are whenever one had been careless enough to scratch Maggie's heart.

Each room was piled from the floor to the ceiling with such boxes, ordered not unlike a brain, with explanatory notes attached, each notion feeding off of other notions, arriving at conclusions, then dismissing what had been thought two feet above in another box. The room wasn't alive: it was a dead body that Maggie was exhuming to autopsy, to diagnose post-mortem.

The explanatory notes read like:

"Feelings about - The Tragic Sound Of Traffic That Wakes Me In The Morning And Tells Me I Haven't Died In My Sleep"

"Letters That Remind Me Of Her"
"Books That Remind Me Of Her"
"Songs That Remind Me Of Her"
"Smells That Remind Me Of Her" ... there was a whole series of these.

"Poems I Read When I've Just Watched The Moon Rise And It Is Strangely Yellow Like The Sun"

"Diary: Cherry Tree Estates parts 1-14"

"Thoughts about Rose's first days at school" (title partially covered by dust)

"Poems Which Make Me Think: What If There Was Nothing In The Universe, And Not Just Some Nothing, But Really NOTHING IN THE ENTIRE UNIVERSE AT ALL, Which Makes Me Feel Really Dizzy And I Can No Longer Tell What's Real And This Reminds Me How Small And Insignificant I Am"

The only leather bound piles were noted as "Rose's Letters", and the letters themselves ran into the hundreds, just like the pictures, each individualised in some way by font or a line from a poem. Inside the binder were different coloured sheets of paper: the blue ones outgoing, the white ones incoming. Maggie was the only person Bertrand allowed to look at these piles of thoughts, meanderings, rants about the smallest aspects about life.

Bertrand sat in his armchair, the armrests faded and worn, covered in holes, looking out the window at the rain. 'Why is it so quiet outside tonight?'

Maggie sat on the floor, cross-legged, her coat still on, hood still up, leafing through the boxes, spinning the lids increasingly high up in the air then catching them. The arrangement of the boxes made her look like campfire wood. 'They don't come out when it's raining. It ruins their trainers. And they have babies to put to bed.' She went on to explain the Jean situation, without really thinking about her words, aware that she was speaking, but doing it on autopilot. That smooth way when you're thinking about something else, like a note in your coat pocket, and you're considering when would be the right time to produce it, to see what your old best friend knows about it.

Maggie finished her piece by saying, 'I saw the flowers you left for Trish. That was nice of you.'

Bertrand didn't answer.

'I need to ask you something.' She placed the note on the armrest of his chair. 'Does that date mean anything to you? I have to ask because it means nothing to me.'

He pulled it closer, then held it back, his eyesight adjusting. '"4th October. 1981. Read me". Hmm.'

'I just thought as it's written very clearly, and you always take pride in your calligraphy.' She looked at it again. 'I thought it strange. The placement of the first full stop. Like it doesn't suggest a year at all. But a separate number. Unrelated?' Maggie tried to remember some significance to all the 4th Octobers she had ever had, but she couldn't think of anything truly outstanding about it. 'Who would send a note like that?'

'Someone obviously wants you to remember something.'

Maggie started getting a headache, the kind when she thought about her real mother. 'I wonder if Jean'll come by. Bill doesn't want me hanging around the house tonight. He still blames me, you know.' She went back to her foraging in the boxes, the one marked "Endgame".

'Do you know what happens when you die?'

'They make a stone with your name on it for the drunks to sit on.'

'That's right.'

'Was that why you were at church, the first time I met you? Asking God not to kill you?'

He didn't answer.

'I'll be fifteen in October, you know.'

'Yes, Maggie, so you keep reminding me.'

'When do you start to feel like dying?'

'That depends.'

'On what?'

'How hard your life is. The things you've seen, the things that have been done to you. How much noise your tears make when they fall. Until it all gets too much, and you don't want to be here anymore. When seeing your footprints in the snow upsets you. None of us asked for any of this, yet we're supposed to be grateful. I'm lucky. I wouldn't upset a lot of people if I died.'

'Me neither. My funeral's just going to be me in the box and a priest talking to a bunch of empty benches.' Bertrand would have taken greater comfort in Maggie's confiding if only her truths didn't remind him so desperately of his own. 'How have you managed all these years by yourself, Bertrand? Haven't you ever wanted to get married? Even just a fling? I could get Jean to have a word with some of the women down the bingo, when she gets back that is. A lot of them still have their own hips.'

'I've got plenty to occupy myself all the time. If I weren't alone how could I write all this?' he waved around at the boxes of books.

'With no one to share it, though. You shouldn't have to be so sad yourself to write about life.' She opened the box marked "Rose's Letters". 'So tell me. Who was Rose? She's everywhere around here.'

Bertrand sat forward and sighed ruefully. 'You know all about Rose.'

'I've seen pictures of Rose. I've read about what Rose's hair smells like. What Rose's feet felt like in your hand. What the back of her neck tasted like-'

'A hard Granny Smith apple dusted with perfume,' Bertrand interjected.

'But I don't know Rose.' Maggie was thinking of questions like, 'How old were the two of you?', and 'Where was she from?' and 'Did you two do it?' and 'Did her absence make you feel so alone that when night turned to day and day back into night you would still be thinking about her? And you would feel so alone you just wanted to curl up under a tartan blanket while Jean watched EastEnders downstairs?'

Bertrand shuffled into the kitchen, not turning round as he spoke. 'I don't deserve someone so very kind to me.'

Maggie fidgeted as teen girls are wont to do when people mention how fond they are of them, no matter how slight that might be. At Pete D's party on the estate once, Jordan Mac and his footballer friends were playing spin the bottle and Jordan was asked who he'd most like to get off with at school. Maggie heard him say her name. She heard it so clearly, so distinctly, like words spoken to yourself under a blanket, insulated and safe and true. She was stood at the living room door and suddenly became remarkably interested in the door handle. She could have written novels about it she thought so hard about its shape and texture, the temperature of the steel on her skin, the life of the person that made it, how he or she was feeling that day, anything to take her mind off the embarrassment of someone saying they liked her. And in public, too. He looked so good in football shorts in PE ... She cursed herself for thinking about such things on a day like today. How long did reflection on death need to carry on? Once her head hit the pillow that night? Or next week? Maybe never.

Maggie took some pages from the box and handed them to Bertrand who had shuffled back into the room with a cup of tea. She implored him, 'Tell me a story,' her eyes red around the rims, her cheeks damp. 'Please. I just don't want to be in my own head tonight.'

Bertrand paused to find the memory he needed. 'I'm not originally from here. I used to live on an island called South Uist. It's just off the west coast.'

'You don't have much of an accent.'

'Ageing clocks eventually ring a different tune on the hour. They get weary and their insides – they're full of lots of different moving parts, you know – they get clogged up with dust and rust. My father taught me how to speak: he locked me in the attic and I found piles of books, towers of them so high the smallest tremor in the house would topple them. So I would light a candle and read until late at night when I heard the latch click off. Sometimes I would just stay up there all night as he sat and listened to the radio downstairs. Once I didn't come down for three days. Except for food or a wee.'

Maggie thought about opening up Bertrand's chest like a grandfather clock revealing an extravagant and complex series of rotating wheels, interlocking through baby metal teeth. She pictured all sorts of mechanisms ticking elegantly by, and on the hour Bertrand would stand up and he would burp the time. Her favourite time of the day would be twelve o'clock. 'Burp! Burp! Burp! Burp! Burp! Burp! Burp! Burp! Burp! Burp! Burp! Burp!'

'South Uist was a fairly typical Scottish island: always raining; always windy; a man's island. This was before the war, you understand. It was nineteen-thirty. Then one day I was in school.' He nodded to himself. 'That was when I saw her. She had a blue gingham head scarf on, and a long woollen skirt with tasselled fringe. Her long, proud neck gaped out from a butterfly collared shirt she always wore. She stood on the edge of the pier at Lochboisdale watching the ferry until it disappeared into the sunset, her skirt blowing about in the wind. I had never seen anyone so beautiful, looking out to sea, hand shielding her eyes from the sun reflecting on the water. Even it seemed in awe, shaking and wobbling with nerves, waves fighting over one another, crashing against the pier for a closer look at her, before rushing back down to the ocean floor to tell everyone of the beauty they had seen.

'First thing on Monday morning I raced to the school house to see which class she was in. I sat in class by myself, nearly an hour early. As each desk filled up come nine o'clock she never appeared. For the whole day I didn't remember one word the teacher said I was so consumed with her. After about an hour I faked a coughing fit and was excused to go to the bathroom. I waited until I was out of earshot of the class then I ran round all the classes, ducking under the windows to see where she was. I found her, eventually. She was standing in front of the class, telling everyone she had just come from Edinburgh because of her father's job: he was a mechanic on the ships. Her eyes were wild and vivid; everything about her had so much vigour, as she explained everything she loved, which was a lot, and things she didn't like, which was nothing. And the things she loved, she loved them with every cell in her blood. She said she loved everything, in fact, except coming to school, and everyone laughed. Even the girls, who hated townies. I had never seen anything like it, someone be so loved so quickly by strangers, and I wanted to be in there, swallowing her eye contact with me whole. I was so overwhelmed I stood up from under the window where I was hiding and started to applaud. Everyone in the class turned round to see what was going on. Then I realised what I had done.

'You might say her teacher was more than a little annoyed.' Bertrand smiled to himself as the memory washed over him, remembering the smells, how the day had felt. 'The teacher thrashed me but I didn't mind. I pictured Rose's face throughout every smack across the hands. With every lash I imagined her giving me a kiss on the cheek. Alternating between each side. I lost myself in my daydream and at the end I asked for one more whip for which she kissed me on the nose. Then I stamped on the teacher's foot to get ten more, from which I pictured a kiss on the lips. It was extraordinary. I mean, I felt it actually happening. I was ready to slap the teacher for something more.'

'So that was-'

'My Rose. Beautiful, flowering Rose.'

Maggie swooned, ironically fluttering her eyelashes. 'So did she fall madly in love with you?'

Bertrand laughed and slapped both arms of the chair. 'Goodness! How every boy on the island wanted to be with her. And I was a small, insignificant child. Sometimes, if my father was very annoyed with me, he wouldn't even use my real name.

He'd yell, Boy! Come here! I didn't know what to say to her. How to say it.

'At lunchtimes and breaks she would have a circle of boys gathered around her like a travelling circus, doing flips, juggling balls, playing keepie-ups, doing press ups, holding their breath till they went purple, reading Shakespeare sonnets from memory in their thick Scottish accents, anything. In fact it got so bad parents were asked by the school to keep a closer eye on their children's activities, after a group of seven boys lined up along the end of the pier one day as Rose sat on a wooden anchor stanchion. The first, a boy called Dougal, announced he was going to dive to the bottom and never come up until he had enough pearls to fill a palace for her. Then he threw himself into the freezing water. His friend Archie went in after him, saying he was going to swim around the world and set a new record, just for her. The four others couldn't think of anything to say, so they just leapt in, scared they would look like wimps. So there I was – the last one left on the pier – with Rose peering over the edge of the pier at them all flapping and flailing about, screaming and struggling just to keep afloat. I stood with her watching them flapping about in the water. I said: "Fancy coming round to mine?" "OK,' she giggled, and we threw a few life rings into the water for them.

'I showed her around my family's croft and went walking along the machair, running up and down the sand dunes. I found myself holding her hand as I explained how dangerous it could get with the tides. I said, "I know I don't really know you, but you have to promise me that you'll be very careful with the tides. To not come out alone." I stared at the ground. "I can always come out with you if you want..." Then she kissed me on the lips. It was the best thing that had happened to me. In a way, it's the only reason I've kept going so long - in the desperate hope of feeling something even close to that again.'

Maggie lilted inside. It was exactly how she wished she could fall in love, how she wished it would happen with Jordan Mac and his big green eyes, late at night under that tartan blanket in her bedroom.

Bertrand yawned, leaving his mouth gaping wide open and accidentally burped. 'Oh, excuse me.'

Maggie went over to him, opened up his cardigan and pretended to look about inside him. 'Is that the time already?' she said. 'I should really get home.'

'Ah, so it is. There is one thing you can do for me, if you wish.'

Maggie agreed, 'Anything.'

'If you like, I can give you some of these.' He reached into the box marked "Rose's Letters". 'It's lucky you're here. It's ... my eyesight, you see, haha ... it's so bad I can barely read them.'

Maggie knew that wasn't the reason he hadn't looked at them. 'Should I start from the bottom?'

'Yes, yes. They should be in chronological order.'

Maggie strained to lift the heavy binders, tipping over the box marked "Letters That Remind Me Of Her". Out spilled a collection of photos, fanning out across the wooden floor, where carpets had once been. Maggie picked up a photo and gasped. 'This is really her.'

'That's her,' he said looking at Maggie. 'That's my Rose.'

'She looks exactly like the pictures you drew.'

'Well of course they do. And most of those were drawn from memory years later in Cherry Tree Estates.'

'What was Cherry Tree Estates?'

Bertrand flinched, he hadn't meant to say so much. 'Oh, somewhere I lived for a while. When I first left the island. I try to forget about that place.'

Maggie replaced the photos into the box and picked up huge clumps of letters. 'Bertrand ... these are all written by you. Didn't she reply?'

'The last I heard she was on an island just off the coast of Uist. I checked most thoroughly with the authorities and there was no one there. Many of the people from the island fell in the war. Just as everywhere else, though. I came close to finding her brother, Nicholas, then I found out he was dead. I chased corpses for years.' He shook his head and a tear filled his eye. 'You can only take so much death in this life.'

Maggie wondered why only his left eye felt sad but not his right. Perhaps his left eye was the woman, the emotional gender, like Bill was always telling her. She liked the sound of some of the other boxes. 'Can I take some of these, too?' she asked, lifting the lid on the "Words That Will Make You Feel Not So Alone, Especially At Night (fragile)" box.

'Of course. I hope you enjoyed all the others from last time.' He added some more pages on top of Maggie's already large pile.

She pecked Bertrand on the cheek, holding his bony door handle of a hand as she did. 'I promise they will make me happy.'

She didn't waste any time in starting the letters when she got home, putting new batteries in her torch. That was much easier than the time she tried to read by candlelight under the sheets, and although Bill wasn't very happy, the firemen found it most amusing. Maggie fell asleep that night with the thought of all the firemen falling asleep with a smile on their faces thanks to her. Bertrand would certainly have approved of the incident.

It had been a long day, her various crying episodes draining her each time, as if exercising on an empty stomach. Maggie had yet again let out more from her body than she had taken. She had negative vitality now.

She opened the binder of letters, keeping a pencil handy to make notes, and started reading, despite how heavy and sore her eyelids were.

It wasn't long before she started glancing at the clock next to her bed every other paragraph. She couldn't help it, counting down the minutes, terrified time was dripping away like an unwatched tap.

4
Desire Knows No Restraints

15th April 1943

Dear Bertrand,

It's been so cold here for so long, it's hard to remember spring is closing in. Being in this part of the country so long, I should know by now there's no spring here. There's only two seasons, like you know: winter, and less-like-winter. And nothing in between!

The island is more perfect than you could imagine. It feels like we're hiding out on some divine property here, that only God gets to have this view, of the sun's play with the waves, sometimes coming down like a spotlight through a hole in the clouds, and it tracks across the Atlantic. I try to will the light out towards you, that it might bring you to me quicker.

Tell me you won't be much longer. I know it's only been three weeks and a few days, but I don't think I can go much longer without the touch of your fingers through my hair wakening me in the morning, or the long baths we take together, when you kiss me across my back and neck (I like it best when I can't see what you're doing behind me. I don't know what kiss is coming next or where. Let's never face each other again. No, actually, I don't like the idea of that. Forget I ever said that. Let's face each other for the rest of our lives. And if we ever lose sight of one another we will yell each other's names out into the sky until one of us returns. Agreed?).

I've wrote a letter to Nicholas (you remember Nicholas, my wee brother, don't you?) in London, and letters I will never send to my cousins, and my granny, and Mrs Peters, and Angus John that helps my dad at the yard, and Mrs McKinnon from the school that used to let me away early, and John Angus and Angus Thomas and every other person with Angus or John or Thomas in their name, just to give me something to do on this island apart from sit on a fence all day long, carving the poems you wrote for me back on Uist into the wooden beams - then I rest to watch the sunset. I love seeing your words etched there, like they're part of the landscape. It makes me forget how much the days are like ticking off boxes just now. Nothing more. The others say I shouldn't rely on you so much. But what can I do? I thought, 'There must be more than this.' Then I remember: I love you.

Last night I dreamt of a Bertrand-shaped silhouette walking towards the cottage with your bag of letters thrown over your shoulder. So where are you? Have you changed your mind?

PLEASE WRITE SOON

Sometimes when I'm lying in bed (I call it a bed, it's some boards with a few blankets laid down; we have to take it in turns for the bed in the cottage and it's always Lindsay and Joseph, or Michael and Emily that get it, for obvious reasons) thinking about what we are all doing here, I get scared that the others will lose their nerve, to not see this through, and get Colin to take them back to Uist and confess to their parents that they'd run away. Well, maybe not Lindsay and Joseph. They are always holding each other, giggling secretly to one another on the fence, just down from me, keeping me company every day at least for a few hours.

PLEASE WRITE SOON

Being here reminds me of when I first came to South Uist. I must have been fourteen. I wasn't used to the constant bloody gale around here. It kept knocking me over (remember when you would see me blow over, then you threw yourself down on the ground just to stop me looking so stupid?). It's even more exposed here. Everything arches in the same direction, facing north-west. From the grass around the peat bogs, to the chimney stack on top of the cottage. Which reminds me. Don't bother bringing a hat. There are too many jobs around here that require two hands.

I know being with someone is all well and good, and that was the point of us coming here, but it's not good when it feels like you're the only person in the world that's alone. On a clear day and straining my eyes, I can just about make out Uist, and I can hear the banter on the pier, the tractors, the cattle, the squeaking gates. It feels like years ago that I arrived with my big clumsy shoes and townie patter. Then you came with your big green eyes and swept me off my feet at the machair. You said I needed to get some wellies, then I kissed you. Although I was only young I knew I wanted to grow old with you.

Let me tell you all the wonderful things that await you. When you get here I'll collect you from the dock and try to carry you up the path through the peat bog to the cottage. I'll end up dropping you in the bog because you'll be far too heavy for me. Then Joseph will pick some of his vegetables – once he's stopped laughing - and we'll have a feast. We'll eat ourselves to bursting, then lie on the floor in front of a well-stacked fireplace. You can run your hand over the curve of my belly, sliding your fingertips under my jumper when no one is looking. Those are some of my favourite times, just lying on the floor with your arms around me, not a word spoken for hours and hours on end. The chill of our feet touching each other would be enough to fill novels a hundred times over, and as I lay there in your arms I would write all the words in my head, ready to put to paper the next day. Only, sometimes I come up with grandiose sentences that actually come close to the feelings inside me, then I think of something else that seems even grander, and before I know it I've forgotten the whole lot, and the words are lost forever. Never to be remembered. That's all I do now. Sitting on the fence constructing as many grand words as I can, then carving it all into the fence next to yours - that way we can always be together. The fence is about half a mile long, so I don't know if it will be a long enough canvas to fill with us. If it weren't for you I almost wouldn't have anything to write about! (It seems all my experiences are based on you. How is that possible? What love does to you). But words just aren't enough anymore.

The last few days have been the best yet, though. Michael keeps telling me that the sheep understand what we're saying to them, they just don't know how to reply. It made me quite sad to think about it, actually. He always let me off from doing my chores because his father would always tell him he wasn't doing his chores properly. He would have been beaten for leaving windows as streaked as I had, but it made him happy to say it doesn't matter. Then he gathered all the sheep around him and told them jokes. Like a good father. We all stood behind him and stifled our laughter.

I sat out on the fence today in the pelting rain with my Swiss Army knife and your poems. (I've started putting a cushion underneath me, as I get a thick indent across my arse cheeks sitting there all day. I'm sure you would find it funny. You always said you loved my arse). I can hardly think of anything to say when I come into this stale cottage to write. It's so cold inside no matter how long the fire burns. No one else seems to notice because they're so busy with each other. That's when I miss home the most.

Most nights I lie with my blanket pulled up over my head to block out all the sounds; the creaking bed boards, the bleating sheep outside. That's when I make up the words in my head. So I make up a list of them and repeat them over and over like a mantra, in the fledgling hope that I will wake in the morning and remember them. The other night I even made a mnemonic of them. Would you like to know what it was? Of course you do.

L for how your laughter makes me cry
E for the ecstasy you make me feel
T for the tears you cry (right eye)
T for the tears you cry (left eye)
(do you still cry out your left eye first?)
E for some more ecstasy
R for how you read Blake to me in bed

This spells L E T T E R. As in, write me a...

Emily said the other day, 'what if someone finds us out here?' It's all Michael talks to her about. The wee lamb is so scared.

I've made a pact that if I stopped eating for as long as I could then you would arrive, but here I am, wasting to nothing and I have no option but to eat some of these rotten potatoes. It's all we ever eat here. I suppose it's really Joseph's fault. He was the one that said he knew how to grow vegetables and sow a field. Then Lindsay said all he knew how to grow was an in-grown toenail. He swatted her on the arm, then they hugged, then they kissed, then they disappeared off to the horse stables. I looked across the field to see the stable doors shaking, and I fell to the ground thinking there was an earthquake (although quite what good it does during an earthquake to spread your entire body across the ground, I don't know). It was only when I looked at the cottage house and it was perfectly still - even the wind-slanted chimney stack that threatens to fall any day now – that I realised what was going on. I just sat there on the cliff edge chewing a length of north-west-slanted grass. If I had to choose between chewing grass and shaking horse stable doors, I know which I would prefer, and I definitely know which one you would prefer, Bertrand (I still think about us that way. Of course I do. What do you think I am? Not human? That I don't have an imagination? That when I'm lying in bed with two other couples out here on a deserted, remote island, the sound doesn't drift up through the walls, that I actually don't desire to feel the same things as them? Or to feel the same things men desire? Desire knows no restraints, you once told me, regardless. That some people say making love is wretched and disgusting when it's really the most beautiful natural thing in the world? That was the point in coming out here. Because no one else understands how we want to live. All I really yearn for is to feel love again and to hear my name shouted by you! It wakes me in the night).

PLEASE WRITE SOON

Your ever loving, bright, flowering,

Rose.

PS Colin will not be here for a while to forward this letter so hopefully you will have arrived by the time this reaches the croft.

5
You Must Remember This

Ha ha! Charlotte the harlot. She liked that. Maybe Bill wasn't so stupid to come up with something like that. It had a nice ring to it, she thought, as she brushed her hair in the mirror, ignoring that ignominious husband of hers floundering with his tie over her shoulder. Oh, come here for God's sake. As if anyone pays the slightest bit of attention to you in that hotel.

He tried to kiss her just on the cheek, but she turned away. He cleared his throat and left for work. The thought of his horrible lips touching her face made her want to vomit. She hated those lips now. So thin and rufescent. And those hands of his. Christ! Those hands. So bony and creepy, crawling all over her perfectly aerobicked body. Did he really think she spent all that time in the gym just for him to climb on top of her with his weedy little ... that thing of his Ha! What a bloody nerve.

The last thing she did was blow herself a kiss in the mirror. She had spent all morning getting spick-and-span, all suited-and-booted for her man to rough up. Her bit of rough would see to that. Give her a right good seeing to!

She got outside the Merc and savoured the wolf whistles from the bin men passing by - a bit of posh, they liked that. Her heart winked at them and she tried to contain the wide smile that spread across her face, but she just couldn't. Then she realised they were catcalling Melanie across the street, just back from her morning jog in vest-top clinging to her breasts (enhanced) and tiny shorts.

Not to be outdone, Charlotte opened the boot pretending to look for something, stretching deep inside so her shirt would ride up and the top of her thong would show. The wolf whistles across the street for Melanie grew to howls of desire and Charlotte gave up. She slumped in the front seat. No one sees me. Why does no one see me? She skidded out the driveway and shouted out the window at the bin men, 'Why don't you do some work. You lot are harassing that poor woman. I shall complain!' and sped off.

At each red light or stall in the traffic Charlotte checked her makeup in the rear view mirror, puckering her lips together, just to reassure herself after the early setback. She looked to each side of her, neither male driver paying attention to her. No one sees me. She opened the top button of her shirt and flicked her hair around. The man to the left looked and smiled. He was ugly. Charlotte looked away quickly. No one sees me.

She turned into the mechanics and was going to give herself one last look in the mirror but knew she didn't need to.

The mechanic came out, filthy already (oh, fuck me!) although it was only about ten in the morning. Some of the guys in the back chuckled amongst themselves, ''Ello, 'ello, 'ello! Back again, eh? Days looking up already, Billy boy.'

Bill turned round, face of stone, and they immediately shut the fuck up. He stood and watched the sparkling Mercedes: the tanned face inside, legs up to her arse, skirt clinging to her thighs as she climbed out. She really worked it as she walked towards them, desperate to regain, desperate for them to want her. The others looked on as Bill stood perfectly still, spanner in hand.

'Is everything alright, Mrs Spence?' he asked.

She pouted, aware the others were listening. 'It's the engine. There seems to be something the matter with it again. Can you get it going?'

Bill – thick as he was – knew what she was up to just by her expression. He could already feel the bulge growing underneath his overalls. 'Maybe I should take a look at it. How about we take it for a little run? See what needs doing.'

She took a deep breath and said quieter, 'I think I know what needs doing.'

Bill threw the spanner along the ground back towards the car he was fixing, and said over his shoulder to the boys, 'Back in an hour.' The laddish smiles and winks from the others filled his heart with pride. Bill thought, If only he could see me now...

Bill loved Lincoln Fields, Charlotte's neighbourhood. Their perfectly paved driveways fronted by bronze statues of lions as if it were a film studio.

'Don't they get nicked, just lying around outside?' he asked incredulously.

The lawns were all trimmed to perfection because the owners had nothing else to do with their time, or nothing better to spend their money on than a gardener. Every house had an extra car sitting in the driveway because... There wasn't a lace curtain to be seen in the windows. No garden gnomes. Not even an ironic one. The whole place was like a giant slate of celluloid; a living movie where Bill could just meld, 2D, into the surroundings. The whole neighbourhood felt distinctly unreal –

they even had their own coat of arms on their wheelie bin, their name wrapped around a fleur-de-lis – as if he were walking through someone else's dream.

Charlotte was already taking off her clothes in the car as the thrill of having Bill's big hands - fixed round the steering wheel – all over her, grew nearer. He was in such control of the car, the way he pressed the accelerator, pushing Charlotte back into her seat, feeling the Gs, the inertia he was causing. She was reminded how unfulfilled the petty lives of her neighbours were. Not like hers, of course. Hers was full of love.

Bill could barely drive she was getting herself in such a state, touching herself, hands sliding up and down her sternum, but he just about managed to maintain control. She guided him out the car, 'come on, quickly, Bill,' taking him round to the back door. She checked that none of her neighbours were at their windows, curtains twitching. Bill caught her eye and she faked a smile. She could relax once they were inside.

The kitchen had all the signs of comfortable domesticity: finished coffee mugs steeping in the sink; 'Golf Monthly' for him, 'Heat' for her, casually fanned across the breakfast table, each skimmed in a minor way when the other was watching one of their programmes.

Bill reached for the coffee to pour himself a cup. Charlotte saw it coming and yelled, 'No! Don't touch that. Just leave everything exactly as it is.'

'He won't remember where it was. I'll put it back.'

'That's not what I mean. Just don't touch it.'

Charlotte undressed on her way up the stairs, casually taking Bill's hand off the banister. She hid this movement well, though, smoothly replacing his hand on her breast. Bill's tongue lunged out at hers and he clawed at her bra. He loved her breasts. They always looked exactly how he wanted them to. Unlike Jean's. He hated her breasts. They looked used up, and seemed to frown at him when she got undressed across the room, she would turn slightly and one of them would peek out from behind her arm, like a scolded child behind a doorway. He wanted to tell Jean's breasts off.

Charlotte ran the shower, where just a few hours ago her husband had been flagrantly beating himself, thinking of the beautiful wife that would no longer fuck him. She just stopped Bill in time before he touched her skin. 'Wash your hands, Bill.' He did so, then she said, 'You missed a bit.'

'Where?'

'There.'

He cleaned his hands to Charlotte's satisfaction and she led him into the shower where he ravaged her as long as he could. For Charlotte it was everything she had been dreaming of since the night before when she had left Melanie's gardener's shed, just before the perma-tanned hunk had left for the day. He had smelled of petrol from the lawnmower he had been fixing.

They dried themselves off and Bill started putting his clothes back on.

'What do you think you're doing? Get back here,' she demanded. 'You haven't finished yet.' She stripped him back down and he threw her on the bed, putting his hand over her mouth.

'Just shut up, you stupid bitch.'

Charlotte moaned in pleasure. This was what she wanted.

Bill just kept banging away as fast and as hard as he could. Stupid cunt, taking the car. Had to fucking walk to work, of course, didn't I. Looked a right spare prick! He went so hard and so fast, and she was so wet, he kept popping out. He didn't feel pleasure or pain, or sadness or happiness or anything, which pleased him. Then he felt annoyed for feeling pleased, and then the annoyance made him feel ... Why couldn't he stop feeling?

'Shut up!' he insisted, banging Charlotte's head against the velvet-covered headboard which only pleased her more. 'Charlotte the Harlot, eh?' He kept doing it, though, annoyed at her constant yakking of 'more this way, no, the other way, up a bit, down a bit'. It's like putting a bloody picture up on the wall, this.

Finally he came, and the relief of being finished was immense. He fell off to her side and she tried to go down on him. That would take far too much effort for him to concentrate on, so he pushed her off and put his overalls back on. He traipsed through the living room leaving dirty footprints across the cream Axminster carpet which she would later scream blue murder about when she discovered it.

Bill stopped at the front door as he was about to leave – hand outstretched for the doorknob - when he decided to go back. He went round the kitchen touching everything he could, moving things out of place. Stupid bitch, he thought ... Tell me what to do?

Bill took the bus home, but it took a while to find one, as Charlotte's estate wasn't the kind that required any running through it. It was a land of second and third cars, sitting idly in driveways.

Bill was most pleased with his morning's work. He felt the voice from his bed the night before relenting. THAT'S A NICE BIT AH SKIRT, SON! He nodded to himself in satisfaction, but he was too satisfied to realise this was also an emotion. A nice bit ah skirt. But this satisfaction was short lived, only lasting until the bus crossed the bridge at Murray Street, where his satisfaction turned to a creeping unease. His eye caught a group gathered around teddy bears and multitudinous flowers tied to the pedestrian railing next to the road sign reading 'Accident Black Spot'.

The bus came to a halt and he knew he was right where the accident had happened. Some old biddies across the aisle from him were muttering to each other, 'oh yes, those flowers are gorgeous. Oh now, would you look at that. What's she up to?'

Bill saw his cherry red Belmont sitting diagonally across the pavement, the driver door wide open, and his wife sitting on the ground against the railing, demanding anyone walking past the flowers and teddies should make as wide a berth as possible. She marshalled them around the memorial, allowing onlookers to read the cards.

'Just be careful and don't move anything.'

Bill pressed continually on the bell to stop the bus.

'Alright, alright, mate,' the driver said.

'Let me out here,' he demanded, never taking his eyes off Jean.

'I can't, mate. This is a busy junction. You'll need to wait-'

But Bill had already hit the emergency open button above the door and he leapt out. 'What the hell are you doing, Jean?' he yelled.

She cowered against the railing and covered her face.

'What's the matter? Do you think I'm going to hit you?'

Jean grabbed one of the teddy bears and held it tight to herself like it would protect her. 'I don't know, Bill. You look like you're going to.'

Bill noticed the scene that, like it or not, he had unwittingly created. 'What you all looking at?' he screamed across the road, only the ones on his side of the pavement moving on. 'Take a fucking picture why don't you.'

Jean brushed the top of the bear's head that had a little tuft of hair, so babies would think it was a person. 'You'd best get away, Bill. Cos Rick's going to be here any minute.'

'Who is this Rick? Who is this fucker?'

'Rick Blaine. He runs the Café Americain, just down from the Blue Parrot.'

'You're fucking him aren't you?'

Jean didn't reply.

He had tried anger, now he felt obligated to look mildly caring in front of so many people. 'Look, just come home, for chrissake and stop making a scene. We'll sort this out.'

An old woman examining the cards on the flowers reached out towards one of the teddies, which Jean noticed in her peripheral vision. She batted the old woman's hand away, adjusting the position of the bear although it hadn't moved.

'Jean? Are you listening to me? Hey!' He snapped his fingers.

But Jean wasn't listening; she was sat there on the damp pavement humming the tune of As Time Goes By to herself, stroking the bear in her arms.

A policeman came by from the 'Fags and Mags' across the road, checking for under-agers buying booze. It was Friday afternoon after all. He put his hand on Bill's shoulder, making him whip around. 'Excuse me, sir. Is this your car? You have to move your car from here, sir.' He enjoyed calling people 'sir' or 'madam'. It was pejorative in his daily context of street scrapings and road tumbles.

Bill stared into the flowers three rows deep. 'It's hers,' he said. 'Tell her to move it would you? She's causing a disturbance.' Then he walked back to work.

6
Madness Taking My Hand

Maggie had been racing her way through Rose's letters all morning, and had even brought them with her to read in the taxi, but she got motion-sick after a few minutes. She had to tuck some of them into the back waistband of her gingham skirt as her pockets were so full.

'Would you like one?' Maggie asked, holding an open box of Tunnock's teacakes that were beginning to melt from the searing heat outside.

Bertrand said to her, 'Did you ever make hats out of tin-foil when you were wee?'

The cabbie adjusted his rear view mirror, bringing Maggie into his line of sight.

'Once on the ferry to Oban, Rose and I made these little hats for ourselves. We promised to wear them forever, in case we ever got lost in a crowd. The sun would shine down on us and we would always find each other. We'd be the only numpties anywhere with stupid foil hats!' He laughed until he snorted. 'We didn't last very long until the wind from the North Sea stole them.'

The cab pulled up outside the Piazza Shopping Centre. 'That'll be £3.40, hen.'

Maggie insisted on paying despite Bertrand's protests.

The cabbie turned around to look Maggie in the eye and asked, 'You awright?'

Bertrand got out first, leading with his cane.

'Of course,' she said, handing the cabbie a fiver and a teacake. 'I'm fine. I know he's old and a bit doted but he's my best friend. You can have this; we shouldn't be ruining our appetite for lunch.'

The shopping centre was playing slow, dreamy Hawaiian music, like they were in some tropical paradise, despite some security guards chasing junkies who had been shoplifting in Poundland, and the air conditioning wafting cigarette smoke around the heads of the committed shoppers, their faces etched with anguish. Their days were filled with indiscipline: they went out with no aim or goal. They woke up and assumed they should leave the house and do something. Buy something. Buy something nice. But they never found anything nice. Only things they picked flaws in, some ill-defined ideal that was hidden in their heads. Their lives were totally pointless. Pointless in a natural-world sense, of endless journeys to find food, and breed, as widely as possible.

Circles of young mothers Maggie recognised who had been in the year above her in school stood outside shop entrances in miniskirts, looking awkward with their prams, and adding to the fag smoke ambience. 'He's fuckin greetin again!'

Maggie tallied what she saw. 'Everyone seems to have electric buggies.'

'And babies,' Bertrand added, making Maggie go quiet.

She watched all the attention the mothers received from strangers, how doting the friends were and eager to help. 'I wish I had a baby.'

'Why on earth would you want a baby at your age?'

'So I could love it.'

'And it could love you.'

'Yeah. Something like that.'

The pair went into Morrison's where Maggie could buy Bertrand lunch as per their arrangement: Lunch For Letters.

'Didn't this use to be a Safeway?' wondered Bertrand struggling to reach the basket from the top of the pile as tall as him, and wobbling as precariously as he did.

Maggie liked Morrison's because it had a pretend street with pretend shop fronts, a pretend butcher, and a pretend baker, and a pretend delicatessen, like they were on some high street from days of yore (when was yore? The people there must have been very happy because everyone wants to go back to then. I looked up yore in the history books at school and all I found were a few wars at the beginning of the last century, and then in between it was very quiet and boring, then a black man with big curly hair took some drugs and plugged in his guitar and made everything exciting again. Then there was another war. And the black man and all his friends didn't like that. [why are there no black people around here? Maybe I should ask those bald men with the table outside with the Union Jacks hanging from it if they know where they are? They seem to know a lot about black people and all sorts of different coloured people with difference accents]. They wanted to play music in a field all day. Then there was a woman who looked like the scary granny down the road and was just as bossy and ugly as her [I tried to sell her cookies once, and she told me I was charging too much. Cow.] on the telly all the time standing in front of a black door with a number 10 on it, next to a weedy little man, and she started another war, then made all the hospitals bad, as well as the ecnomony, I mean, economy [I always say that wrong when I try and speak too quickly. If only my brain automatically changed words before I said them, like when I type words badly into the computer at school and it changes them, even when I spell 'obviously' 'obviuosly'. It makes me really lazy and a bad speller]. Then she lost the election, and two men who were very similar won the next elections, and they stood in front of the door with a number 10 which meant they were in charge of the country [maybe I'll go to London and stand there and then I can run the country along with Bertrand], and they both fought wars in a desert [though not themselves, because they're rich and lazy (or so Bertrand and someone called George Galloway says. You know, that one on Big Brother.)] for the same reason [though the second one had to go back and finish off what the first one was rubbish at] and now no one likes any of them and the second one is about to retire to much applause, though they aren't clapping for the reason he wants. And now we are here. So maybe yore isn't as good as it's meant to be?) and everyone knew everyone else's name (apparently), which must have been very difficult to remember.

At the Deli counter Maggie asked for two little tubs of pasta salad, which was easier for Bertrand to eat and digest.

'No problem,' the Deli boy said.

Bertrand rubbed at the fake wooden front of the counter. It seemed to depress him further. His eyes wandered around the speckled white floor. Bertrand leaned down to whisper to Maggie, 'why would it be a problem? I wouldn't have expected it to be a problem with him being a Deli worker. Why do people say such silly things?'

Maggie hit him on the leg. 'Bertrand, you're being old and a fogey.' It was the sort of thing he used to say all the time as a petulant child, before Rose had come to South Uist and swept him up: Why does the wind always have to blow in that direction? Stupid wind. What's that stupid dog barking at? Like it's laughing at me. Why does it have to shit all over the pavement like that? Everything is so stupid.

'Actually, do you want just one tub altogether?' the rather confused boy asked. His face was a Panavision of acne which Maggie thought was the reason he didn't look people in the eye; he was – unjustly - shamed.

'No,' Maggie said. 'We need two because we don't like to dig into each other's food because sometimes you drop food off your fork and you leave tiny little bits of drool that you can't see on it. And as much as I like Bertrand, here, I don't wish to get his invisible drool in my stomach.' She turned round, 'Sorry, Bertrand.'

He gestured it was alright.

Maggie turned back to the boy, speaking behind her hand, 'Plus, he's a little old and drools more than most. I know. I've seen him with a tin of beans.' Then she resumed her regular volume. 'So to answer your question, no, we would like separate tubs, please.'

The boy sighed, 'Here you go,' and handed Maggie the tubs.

'Thank you,' she said cheerily. 'By the way, you have lovely skin.' Her compliment was taken with irony and the boy stormed off into the back, convinced she was mocking him.

Maggie's threw her hood up in disgust at herself. She trudged ahead by herself, calling back to Bertrand, 'Why am I so totally incapable of making people feel happy?'

Bertrand trailed behind, dragging his feet like a little boy scorned, lost all over again in this New World, mumbling no thank yous to people selling things that required them to hold out long, winding manuals of small print, asterisks next to every second word, every letter another Term and Condition.

Outside the supermarket they sat on one of the benches placed down the middle of the main avenue of discount and charity shops. In the window of the British Heart Foundation was a long Doctor Who-type scarf.

'Do you see that scarf in the window?' Maggie asked.

Bertrand squinted, which he had to do for most things that weren't right in front of him. It made his whole neck rise up in rubbery tide. 'It looks nice and warm. A nice old man scarf.'

Maggie skipped over to the shop and bought the scarf. She liked the way the lady assistant carefully unravelled it from around the mannequin's neck, as if trying not to waken it. When they walked towards the till, the woman felt something in her hand, something freezing cold. It was Maggie's hand.

The lady smiled awkwardly as she tried to let go, only for Maggie to cling for a second longer. 'Very hot today for a scarf, isn't it?' She spoke like her English teacher, Miss Gray. She and Bertrand were the only people Maggie had met that had never shouted at her at some point.

'It's actually for my friend over there.' She pointed to the bench across from the shop.

The woman searched for him. 'That's your friend out there, is it?'

Maggie was used to this reaction when introducing Bertrand – him being an old man, and her so young. 'That's right. He's my best friend actually.'

The lady smiled in a kind of pitying way which Maggie didn't like. Miss Gray never did that. Maggie said, 'I ... I have other friends as well, you know.'

'I'm sure you do. You know, you have such a pretty face, why are you hiding it under that big red hood of yours?'

Maggie's face went the same colour as her coat and looked down at the ground. 'Bill said it will make the whole world happier if I do.'

'Really? And who's Bill?'

'He's not my dad.'

'I see...'

'I'm going to have a baby, you know.'

The lady nodded, in two parts. 'Really.'

'Yes, really,' Maggie said indignantly. 'I'm going to show it just how much love there is in the world.' She skipped back towards Bertrand, twirling the scarf around her neck, it dangling down to her ankles. She shouted to him, 'Do you like it? I got it for you. I've been stealing pennies from Bill's jacket the last few days when he's passed out on the sofa. It's better the British Heart Foundation has it than him.'

Then, a few feet from the bench, the scarf wrapped itself around her left foot and she tripped over, tumbling spectacularly like a bottle half-filled with water, her momentum gathering with each roll. Her hood fell down and her face started to burn again, feeling the stares of a group of boys bouncing a football, passing through the centre. One of them was Jordan Mac. He was laughing with the others. Everything was hilarious when you looked like Jordan Mac. His lovely arse and sunbed tan. And that lovely gel caked in his hair.

Bertrand tried to help her up but Maggie wouldn't budge. She kept looking at Jordan Mac until he got lost in a crowd at the other end of the centre. She sat back up on the bench and flung her hood up over her head again, and started scoffing Bertrand's unwanted pasta, shovelling it violently into her mouth.

Maggie forced her words out solemnly, between chews, pulling out a piece of paper from her coat: "Feelings about falling in love with Rose". 'Tell me something nice, Bertrand. About you and Rose, when you first fell in love.'

'I was always falling over when I was your age,' he said. 'It's how I first got talking to Rose. She was swinging on the gate of our croft, when my dad – he was in the army – he told me to go out and tell her to stop. So I went out with my walking stick and my dog, mad Bruce spinning around my legs, barking like a banshee, and just when I was going to ask her why she was sat on our fence, I stepped on a pothole, and fell on my face right in front of her. She laughed so hard, I just joined in with her. She was chewing a bit of grass, swinging one leg back and forward, and when her leg went back it showed the flesh of her ankle. I nearly passed out.'

Maggie put down the pasta tub and letter, and peeked from under the hood to see the lady from the charity shop watching her, craning her neck, peeking over the shoulder of the mannequin.

'She wiped the mud from my face and told me she had seen me at school and wanted to be friends. I looked back at the house. My dad was standing at the window with his arms folded. I said, "Meet me on the machair in two hours".'

'And that was it? It was that easy?'

'It was never easy. My dad never liked me going out, especially at night. But you find a way. Lovers always do.'

Jordan Mac and the others were walking back towards Maggie, carrying brown bags of McDonald's, like the ones that carry dog shit.

'Let's walk for a bit, Bertrand,' Maggie urged him, taking them off in the opposite direction, stopping for a second to wave to the lady in the charity shop. She hesitated for a second then simply raised a startled hand. Such a strange little girl, she thought. Maggie stuffed her hands back in her coat pockets filled with Bertrand's words. 'Why didn't you write to her?' Maggie wondered. 'On the island. Where were you? Did you not love her anymore? That kind of thing?'

'I was never in love with anyone else. Rose and I were always faithful to each other. And I couldn't write to her where I was.'

'Where were you?'

Bertrand looked away.

'Words were really important to you two, weren't they?' Maggie said.

'I should think if I didn't have words I would be all alone in the world.'

Maggie touched his arm. 'No you wouldn't. I would be all alone in the world if I didn't have you.'

'Let's just say we have each other then.'

She nodded in agreement. 'Do you remember that poem, the first thing I took away of yours? From "Words That Will Make You Feel Not So Alone, Especially At Night" box. "The Immaculate Heart". It was everything I have ever wanted to say.' She took it out her pocket, folded in perfect quarters and noticed Bertrand was trembling, looking at the words but trying not to be seen to. He was wheezy, so they sat on the floor behind an enormous plant pot holding a palm tree, where no one would bother them. From under the hanging leaves, all they could see were passing feet and prams.

Maggie let down her hood and started reading "The Immaculate Heart".

'"Farewell, then, love, I barely knew you.
Let me not fight this solitude, this desolation,
give me her arms, give me words to catch them.
In my dreams, that's when I miss her most.
Her tender breast, it was my pillow,
and not even God can
lift this devil from me:
it is my nightmare.
My dream: a wish I had: to love and be loved.
All I ever wanted was to dance
through the corridors of your delicious heart.
This rusty heart of mine,
that immaculate heart of yours,
I was so scared I'd never find."'

A tear filled his eye again, but this time the right one went as well.

Then they said almost in unison:

'I must be pretty pathetic. A scatty old man that no one except a little fourteen-year-old girl can love.'

'I must be pretty pathetic, a scatty young girl that no one except an eighty-year-old man can love.'

Maggie wrapped the scarf around their necks, and squeezed their shoulders together, hugging herself more than anything. She let go to get a good look at his face. He looked like someone who had been told the meaning of life, then forgotten it the next day, never to rediscover the secret. And every day he had to live with the torment of knowing he had found 'it', only to lose 'it'. The tufts of hair missed when shaving, just below the corners of his eyes, made him look more lost to Maggie, more confounded with this life; that he spent all his energies on prodding sticks between the whizzing spokes of his brain; all that turmoil he was too old to do anything with.

Every few seconds there was a light drip sound as tears dripped down on to the Morrison's bag filled with the teabags and milk and biscuits Maggie had bought him.

Bertrand's trying to fight his tears. He's losing.

'The fear has now hit me. What if she got married? What if everything she made me believe in stops? How can someone make you feel so much joy when everyone else is so joyless? I'm afraid I'm starting to doubt.'

Maggie realised it was her that was crying now. 'You don't have to be scared.'

'The truth is I'm scared because I think I might be going mad again. I can feel madness taking my hand and it's running me away from myself. I can see myself becoming just a dot on the horizon, and the worst part is there is nothing I can do to stop it. I'm helpless to do anything but watch it unfold in front of me, like I have no say in my own sanity! I just sit in my house all day and write about how much I loved her. It's all I do. And now even words are becoming my enemies. They're conspiring to keep us apart.'

'What's brought all this on? It's not the scarf is it? Because I can take it back...' Maggie watched him leaning round the side of the plant pot. He's not listening. He's looking at that little girl over there, talking to her doll. I used to have a doll like that, before Trish threw it out. An accident, she said. I loved that doll. It would talk back to me, sometimes. Telling me how pretty I was.

'I can feel love slipping away from me. I need my Rose back. My ever loving, bright, flowering Rose. No one can go without love like that. It doesn't matter how old you are.'

'I'm going to help you find it, I promise. Once I finish the letters, looking for clues, I'll help you find her. As long as you promise me something.'

'What's that?'

'You have to promise to keep showing me how beautiful the world is. You're all I've got.'

'You're all I've got,' Bertrand echoed back.

'Then we're even.'

He laughed at himself, 'I feel like I'm unravelling. And in such a public place.'

'I'm going to find Rose if it's the last thing I do,' Maggie promised.

'You swear?'

'I swear on my own soul.' Maggie wondered if she failed, would God really take away her soul. Would some 'soul repo' guys show up at her front door one Sunday morning when she was least expecting?

BORED SOUNDING FAT MOUSTACHIOED MAN: Soul Repo. You swear it, we collect it. Are you one Maggie Burns?

GIRL: (wiping sleep from her eyes) Yeah, that's me.
BORED SOUNDING FAT MOUSTACHIOED MAN: How old are you, miss?
GIRL: I'm fourteen. Why?
BORED SOUNDING FAT MOUSTACHIOED MAN: Just seem a little young to be losing your soul. Sorry, but we've got to do this...

A security guard bent down, leaning on his knees. 'Hey, missus, you can't sit down here. Come on, it's a beautiful day. You should be outside.'

Maggie adjusted her hood even lower and clung to Bertrand's arm until they met the blazing heat air outside.

The people with the Union Jack table were still there. One of the skinheaded men - trying to pretend he was really a respectable gentleman by wearing a suit - handed out leaflets saying Blacks and Pakis should 'go back where there from'.

Bertrand handed him back his leaflet. 'From one bald-headed man to another: you, sir, are a buffoon. They should bring back capital punishment for spelling like that.'

Maggie turned back and nodded at the skinhead to say, 'that'll-teach-you'. Bertrand's hand was trembling as Maggie took hold of it. 'I thought that man might punch me at any second there.'

'That was the right thing to do, though. My English teacher says the same thing about people like him. I liked hearing you say it.'

Bertrand took her back towards the taxi rank.

'There's just one thing from earlier that I've been wondering about.'

'And what was that?'

'When we were talking about Rose and how much you missed her. Why did you say "I think I might be going mad again?"'

7
A Love Which Knows No Beginning

There was always someone having a party on the estate. Parents would flee the coop for a night or two just to get some FUCKING PEACE AND QUIET from you little bastards! It being a Friday night, there was no shortage of places to party, and Maggie was convinced Mick J's was the best. He was 'a bucktooth fuckwit' as Jenny Spanner put it, but all the drink was free (Mick's dad was a pub landlord). Besides, Jordan Mac was going to be there with those great big green eyes of his. Maggie knew he would be looking out for her – trying to play it cool. She pictured him giving himself a little speech before he left his house – reminding himself to 'just be cool', which was easy for him. He picked out his best underwear knowing that some girl was bound to see them at some point, then he would sharpen the prongs of his fringe with a touch of 'hair sculpting wax', give himself a slap on the face, to pick himself up. This is Maggie we're talking about! The Maggie I'm In Love With. That was Maggie's ideal full name, no matter who it was coming from. I've been waiting for this since Pete D's pill party. Don't mess it up, don't be ugly, Maggie said out loud as she closed Mick J's front gate behind her, banging her fists on her legs, her own voice and Jordan's overlapping in her head.

Lovely, sweet (she didn't actually know if he was sweet, but she was sure he was because he had a lovely face and nice footballer's legs) Jordan Mac. So what if he had a reputation! People make up such horrible lies about people. No, Jordan was different. She could tell.

Only the week after Pete D's, was Lesley L's party. Maggie would replay that scene in her head as she lay in bed with the covers over her head. Bertrand's words came back, 'My dream: I wish I had'. Another spin the bottle game, same result. 'Jordan will tell me he wants me,' Maggie said, looking up at the front of the house, dance music pounding through the walls. 'Finally, tonight is the night.'

It was like Bonkers in the living room as Maggie walked in. Crazy banging fucking tunes. They all shouted, and hardhouse whistles went off like a football referee's nightmare. Or is that a referee's dream? Maggie laughed to herself in the hallway.

No one noticed Maggie as she wandered between groups, trying desperately to catch on to one of them. No one had noticed her yet. 'Hey, Jenny Spanner!' Maggie beckoned, but all she got in return was a hefty growl and an upturned gurning lip. What a boot, Jenny thought, convinced Maggie was taking the bucktooth fuckwit out of her name. She was babbling away, her mouth juddered around from the Ecstasy she had taken an hour ago. Du hear bout the study nxt dr? Get this rite Alison P n me r n Fury's rite n I wz like th@ hiv U herd bout th@ bcktooth fckwit Micks room? n she was like th@ naw av no rite n I was like th@ rite thrs ment 2 b like shitloads o porn n there bhind the bookcase like all the books r jus fake n bhind thems all pornos n wen a herd a wis like th@ ... geez anair chewin gum ma teef r mad n at ... ta ... pure mad wi it :)

Everyone in the living room was Jenny's friend, and most of them had coalesced into the middle, forming one bigger circle, all munching their gums. If only I'd brought some Wrigley's, I could have given them some, Maggie cursed herself.

So that was one room out the question to begin with, as was the study which had been appropriated by the stoners – in blissful hope that Mick would get his dad's pornos out. Maggie tried the kitchen next and found only more stoners using the sink to do buckets in. 'Here Maggie, take a hit if you want,' offered Wee Concho. Del S said Conch's dad had taken so much acid once he could only walk sideways, like a crab, for about two months. Del S was something else.

Maggie looked over at Jordan Mac and some of the other footballers who were sitting on the floor up against the dishwasher and the kitchen table, eyes red as fuck man! and each with a stupid smile on their face, none of them looking at her. Jordan nodded and raised his bottle of Miller to Maggie, whom he had mistaken for some girl that had went down on him a month ago. Maggie erupted inside, an acidic heat penetrating the surface of her skin. She wondered if he remembered her falling over in the Piazza the day before. Had he even seen her?

Then Jenny Spanner appeared behind Maggie, and Jordan led her away upstairs, the pair unsmiling, wordless. His big green eyes all over her arse.

Maggie took the adapted Irn Bru bottle (a glass one which was better, as Conch said) and held it over the sink water, lighting a little bit of bud in the holder. The smoke drained from under it, forming a tiny cloud storm inside. Then she plunged the bottle, cut off at the bottom, down under the water and the smoke rushed up to the neck which Maggie's lips were wrapped around. Nicky O – Jordan Mac's best friend - suddenly liked the look of that. He stood up, finally paying attention to her (what's her name, again?) as Maggie sucked up the smoke as hard as she could and staggered back two steps, falling into Nicky's arms.

'Whoa! OK there, spacegirl?' he glowed, sensing another easy point on the team's scoresheet. Lucky, seeing as Jordan was probably getting at least a blowjob off Jenny Spanner (is that ten points or twenty?).

Maggie looked up into those big dim eyes of his, that seemed to be looking back inside his own head rather than outward. She could feel him growing against her thigh. She just took his hand and led him upstairs, the pair unsmiling, wordless.

No one else knew, but Nicky had an unfortunate and vast catalogue of sexual encounters. The earliest being – and Nicky himself probably couldn't even remember this –the time he came home from school early, sick. Wondering where his mother was, he followed a rumbling and rattling sound coming from the basement. He peaked down from the top step to find his mother astride the washing machine going like the clappers on full spin cycle and she sounded in some sort of pain. By the time he was old enough to have realised what she was doing he had forgotten.

I have to go do some washing downstairs, Nicky.

Again? That's the third time today, mum.

The last encounter was when he had Vicky F pinned against his bedroom door, as both of them pretended they knew what they were doing. Nicky was humping away and was almost done when Vicky's unsatisfied face looked down and she said, 'Yer no in me yet.' He had been fucking the pocket of his dressing gown hanging from the door behind her.

And now Maggie dropped to her knees, drunk and stoned butterflies fluttering in her stomach, the thick pile digging into the crowns of her knees. Nicky dropped his trousers. Nicky kept gripping the back of her head. Nicky kept telling what to do and how to do it.

'Ow! You're biting it.'

'Fhoghy.'

The crease between the tops of his thighs and his arse cheeks had formed an anticipatory film of sweat, which Maggie recoiled from when she found it with her cold fingers.

Nicky was now too close to getting his hole – and another twenty points closer to Jordan and the other lads - to just spray all over the place, so he pulled out and took off Maggie's clothes like she was a mannequin. She didn't like being naked (it felt like being outside; somewhere unfamiliar) but she reminded herself what she was doing it for and set to the task at hand: lying there as perfectly still as she could. She had found through experience it was the best way to make it less painful. This was always how sex had been for her. Sexuality wasn't something innate inside her, waiting to be unlocked. It was something given to her, something someone else would inform her of, namely teenage boys, lusty. Even her – wildly premature - sex didn't feel like her own, but then she had never dreamed of her first time being perfect. She had heard through her bedroom wall late at night, into Jean and Bill's bed, what sex was all about: a man and his anger.

Maggie hadn't told Bertrand, but when he gave her the pile of Rose's letters, there was one that she remembered – entitled "Inside Sheila's Bakery".

Making love wasn't a big deal in Bertrand's eyes, back then. As a youngster he, rather unusually, hoped the whole unpleasantness could be got out the way sharpish so he could move on with his life. Once that rotten question – when did you lose your virginity? – could be answered he would deal with more pressing matters of the world. Fourteenth birthday. 'Gainst a wall in Sheila's. There wasn't much to do on a remote Scottish island like South Uist, whose only connection to the mainland at Oban was a rolling six hour ferry journey that would challenge a tin stomach. What he didn't count on was Rose's sweet little belly hopping off that ferry one day. Suddenly the question changed to when did you fall in love?:

Fifteen. After climbing to the top of Ben Kenneth one night in my dressing gown, then watching a burning ship on the ocean.

Now Bertrand found there was a whole range of possibilities opening up before him. Sex no longer seemed like a sticky mess of bodies colliding together in, as far as he could see, quite an unnatural manner. (Bodies seemed to have been designed to keep the sexual organs as far apart as possible.) To speak of such thoughts would have made his life a misery, especially on such an island where boys would be boys, and boys are cruel little sods.

Now, Bertrand's second time would change everything. Where was your second time?

In the marina shed.

He had grown bored of the unnatural act after just two goes (and Sheila was a wily old minx, demanding several satisfactions from her toy boy), in the same way a child is adamant about hating vegetables having only smelled them on their plate. With Rose, it was an altogether different story.

Bertrand wrote about how she nibbled on his ear lobe as he thrust against her in the reserve lifeboat docked in the marina shed. The bodily collision he had thought so ridiculous and unwieldy was now a beautiful coercion of two people sharing a secret, transporting it directly from one to the other without it even meeting the freezing cold air of the dock. It was indubitably, incontrovertibly, between those two, and those two alone. Rose jammied down her britches and climbed on board Bertrand who sat in the captain's seat kissing her ears. He felt hers to make into whatever she wanted, then. He was a blank sheet of music, eager to play her melodies and crashing crescendos. She fell onto him, him into her, and she spun the chair round to get a look at the outside world as they shared another secret, their body heat in the dingy old cavern steaming the windows. Rose reached for the window, pressing her hand against the condensation and dabbed it over her burning face and neck, watching two ships steam alongside each other on the sea outside. Bertrand ran his hand through her campanulate hair. They shared several more secrets, which for Rose ended up very loud indeed. So loud, in fact, they rocked the boat off its stocks, sending it sliding down the barnacled ramp, bursting out through the boathouse doors, into the shallow sea of the pier. The windows safely steamed, they just carried on, rocking with the ocean. They had to radio Rose's dad to get a trawler to tow them back.

They went back only the next day, and tried to rock each other a little gentler this time. Bertrand remained in the captain's seat watching Rose; her figure hazy through the condensation of the window, walking away sultrily after they were done, zipping up the back of her thick woollen skirt, ready to brave the storm outside. It was as she shut the boathouse door - that was the first time he felt the twitch inside his head. Like the fibres of his brain were slowly disconnecting one by one with consummate ease. He could already feel he was no longer being himself. It was unmistakeable, how easy it was to leave his insides behind and become no one, locked inside a body but with no connection to his thoughts therein. She had changed him forever. He was not there anymore.

But Elliot C was not Maggie's idea of an ideal first time. Then again, he said he loved her. 'Well, if you love me then...' Maggie had said with a pleased smile.

Elliot was a conniving little sod and had worked Maggie out. Leaving gym class one morning he heard her talking to herself: '...and then he'll take me up in his arms and carry me away...' This was a daydreamer, and Elliot (that conniving little sod!) knew it. Eventually he wrote her enough poems and sonnets (cut and pasted from a John Keats website page) to worm his way inside her and as soon as he was there, Maggie knew it was all wrong.

First of all, he didn't want to wear a johnny. 'It's fine. I'll tell you when I'm coming and you hold your breath for thirty seconds, and you won't get pregnant. Danny W told me.' Luckily Maggie insisted (it's amazing what a girl that refuses to open her legs can get away with). He was inconsiderate. As soon as he was inside her, he just banged away as fast as he could, clutching Maggie by the face. He had the same utterly vacant, blank expression on his face the whole time, and he had been drinking, so the faster and harder he went, the hotter he got. The sweat ran off the tip of his nose on to Maggie's face as he groaned in something like pleasure, which meant it was all over. Thank God. Elliot pulled out and looked down at the bloody blankets.

'Eugh,' Elliot groaned, doing up his flies. 'I'll leave you to deal with that, eh?' and walked out the room, leaving Maggie lying alone in the dark to curl up with her tartan blanket, still feeling him inside her, and she couldn't exorcise him.

This time is different, though. I can tell. Nicky was really in love with her – she was sure of it - and she felt it for him too. This wasn't going to be like all those other times that were so similar to Elliot (twelve, thirteen times? Maggie had lost count to be honest, as after each one she tried to forget about it). Before, she had used her body as a plumber tries different tools to fix a pipe. Now she had found the most optimum tool in the bag for the job.

Nicky pulled out a condom from his wallet.

'We don't need that do we?' Maggie asked.

'You serious?' Nicky was amazed at the question. 'Cool. Don't worry: I'll pull out.'

'No don't. I want to get pregnant,' she cooed, pushing herself onto him.

Nicky was too excited at not using a condom for the first time to complain. He gripped her by the side of her face and proceeded to bang away as hard and as fast as he could.

'Nicky,' she said trying to manoeuvre away from his shoulder that was pressing down on her face. 'Nicky, take it easy. Go slower. Make love to me.'

'God, you're so hot!' he moaned, thinking of Jenny Spanner.

By this point Maggie had resigned herself to losing this battle. Why was Nicky not everything she ever hoped he would be? Granted, she hadn't given it any thought whatsoever until about half an hour ago, but she had done a lot of thinking since then. She could see it all, it was going to be so easy:

Nicky, or whoever, would get her pregnant, marry her, getting down on his knee when he proposed - of course - he would be such a gentleman. He would tell her how much he loved her as soon as he woke up in the morning when one of them would roll over and initiate passionate lovemaking – because love-making in the morning was the most passionate and beautiful of all. Not that Maggie knew this from experience, but she had read about it in lots of magazines and fat women with bleached hair and talk shows would discuss it bawdily on national TV just to prove how full of love their lives were, when in actual fact all their clinging desperation to show how much experience they had of love and the 'wonderful little things' that couples do like making love in the morning, only proved the opposite. They were too busy trying to convince themselves they were happy that they forgot to ever question it.

Nicky need never question it with Maggie, though. Their marriage would be a picture of serene coupledom. The couple at parties that everyone comments how happy they look, and they giggle between themselves, as only they know they look so happy because Nicky just pulled their car over in the hard shoulder of the motorway to make love before they got there, and they would arrive at the party smelling of sex.

Nicky was quickly becoming everything in Maggie's mind. He was the Athena poster of the man holding the little baby: both brawn and nurturing. He was the valiant hero that would teach her incredible, mind boggling things about the possibilities of just two people in a room together with nothing but their desire and a locked door.

And here was the room.

With the supposed man of her dreams - whom she had been in love with for over sixteen days now – next door, shagging her nemesis. And she was stuck with his best-mate Nicky: his legs tensed out, feet dangling over the end of the tiny bed, it should have been different.

He was still banging away, prostrate. It had been four minutes and was now worried he was too drunk to come. 'God, you're so hot!' he repeated trying spur himself on.

Maggie by this point had given up so monumentally on their shady grass-induced little tête-à-tête in Mick's little brother's bedroom she started playing games with Nicky's words. I wonder if god really is hot? Jesus always seemed kind of cute to her. That long flowing hair like a lion's mane, and all those miracles. Who couldn't fall in love with that? Plus, on every crucifix she ever saw Jesus always had a raging six pack. It must have been all that farming, back in days of yore.

Maggie giggled to herself.

Nicky screwed his face up. 'Shut up. I'll be done in a second,' he said.

Oh shit. She had forgotten about him. Isn't he done yet?

Maggie tried one last time to get into it. 'So you really love me, Nicky? You do, don't you?'

'I'll be done in ... a ... SECOND,' he pulled out and finished himself off onto the Buzz Lightyear duvet. 'AAAaaahhhhh. Oooooh. Ah...' Nicky was happy. Eddie P would have to get two blowjobs AND a fuck to knock him off the top of the table now.

Maggie looked across at the toys on the shelf across the room. The 'War on Terror' Action Man caught her eye. Maybe Action Man will come and rescue me. Then she dismissed the idea. Girls don't need rescuing. 'You didn't come inside me,' she mumbled. How was she supposed to get pregnant and have a baby that would love her if Nicky didn't come inside her?

He fell on top of her, his hairless chest damp with sweat, his hairless legs untensed. 'What d'you say your name was?' Nicky asked, folding the duvet over the wet patch.

Maggie was looking around the pale blue décor of the room - the rows of stuffed animal toys lined along the skirting board, the striped wallpaper with Power Rangers border. So far away. 'Doesn't really matter,' Maggie said.

Nicky stood up and shook his penis free inside his jeans. He opened the door, letting a crack of light shine on Maggie's face, then he stopped. 'I'm away to Marisa B's party with Jordan. Let's keep this to ourselves, yeah?'

Maggie went back downstairs to find Jenny Spanner and all her crew, gone – only the stoners and strikeouts were left, the music quieter, more mellow. Maggie heard the song at the end of that Romeo and Juliet remake she liked, with all the bling guns and transvestites. It was about Juliet being brave enough to run away with Romeo, and it had the most terribly sad strumming of a guitar she had ever heard, like it had been recorded through someone's heart valve it ached so much. Maggie took a long drink from a bottle of vodka lying on the kitchen table and tried not to throw up. In walked Tommy J.

Tommy was a handsome little tramp. Never hurt a fly in his life. Or touched a girl. 'Hi, Maggie,' he said wearily, holding a bottle of Bud by the neck.

'Hi, Tommy. What's wrong with you?' she asked.

'Oh nothing. Actually, I don't know if you noticed but Jenny Spanner's left for Marisa's.'

'Yeah. Someone just told me they were going there.'

He slurped down the dregs of the Bud and immediately opened another, skidding the top across the kitchen surface like an air hockey puck. 'Ach, I have this stupid thing for Jenny Spanner. She doesn't even know I exist.'

Maggie touched his arm; they had been screwed over by the same couple. Suddenly they had something in common: the need to deal with their mutual rejection as quickly as possible, to Band-Aid the amputation. Tommy realised, with no other guys around to steal his prize he was right in there.

Maggie slurred drunkenly, 'Jenny Spanner is a stupid boot.'

Tommy smiled. 'Yeah. Yeah, she is. Fuck her!' Tommy passed her a bottle and they chinged them together in solidarity.

'You wish,' Maggie grinned, revelling in how wickedly she was flirting; a belief grew in her, that she was actually capable of being alluring.

Tommy was on top, clutching her by the face. Maggie asked him gently, 'Tommy. Can you take your hands down, please.'

Tommy, in such shock he had barely realised he was in the midst of losing his virginity, said, 'I'm sorry, Maggie,' and kissed her with concern.

Yes, Maggie thought. This is more like it. I can imagine making love to sweet-little-Tommy-who-never-hurt-a-fly-or-touched-a-girl, in the marina boathouse. Or sitting on top of him on the captain's chair.

Tommy was doing a sterling job, managing to maintain for such a long time without a condom. Maggie thought about how Bertrand would describe this if he were Tommy. We're sending that boat out to sea now.

Maggie closed her eyes and said, clutching for breath, 'Do you love me, Tommy?'

Tommy's hips slowed their rhythm. 'What?'

'Tell me you love me,' she pleaded, digging her nails into his back.

'Ow! That's fucking sore! Stop that.'

'No. Not unless you tell me you love me.'

'I don't fucking love you!' Tommy confessed, adamant, barely moving now. 'What do you think this is?'

'I want to get pregnant,' Maggie suggested, as if it were the most obvious thing on the earth. 'So people will love me.'

'What are you, some kind of psycho?'

Tommy didn't want to lose his virginity to some kind of

psycho. Even then, against his better judgment he pulled out and put his trousers back on. He could still say he had lost his virginity. He had been inside her for a few minutes at least. That counts, surely? he told himself on the way downstairs.

Maggie followed just in time to see Tommy running out the front door. He'd have to finish himself off back home in bed, but no matter, he was used to that.

The party had whittled from a grand loud party down to a mere gathering of friends, then down further to just Maggie and Mick, the bucktooth fuckwit, sitting in the study by himself, barely still awake.

Maggie swigged from her beer and startled Mick by straddling him in his chair. The breeze from Tommy opening the front door was still whistling past Mick's chair when Maggie started fumbling with his flies, pulling it out, and getting on him. She covered Mick's mouth, in case he ruined the whole thing by talking. She shut her eyes and imagined looking in through that steamy boathouse window. 'Do you love me? Tell me you love me!' Maggie cried desperately. She was now getting quite sore.

'What? No, I don't love you!' Mick said.

Maggie got off him immediately. She slapped Mick on the face so hard the momentum of her swing toppled the pair of them back into the shelves of books behind them.

'Shit!' cowered Mick, covering his head as the locked shelf door broke off, spewing dozens upon dozens of pornos out on top of them.

Mick tried to gather them up. 'Oh shit, oh shit! How am I going to explain this? This was not meant to happen.'

Maggie thought exactly the same thing as she picked her coat off the floor, and put the hood up as she met the summer night rain outside. She had failed in the modest task she had set herself for the night. She was desperate to hear something from Bertrand, something that reminded her how beautiful and wonderful life could be, but there was nothing out on the streets that night that could convince her. Not the teens in the park with all their friends, the squabbling middle-aged couple waiting on the night bus, both paralytic, in their Friday night best Topshop and Ben Sherman, yelling insults at each other, their bickering ending their night out early. Maggie sat on a wall across the street sucking a lollipop, watching them turn quiet. Not a word to say to each other anymore. They had said all they could, and now just stood a few feet apart, him lighting a cigarette then gobbing on the pavement. Maggie contemplated going to Bertrand's house when she realised it was almost midnight. No matter. She always had Rose's letters whenever she was short of belief in the world.

The car still wasn't back in the front of the house and Bill was still not in bed. There was no light on in the living room, no blue glow of Adult Channel Freeviews on the TV. Maggie hated coming in at that time because Bill would be passed out on the couch with his shirt off, his big tufty-haired belly stuck up in the air, his trouser barely reassembled around his waist, his lust hanging in the air like burnt potatoes.
She slipped the lock in the door.

Bill had been sat in the living room with the lights off since he got back from Murray Street. He held a framed photo in his hand of all the women in his life sat in that very living room several Christmases ago: Trish sitting on Jean's lap as a five-year-old, his mother with a big smile, in the single seater he was in himself now (his father deceased that summer). All the women, that is, except for Charlotte. She had never made him feel as small as he did earlier that afternoon. How furious his father would be, letting a woman treat him like that. Then he looked again at the photo - there was Maggie crawling along the floor as a toddler in her second Christmas with the family, to everyone else's complete indifference, their eyes looking somewhere else, Maggie almost out of frame altogether.

She tip-toed past, grimacing as the second stair creaked with the weight of her foot. Bill's head shot up and he quickly put the photo down. For once the pair actually looked at each other, the whites of Bill's eyes piercing through the darkness into the orange glow from the streetlight outside, drenching Maggie on the stair.

They were both too drained to broach the subject of Jean and her current location. She was in the world, in her head and out her mind, that's where she was. Out there. Dealing with it the only way she could.

Maggie paused, crouching out of the orange light for a moment on the stair, looking at him through the banister supports like prison bars. He looked away and she went upstairs without a word.

The pile of letters she had read lay on the floor beside her bed, easy enough to poke her hand out from under the sheets and grab another. The more she read the more she wished she could run away to her own deserted island. Cut adrift, at a loss, losing her way, and everyone trying their best to leave her behind. What she needed, above anything else, was to find out if Bertrand made it to that island and saved Rose from – what seemed like – a hopeless situation. The letters were a documentation of a young girl's madness. So desperate for love in a loveless world that the only thing keeping her going was finding out that her true love would make it to that island. Actually, not just to make it to that island, but to survive it. Maybe then, Maggie could start to believe again. But as she worked her way through the correspondence – the Read pile growing, the Unread dwindling – she sensed an increasing desperation in Rose's voice as well: crying out with nobody listening. If someone didn't come soon she feared that Rose's life was going to deteriorate to a place where she couldn't be saved.

She kept reading until her eyes were so heavy she was falling in microsleeps, tiny fractions of a second at a time, only capturing every third word.

I. You. Love. You. I. Bright. x.

Maggie finally realised she could no longer stay awake despite how harrowing the next letter was proving to be. The torch fell to her side and her skinny arms tired from holding the thick duvet over her head for so long, gave way. She would have to wait until morning to find out Rose's fate now that the island had descended into chaos.

She took the pillows out from under her head and shaped the two of them into the length of a body. She wrapped her legs around the Jordan-shape and held them close as she fell asleep.

8
We Shall Overcome

16th June 1943

Dear Bertrand,

'I love you. I can't make it. You would understand. x'

IS THIS REALLY ALL YOU HAVE TO SAY, BERTRAND? YOU LEAVE ME WITHOUT WORD FOR OVER A MONTH AND THIS IS ALL YOU HAVE TO SAY! AND WRITTEN ON A MATCHBOX? I COULD BARELY READ IT!

Right. I'm sorry, I had to write that down, my love. In the past weeks I have grown so temperamental – maybe it's the blazing sunshine. It's been scorching the island from dusk 'til dawn. To think of all my winter talk last time. However, mostly I stay indoors in this study, staring out the window. Having no one to yell at, I am forced to take it out on this pen and paper. I swear I have to because this damn island infuriates me so much at times, there seems nothing else to do except abuse words for my own end.

It's as if I am in some unspoken battle against this island; it's like it's conspiring against us, to somehow keep us apart. There is a copy of Margaret Leigh's novel Love the Destroyer in the study here. It had me thinking about the difference a comma can make. Love the Destroyer. Love, the destroyer.

Before the war, people back home would tell me as long as they had their health, their family, and a little bit of love they would be fine. And now they're chopping wood all day, remembering to blackout at night, and today I heard the first gunship firing. None of us could see it, but we all ran to the house and speculated. The sheep raised their heads and Baa'd in consternation. Turns out the war has reached us too.

But of love: Of course I love you I love you I love you I love you I love you I love you I love you I love you, a million times over because you make me forget myself. I would write this for as many times as I really feel it, but there is not enough ink to allow me to write just how many times I love you over. You just torment me.

About your 'note'. Why can't you go on? Where? When Colin gave me the matchbox he said you had no other message, but that Colonel Pinter was there. Is that why you didn't tell Colin what the matter was? I wondered if the army had got to you. Your stepfather is a bastard. But if it comes to it, I'll come and rescue you myself. We all had a meeting about it last night in front of the cottage. The others were all burned to a crisp having lain in the sun all day while I sat and watched them from the study, hunched over sheets of paper making a list of things we could do for you, wherever you are. It wasn't a very long list.

I thought we could radio Colin out more frequently but he's finding it harder and harder to get fuel to come out to us. Joseph suggested that your mail would still reach you if you'd been sent abroad, eventually, and if I am right, and there is even the slightest chance you could still make it, then I beg you to try. Michael says war is man's death-instinct. That we shouldn't really be surprised at how the world falls apart; there's nothing special about humans, he says. We should be amazed we all kept ourselves together this long. Now when I look out at that spot of sunlight tracking across the sea, it feels like God's eye is searching more and more randomly.

If only there were more people like you, Bertrand. My dear Bertrand. I miss saying your name. I sit here saying it aloud to myself like you're the only person I trust. But I can see your tired eyes, wherever you are.

Sadly, we all agree it's too dangerous to ask Colin to take me back to Uist to look for you, if only for his sake. You could be on an army base in Inverness or France for all the difference it makes.

Joseph chopped some firewood tonight and we sang songs, reminiscing about the old times until we all fell asleep. In the middle of the night I thought I heard Michael talking. Then I realised he wasn't asleep. He was sat outside on the front step, rolling blades of grass between his fingers and talking up to the stars. Everyone's starting to worry about him.

Around the fire, I told everyone about when we would take it in turns to sneak out of our houses to see each other in the middle of the night. Do you remember how you couldn't sleep at night, and how alone it made you feel? Then you would hear me pulling the cattle gate open, and the squeak would ring out around the croft at silent night. You would jump out of bed and meet me outside the dog kennel where mad Bruce barked like he was deranged (he was really, wasn't he?) so we would make a run for the stream at the end of your family's croft, the one that fed into the loch, before your father or mother would waken up. Then we would run around in the middle of the night: both of us in our dressing gowns, and you with your father's bunnet cap on - which was far too big for your head - and your walking stick. Sometimes I wish in all those nights I had been caught by the bobby, running down the road from my house to yours, counting the 'Passing Place' signs to keep a log of where I was (thirteen to yours). There really was nothing like the darkness of Uist.

Then the night before we were to leave for this island, you took my hand, marching me out across the peat bogs towards Ben Kenneth. I was scared to death that we would fall in the peat bog – dad was always telling me not to go out there, even in the daylight! But I let you take my hand and guide me further and further into the darkness, stepping wherever you stepped. The only sound was the squelch of the marsh from the water rising up through the peat into the soles of our boots.

It wasn't even that cold. When the clouds parted, a full moon burst open, showing the lead black outline of the hill towering over us. I stopped and said we couldn't. You didn't even hesitate and pulled us on.

Like everyone else, I had climbed Ben Kenneth a few times. The wind had been so strong at the top, I didn't even dare to stand up, and crawled through the heather to get off. Even my father, who was a brute, was almost blown off trying to stand on top of the cairn. You just smiled knowingly. Trust me, you said, it'll be worth it.

We climbed and climbed for what seemed like hours. The smell of fresh heather rose up, the night reminding me of the spectrum of its greens and purples and yellows – I could smell those colours - with every step I took, feet sinking down. I was worried that dawn would break before we even made it to the top, if we made it at all. You looked towards Lochboisdale and started running, dragging me behind. Hurry up, we'll miss it! you said.

Finally I saw the cairn, the pile of rocks that signalled the peak and the burning in my thighs subsided. Almost the entire island could be seen from there, the distant lights of kitchens filled with people having midnight drams, and ten miles or so beyond the coast, a hint of the island I find myself hidden on now. We had won. It was our way of saying that no matter what that beast of an island threw at us, we would overcome it. And how.

We sat on top of the cairn watching the moon slow-waltz across the Atlantic as the sky cleared. What are we waiting on? I asked. Just wait. Any second now, you said.

Then you pointed towards the pier at Lochboisdale. You told me how one of the fishermen's boats had taken a pounding in a storm – the mizzen-mast ripped out the deck like an uprooted tree. You told me about the tradition of setting the boat facing out to sea, locking the steering in position with a rope. Then they would set it alight and let it go free, to let the ocean have her.

You pulled me close. There it is, you whispered. You felt me shivering and pulled me closer, wrapping your hands around my stomach, my hair blowing back into your face. Beautiful isn't it? you said. She was called Marilyn.

The water was rippling, breaking up the moonlight, then the fire stretched, climbing up through the darkness, and we sat on the cairn, watching the boat float out to sea in absolute calm. Even the wind seemed to stop, just for us. The waves around the boat shimmered orange as far as we could see.

It was all this that flooded back to me, sitting there at the campfire, the flames flickering up, spitting embers out. The others started to sing 'The Dark Isle', the orange glow in their faces and Joseph's folk-singing voice crackling. I thought about how long we waited for you the next morning on the far side of Uist, but Colin just couldn't wait any longer. He told me not to worry, that he would bring you here the next day. And the days just kept passing...

We are all far too young for this. All this war. All these voices. All this madness. All this love. Why won't it just stop? I thought coming here I could forget about it; I could get away from it all, but it only makes me pine for true freedom even more. We're only twenty and I think about how much freedom we had on Ben Kenneth that night. Ours came deep from within our very souls, and we had both just turned fifteen that October.

Maybe our age is when you feel like your place in the world is in jeopardy. Nothing feels special anymore because all that magical beauty you thought was so unique when you were young is just an illusion. You know all the world's games and cheap tricks. Well, Bertrand, you showed me true beauty that night. We shall overcome.

Colin asked us the other day if we worry about whether we will be found and what our families would do to us. Especially the men, who are now officially deserters. What if the Germans land nearby and the war spreads? he asked. I say let them come. What if the Allies start to lose badly, and we have to go on knowing we never helped? Lindsay threw another log on the fire and said, 'let them lose! If we abandon each other we have lost anyway,' then Joseph kissed her on the cheek, so proud of his angel. You would never have seen me smile wider.

I'm sorry if my writing is shaky now. I've just stopped writing for an hour to run to the cliffs then to the opposite side of the island to check that indeed you are NOT sailing towards me right now.

But speaking of sailing, Michael keeps saying that he sees a navy boat sailing nearby, flashing its light towards us. I told them not to worry, that the island has long been abandoned, but he seems adamant. He worries too much. Anyway, I won't run away from fear of getting caught. Unless Colin has told someone back on Uist.

Then Emily points out that we cannot sustain ourselves here forever: eventually we will run out of supplies and Colin won't bring us fish for years to come. I've got hope - and the tartan blanket I have come to call home, and indeed is more of a home than was ever made for me back in South Uist, and also for yourself, where we tolerated such violence, from both our tyrant fathers, who felt so compelled to leave a memory of the shape of their hands against our faces - despite all we could give in to fear about. Still. Even a week is too long to wait for you. Still. We shall overcome.

I had a horrible dream that you would leave me, and so would the others, running away in the middle of the night, taking the radio with them to let me stay here, resented by the glowering limestone cliffs and the scowling grass (I swear every slanted blade curses me, perhaps because I trample their relatives day after day on my trek to the cliffs to look for your boat, or perhaps even your flailing body in the ocean).

Michael is starting to behave strangely, withdrawing even more than he has been. It came to his verse of 'The Dark Isle', and he didn't even realise, he was just smiling stupidly to himself, staring deep into the fire. He spends long periods of time by himself, sometimes disappearing for hours and hours on end. When he comes back and we ask him where he has been, he says, I've been sitting at the cliffs.

All that time? I asked.

Colin has been talking about the possibility of the army coming here soon. He says it's a question of when, but I don't know why they would bother, Joseph and Lindsay have never been happier. I wish you could have seen him toiling in the field. He put the plough over his shoulder and was trying to drag it around himself like a Shetland pony. Lindsay was rolling about in the dirt laughing at him. Joseph kept pulling and laughing, pulling and laughing, 'If it's so damn funny why don't you help?' Then Lindsay pulled him to the ground and they rubbed each other in dirt. I did a carving on the fence of them, just little stick figures holding little stick hands together. We'll just do the crops next week, I suppose.

I planned on writing more but I'm running out of ink, and Colin's boat will be here soon to take the mail to the mainland. So I have to leave you again.

Your ever loving, bright flowering Rose.

PS. You make me forget myself, and that's all I ask.

I'm just going to finish the ink that I have here. Colin can always bring more. I love you. *I love you.*

9
The Dark Isle

7th July 1943

Dear Bertrand,

So much has happened since my last letter. Colin says your croft is now deserted. The house has been abandoned and the cattle are running mad around the island, across the roads and cartways and into the middle of Lochboisdale, as the Colonel let the farmhand go to sign up for the navy. Colin said a sheep found its way into the post office the other morning. He's sent your mail for the army to forward on to you. I know you can get away.

Meanwhile, I'll run through things in reverse order of importance – which is also, rather helpfully, in chronological order starting with two weeks ago – and would appear to make more sense. Or does it? What difference does it make now? Nothing makes sense on this island anymore. God's eye has left us. He is no longer tending the lighthouse.

Michael is now barely ever in the cottage. Even in the evenings when it gets so cold. He has hardly spoken a word to us, apart from Emily, in the past two weeks; the last time must have been when he handed our letters to Colin to take to the mainland. The others were in the cottage, and I was on the fence as usual, watching them at the end of the pier, beyond earshot. Words were exchanged that seemed of much greater importance than usual. Michael was animated about something, shouting something at Colin. Then they shook hands rigorously, and hugged each other. And you know what it takes to get a man from South Uist to hug anyone.

I had no idea what was going on between them, but I was afraid Michael had made plans that the rest of us were going to end up paying for. Witnessing Michael's odd behaviour before and since, the concern for our well being grew by the hour, by the minute, by the second. At first I thought he was planning some escape for himself, but as it turns out, it's much, much worse than that.

The next day he and Emily lay in the grass all day; he was completely drunk from the whisky Colin had slipped him. They ended up arguing after he refused to tell Emily what he and Colin had discussed. He promised her everything would be even more perfect than it had been.

Emily just sat beside him, picking daisies while Michael wandered off, breaking sticks in half, then again, then again, until they could no longer be snapped. Then he got another stick and repeated this all afternoon. He's been sleeping outside in front of the cottage, which Emily has reluctantly been too. I watched them from the study window last night; she sat up and stroked his face as he mumbled things in his sleep. He eats in complete silence, standing up, looking out the window with his back to the rest of us – we all let him be: we knew he had never been away from home for so long. He hadn't even left the island before, unlike the rest of us, who have at least seen the mainland. Sometimes he cries in his sleep, saying that his father is coming to get him. He'll look out to the ocean - which is completely empty - and point at imaginary navy boats he says his father is on, looking for him, ready to beat him.

Then round the fire last night as we asked why Colin hadn't been that day, Michael told us, 'Everything is so perfect here. I don't ever want to leave. I was speaking to one of the sheep about it today.'

Joseph cleared his throat, realising the onus as his best friend, and said, 'We all need to know what you and Colin were discussing yesterday, Michael. Why didn't he come today?'

He said that everything was taken care of now. That we didn't have to worry about Colin getting caught coming to the island. That he had shown him an advert in one of the Uist papers his father had taken out, offering a reward if anyone had information on where he was. That the islanders were starting to whisper about where he was going, even that someone saw him leave Lochboisdale with a slaughtered cow onboard for us and came back without it. 'He thinks someone is going to follow him one day and track us. I can't risk my father finding out where I am. I won't live with it anymore. So, I've asked Colin not to come back. It's the only thing to do. He can't support himself, just coming back and forth for us all the time, giving us his fish - and what if people find out what he's been doing for us? And if my father finds out, it doesn't bear thinking about. This way we'll all be a lot safer. I promise.'

We all went mad. How could you do this without asking first? and You can't be so scared of your father like this! It's not right.

He said circumstances had changed. He said he finally understood what love was - like the time Emily and him made love up a tree because she said she wanted to feel closer to God, and after they were done she said she never felt the need to do it up a tree again. 'I'm no theologian, and can't pretend to know what God is. I have a sneaking suspicion, though, that it's inside you.'

How he loved the red tinges at the top of her ears when she got embarrassed; the crevice under her ankle bone; the way she sometimes ran her tongue across his teeth when they kissed; the way she groaned when he ran his tongue around her ear; the way she yawned; the way she would slow down her walking pace if she was passing an old man just so he wouldn't feel quite so ancient and decrepit and like the entire world was rushing past him at one thousand miles an hour; the way she loved her little brothers, lining them up in a row in front of her at Christmas time and kissing all six of them one at a time on the forehead to let them know she loved them just as equally as each other.

Emily had reminded him how they had been the only thing that stopped all the pain his father made him feel, calling him a wimp all his life. We could all see in his eyes: Michael was gone. He kept saying how he understood what love was now. How it was the meaning of life, and now that he had found it, he realised it wasn't enough. He had been playing a game looking for infinities, and now that he had discovered that 'love has a ceiling' he couldn't go on. He understood life. He understood love: He had truly gone mad.

He walked off towards the cliffs. Emily told us she would talk to him and sort everything out. They still had a radio for Colin and he would come back if they asked. So she ran after him, and he smiled in surprise like he hadn't seen her in weeks, putting his arm around her, and shouting out towards the ocean, 'You see, you couldn't stop us getting here! You lousy, pathetic, puny waves!' Emily dropped her head on his shoulder and rubbed his back in consolation.

We had an emergency meeting, leaving them alone for a while for Emily to make him see sense. We talked about convincing Colin, if he came back, to take Michael to the mainland - that the isolation wasn't helping him, that he was just going to get worse out here. 'We have to do something!' Lindsay yelled. I had never seen her so angry. It was maybe harder for her and Joseph being now the only couple on the island when there should have been three. Somehow our dream was falling apart. The only person, apart from my Nicholas in London, that knew that this island wasn't abandoned, had been told never to come back. All our supplies cut off in one fell – mad - swoop.

What was discovered in the morning, and the actions of certain people that followed, made a mockery of any possible solutions we might have concocted the night before.

Joseph was stood against the barn door smoking a cigarette, when he saw Colin's boat slowly approaching. Lindsay jumped off the fence next to me and tapped me on the shoulder, to look at what was coming towards the pier. 'Colin's coming. Look.'

I put down my knife and stopped carving. 'He's going awful fast, isn't he?'

'He's going to go right through it.'

I paused. 'Wait a minute. That's not Colin's boat.'

It crashed straight through the pier, and, right enough, it wasn't Colin's boat. His was painted red and white and had a mast. This boat was brown, completely burnt, actually. Joseph was first to run down to inspect it – Lindsay and I followed.

Joseph touched the body. 'This boat's been set alight. It's a miracle it got here. From Lochboisdale, no doubt.'

I looked closer at the side, and could just about make out the name on the scorched wood: Marilyn. I shut my eyes and realised you had sent me a sign. To let me know you were coming – like the waves crashing into the cliffs, you'll keep coming back for me. I didn't tell the others where it had come from, they knew what Uist fishermen did with old boats.

'And I thought Colin had come back,' Joseph commiserated. 'Come on, I'll get the radio from Michael. He had it last.'

'What time did they finally come in at last night?' I asked.

We each looked at each other in confusion.

'I thought you went to get her?'

'Me? What about you!'

I ran to the cottage to check but there was nothing, and each of their belongings were as they were the night before. Lindsay checked the barn, and we met in the field with shrugged shoulders.

'The radio's definitely gone,' I said.

That's when we heard Joseph shouting from the top of the cliffs, waving us towards him. He had spotted something, or, at least, some body.

I think we both knew what we were going to find when we got there, because Joseph stopped Lindsay from looking over the edge. If she had looked, she would have seen two bodies lying in the shallow waters, side by side, Michael's arm still draped over Emily's back as the waves crashed over them.

We were all catatonic. Joseph kneeled down and hugged Lindsay's legs. She just stared out to sea.

'What's going on, Joseph?' she asked, as if in a sleep-state.

In the end, the isolation must have got the better of them. It was the only way they could truly be together forever without Michael's father's interference. The thing that really turned my stomach was imagining Michael trying to convince Emily to go through with it, because she wouldn't have thrown herself over easily. At least their final act had been one done together.

Lindsay suddenly emerged as the leader: 'We should go down and pull them out before the tide comes in.' It seemed so practical; it was another job to be done on another day on the island, like sweeping the barn.

When we got down, the waves lapping around our feet, their faces were blue as the freezing water. We managed to pull them to the shore, and went through their pockets to find the radio. It was in Michael's pocket alright, but smashed to pieces. A note had barely survived from the water. From what could still be made out, it was a suicide note, written in both their handwriting, which at least did us the favour of not having to debate whether Michael had simply dragged Emily over the edge. It spoke of how it was the only way they could be sure we would all be safe. Emily's part said the radio could be found safely in the cottage kitchen, but Michael's part (which was written below Emily's) said that he had taken it with him because he didn't want to risk us calling someone, and his father finding his body. He repeated it was the only way to be sure. The rest was indistinct or smudged from the water, but many Xs were at the bottom of the paper. So much love in death.

And that is where you find me now. Helpless, even if I scream my loudest. Too far from Uist to swim, and nothing to do but bury our best friends, which we did, behind the barn, surrounded by our few remaining sheep.

Given the events I have documented above, I don't expect this letter to find you. Still. If anything I write it for my own comfort. I also know that it will change nothing of what has happened but what else can I do with these feelings of melancholy when I should be joyful and exuberant with you, my love? Maybe by writing these things I learn a little more about myself. Also, if I don't write these words then when they discover my body they will have no idea of what took place here.

Once, you told me an old Uist saying. 'Fast runs the slattern's husband on the machair of Uist.' How you need more than warm clothes to make it here: you need a robust heart. And if you no longer have either warm clothes or a robust heart, then you must run to keep warm. That's what my love is now. Cold and tired. But still somehow ready to run.

Still. My only wish is that I could have died as happily as Michael and Emily did.

I now know I will never get off this island.

10
Dear Diary

20th June 2005

Of course, I wasn't always called Maggie. There was a long time when I was in my mum's stomach that I was called It. Maybe that would have been better for me because any time I filled out a form with my name on it, it would take less time. I only sign things 'Maggie' now. When I think about how many times I have had to write my full name down on pieces of paper ...
It's a lot.

I never knew my real mum and she never knew me, her real daughter. But if she thought of me as a real daughter then she wouldn't have passed me over to the people who wear navy suits, chew the end of biro pens, have greasy hair and work in the hospital. Their job is to take children away from their parents.

I never got a chance to ask my real mum why she got rid of me, or if she thought she didn't want me then why did she shag whoever my dad was? 'Cos of the smack,' Bill says. Apparently she was very young when she had me. Only a few years older than me. I'll be fifteen in October, though. I can't wait. I want a baby just like she did. And I don't want a sausage supper for tea again tonight.

Once I got taken to the Burns' house there were plans afoot to change me. Bill being the lazy son-of-a-bitch that he is, called the Registry Office to try and change my name, because he hated Rod Stewart (fucking poof! he said) and his song about Maggie May. My English teacher says it's a great song about loss of innocence or something, and asked if that was what I had been named after. I didn't know. Anyway, he ditched the whole idea when he realised he'd have to pay the £10.50 to change it. It was the nurse that looked after me that choose my name. My real mum never got round to it. I met the nurse last year. She was lovely, with red cheeks like Mary Poppins. I asked if I could fly away with her but she said sadly no. She told me I had an irregular heartbeat when I was born, 'a speckled heart' she called it, as if my body wasn't ready for the big wide world. Then one day the x-rays went clear and the tests were fine. I'm glad I'll always have the same heart, I said.

My favourite class is English this year because the teacher lets us use our imaginations, unlike our crummy maths teacher, Mr Wilson, who doesn't. Once he asked the class what Pythagoras' theorem was. I said it was an equation that said if you take away the amount of times in your life you have cried because you are sad, from the amount of times you have cried because you are happy and you get a positive number, then you are as happy as an old Greek man called Pythagoras who was most famous for being the happiest person in the world. The history books (which are totally huge. Bertrand has some of them on the floor in his house) says he lived from 580-500 BC. BC stands for Before Crying, so Pythagoras was definitely the happiest man in the world. Or maybe it was Began Crying, so Pythagoras was definitely the saddest man in the world. I know which I am. Mr Wilson tried to stop me at this point but I carried on anyway. Pythagoras' theorem said as you get older the more likely you are to end up with a negative number. After I was done I swore I saw Bertrand in one of the empty desks at the front of the class turn round and smile at me and then he was gone again. Mr Wilson said that wasn't exactly what we were looking for, Maggie. Don't I get a gold star anyway? I asked, and that led to an argument.

But in English class you can do anything! OK, children. I want you to imagine you are a flower looking up at the sun and you have to write a poem about what it is like having clumsy people trampling over all your friends. Bertrand is always a good help when it comes to things like these. I put my hand up and whispered to her, What if you only have one friend? Can I make him as big as a tree? Bertrand would prefer that.

Anyway, to get back to my real mum. It's hard to feel anything for someone you have never met. She might have been lovely, she might have been horrible. That's why I don't understand people in churches who pray to someone they've never met. What if he was actually not a very nice person? I asked the school chaplain once. What if you pray and something bad happens to you and someone who doesn't pray has lots of good things happen to them like Jenny Spanner and her happy mum with that cool Burberry jacket I wanted for xmas. What if you think god is an idiot with a tiny dick. I wasn't allowed back in the chapel at lunchtimes after that. Which was a pain because that meant I had to go outside and hide from the people who call me names. Before, the chaplain asked me why I had stopped praying, considering I seemed to enjoy talking to myself so much. I get the answers I want that way, I said.

I suppose I should say why I have started to keep a diary

then, in case I forget later. Ten days ago, my sister Trish was knocked over by a car. She didn't see it coming. Or maybe she did. People always say that. But how do they know unless they shout out, Oh my god, I can't see that thing coming towards me!? But that would mean they had seen it coming, and the other person is a liar. Anyway, she just ran right out. Was I chasing her? Yes. Do I feel guilty? Yes. Is there anything I can do about it now? Yes. I can find Rose for Bertrand and maybe I won't feel so crumby about this world. Bertrand tries but it's not always enough. If it works out, I can die with a big positive Pythagoras number. I can't remember every time I've cried, so I'll start my number from zero. Starting ... NOW!

I've just finished another letter from Rose, from the pile Bertrand gave me. −1. That didn't really count. For real this time. Starting now! I have to ask him and find out what happens. But the thought has just entered my mind. What if Rose never made it off that island?

I can't sleep at night for thinking about 4th October 1981. What am I meant to read? Surely the person will write back.

25th June 2005

I have lost 2.37 days because my name is Maggie and not It. But unfortunately I have wasted 4.78 days trying to work that out. There is never enough time.
−1.

11
There is no cloud/Memorial

Jean had now been sleeping in the Belmont for five days. She had grown used to the feeling of the plastic interior on her bare feet at night (they threw the floor mat out after Maggie threw up on it once). The horns of angry men in white vans would waken her first thing in the morning, when the light was still a hazy blue, like the sun couldn't quite bear to illuminate the angry landscape. The first thing Jean would do was crack the window down and light a cigarette. It was handy now living across from the 'Fags and Mags'. She would never run out of fags. Or mags. Her legs were always stiff, and no matter how used she was getting to bending them a certain way to get the optimum amount of space for herself, when she did walk around the memorial site it was like she was having to learn how to walk all over again. It was strange feeling one leg following the other.

The worst days were rainy ones, because all she could do was sit in the car and watch for people trying to take away the flowers. If the rain was heavy it was difficult to see out the windows sometimes, and she couldn't turn on the windscreen wipers, as it would run down the battery of the car seeing as she was driving nowhere for days at a time.

There was never any respite. It was at night that the memorial was most under threat, from rampaging drunkards and thugs. Trying to get some sleep around such carnage was almost impossible. And she was never sleepy anyway. She wasn't doing anything except sitting and waiting. That didn't make her job any less important in her eyes. Actually, it was a test of endurance for her, and she swore she wouldn't let this one go. This was about more than boredom.

Every third or fourth day, depending how busy the street was, she would drive back to the house for a quick wash while Bill was at work and Maggie was at school. Not that Maggie went every day. Sometimes Jean would run inside to see Maggie through the frosted glass of the living room door reading pieces of paper on the floor - sheets and sheets of paper laid out, covering every inch of the shagpile carpet. The two would look at each other, their warbled body shapes exchanging silent dialogue: if you don't tell, neither will I.

Every second that Jean took undressing, working the soap into a lather, she imagined a group of people in dark sunglasses jumping out from behind the bushes and quickly sweeping away all traces of the accident: the last proof that her daughter had indeed walked the earth for the past seventeen years. She simply had to wash her hair because the itch in her scalp would get beyond unbearable by the fourth day. She emptied some shampoo in her palms, the bare minimum she could get her hair clean with. 'If I don't get my hair rinsed and out this shower in fifteen seconds, everyone in the world will die,' she said out loud, hoping that saying it would make her believe it more. She was still rinsing the cold water from her hair on her way downstairs. It had taken thirteen seconds. She was jubilant. She had saved the world! yet no one would ever know it except herself.

She burst out the bathroom, running headlong into Maggie on the staircase.

'Jean,' Maggie said blankly. 'I was just going to my room to leave you in peace. When are you coming home?'

She barged past to check the drinks cabinet. Bill still bought her usual bottle of gin and left it there for her. He knew she was coming back when he wasn't there and taking it away with her.

Maggie remained halfway up the stairs. 'Jean?'

'I don't have time,' she would say opening the front door. 'I have to get back to Trish. Your dad knows where I am.'

'He's not my dad!' Maggie shouted as the front door slammed.

Jean rolled down all the windows to help dry her hair. The air was warm against her wet face, rallying back to Murray Street. Got to get back in time, Got to get back in time, she said constantly, banging the steering wheel impatiently, waiting for the lights to change. If I don't make it across the bridge in twenty seconds then I've not been a good mother. This was enough to make her foot suddenly stamp on the accelerator, the car lunging through the red light to a barrage of car horns and waved fists and dropped Poundshop bags by crossing pedestrians. I'm sorry, but I just can't be a bad mother. I can't be a bad mother. She checked the clock on the dash. She had five seconds to cross the bridge. On the other side, on Murray Street, all the flowers and teddy bears were still there, still tied to the railing and on the pavement, just as she had left them seventeen and a half minutes earlier. In fact someone had now written in chalk on the wall, 'WE MISS YOU'. Mistaking the message for herself and not Trish, the relief of someone apparently acknowledging her atonement was enough to make her rest her head against the steering wheel.

The remainder of the day was slow. She was having trouble finding enough containers of water to keep the abundance of flowers in. Too scared to waste time at home filling endless empty bottles of Asda cola, she got what make-shift vases she could, and crammed all the flowers that would fit inside. Most of the flowers being cheap from the Texaco garage down the road, they were already starting to wilt. The recent heavy rain helped, but not much.

Also she couldn't prevent the teddy bears getting dirty. They were only a pavement's width away from one of the town's busiest roads. Some had come with play outfits, like Policeman Bear and Doctor Bear, and now those uniforms were starting to become solidly black. There wasn't any time for her to take them home and put them in the washing machine. That would take hours, and God knows what would be left when she came back.

She lit another cigarette and rested her head against the window, the heat from her temple slowly blossoming a cloud on the glass. When would Rick come back? she wondered. She looked to the side out the window, and noticed the rain slowly washing away the chalk sign that had been written on the wall just a few hours before. There were some things Jean couldn't stop from fading away.

As long as the flowers and teddy bears remained, she could be sure she had done what she could, even if that meant sitting in a rusting Belmont all day. She had to do it for her daughter. She couldn't be a bad mother any longer.

It was about five months into the pregnancy that Jean had started feeling something she couldn't describe, close to a terrible hangover after a big night out, and as the memories of what you'd done seeped back into your brain banks, the full horror made itself known. Jean didn't know what she had done, but the feeling was there.

Cashiers at the supermarket would give her and her belly a knowing glance and pursed lips, the pursed lips of assumption that everything in your life is good because you're expecting. Jean never understood the term 'expecting'. What am I expecting? Anyone else might have pondered, What's happening to me, exactly? What are these feelings of darkness taking over me? But all she told herself was, 'No, no, there is no cloud, remember...'

'Which one, Jean?' Mary pondered, holding up a pink all-in-one outfit, Tina holding a lime green one. The two argued about what one would look best.

'Don't be daft,' Tina exclaimed. 'She doesn't want that tacky wee thing.'

'What you calling tacky?' Mary belted back, as if she herself had been insulted. 'You'd need to be mad to put that on a wee one.'

'It's called class, Mary, fucking try it sometime...'

'Any of them's fine,' said Jean, staring blankly out the shop window, in her peripheral vision and hearing: all the love and devotion the other women in the shop were showing the bumps in their stomach or tiny frog-like babies in their prams, the metal spokes sparkling fresh. And the other mothers with their glossy hair, gleaming nails, and Marks and Spencer clothes. They looked well rested; looked after at home. They were actually enjoying their whole pregnancy experience, taking it on like some travel writing project, the sort of thing that people claim to have been changed spiritually by at the end.

She looked at herself: the unmatching trackie bottoms and top, and her filthy trainers; greasy hair scraped back into the same beleaguered, out-of-ideas ponytail every day; she saw their smiling faces and wondered how they could possibly be enjoying all this? Cutting back on smokes and cutting back on booze. And why were all their husbands with them, leafing through the racks of clothes and activity centres and twinkly music mobiles, and showering their woman with hugs for no apparent reason? Why weren't they at home, drinking, or out with the boys, like Bill?

It could best be described as a black cloud that covered the sky when Jean went outside, and no one else could see the cloud except her; she put her Mothercare bags down to point skywards, asking Mary and Tina, 'Don't you see it?' They couldn't see anything except a sky that looked quite normal to them. Normally black. There is no cloud.

Jean would lay in the bath, looking down at her swelling belly, feeling the warmth of the water slowly fade until she was all goosebumps. Fat little Jean from Murray Street. She couldn't understand how she could feel so far from something that was actually growing inside of her. It didn't matter about the umbilical cord that kept the baby alive in her stomach, with the food that she put in her mouth. That was no real link. Connecting things merely through tissue wasn't enough for Jean. That was what Bill never understood about pregnancy. She tried to explain it to him but her inability to articulate what she was feeling only drove them further apart. His father asked him if he had tried giving her a quick slap. 'IT WORKED ON YER MAW,' he cackled from his care home bed. 'I know,'

Bill said. 'I heard. I saw. I remember.'

Bill tried pretty hard to convince her to speak. Sometimes convincing her until her eyes were black. The poor bastard couldn't even get a hard-on from her anymore. What a Selfish Fat Cow.

As the months went on Jean convinced herself the feelings would pass because she realised how impossible it was not to feel love for your unborn child. No one does that, she thought. It's just not possible, is it? Only a wicked mother would think such a thing.

The idea would cross her mind and she would try to pretend it hadn't happened. She had done the same thing, feeling guilty for lusting after certain boys when she was young. I can't think things like that, she thought. But she did.

Bill was annoyed at these, what he called, attempts for attention. ALWAYS PISSING AND MOANING. WHAT THE FUCK'S SHE ALWAYS SO PISSED OFF ABOUT? YOU'RE PREGNANT AREN'T YOU? YOU TOLD ME THAT'S WHAT YOU WANTED. HAVEN'T I DONE ENOUGH?

Yes, yes you have.

Jean couldn't hide her resentment for Bill any longer. After all, it was his bastard seed, his desperate humping, that had put that thing in there. Now it was her that had to deal with it.

Five months turned to eight, eight turned to nine, and nine turned to nine and a half. The doctor decided to bring her into the hospital. Jean didn't want to. She was happy to put up with the bump for the rest of her life, as long as it just stayed in there and never came out to impress upon her life anymore; that was all that she asked. Every fibre in her body strained to keep that baby in there. After nine hours in labour she couldn't hold it back any longer and baby Trish was finally born. She wept as the baby came out.

Look how happy she is, the nurses said. She's crying.

There was no going back. For months and months she and Bill had tried for a baby. It was the only thing in the world that meant something to her. Something for her to devote herself to - instead of cooking and cleaning all day long. A way she could show just how much love she had to give. It wasn't meant to be this way. She didn't deserve to have all that hope taken away from her, she thought.

Jean wept as she held Trish in her arms. When Bill told her to stop being so emotional, the nurses looked at each other in amazement. Another amazing tale for the staff room.

It was in the months after, Bill started spending more

and more time at the garage, frittering away his time on cars that he knew would never run again. He changed gear boxes, transmissions, winch out entire engines and rebuild them, working late enough into the night that he could be certain Jean wouldn't be awake when he got home. His hands would ache and blister from all the work. He would tidy up and get to the door, ready to go home, when the thought of seeing Jean still sitting at the kitchen table just as he left her in the morning (except the bottle of gin would stand empty now) staring at the free calendar the butcher's sent them every year (every day a colossal push through the thick black line into the next numbered box) was too much to bear. He switched the lights back off and watched TV, turning the volume up. He couldn't take any more monosyllabic answers. How was your day? Fine. How's Trish doing? Fine. What's for dinner? Fine. He felt so cheated. She said she would stop complaining. It was a violation of the whole agreement. He tried to convince her to speak again - for quite a few hours. He tried so hard, Mary and Tina couldn't see Jean the next day. She was EXHAUSTED from all the convincing.

When her face was better, Tina and Mary took her out shopping on a Tuesday. Jean always dreaded that day most. Having a tiny baby in a pram seemed to give strangers licence to do whatever came into their stupid little heads.

'Aw! Look how cute,' they would tremble, touching Trish on the chin which made her giggle.

'It's just a baby,' Jean pointed out, looking away with utter disdain. 'You can have it if it's so cute.' She didn't so much walk with the pram as appear to be driving it away from her.

She would spend most of the day sitting at the kitchen table as Trish bawled next door in the living room in front of Richard and Judy on the TV. Only when the weather man who hopped around the floating British Isles was on did Trish stop to gurgle her first laughs. But the sound of laughter did nothing to clear her black cloud. The endless back and forth of the hand to the bottle; the tipping; the constant awareness of how long it's been since your last mouthful and that to raise the pace this early in the a.m. would be foolish. Somewhere into the third of fourth glass, the cloud would break, and she could safely repeat 'There is no cloud' and believe it, because she had gotten rid of it. That was what her day, every day, was always about: a constant, never-ending examination of her state of mind and mood; a sizing up of where she was, and how to get out. As the drunkenness came, so did the self-loathing. Jean didn't understand how people could go out on the drink and "have a good time". Booze was always there to get something out; to commiserate with herself. She'd turn on music that moved her, usually something with banal lyrics and basic chord progressions, minor ones usually pinged her heart just the way she liked it, normally Bryan Adams ballads. She needed something that got right to the heart of things.

One day as she sat smoking endless cigarettes, tapping her leg in the air, staring at the mantelpiece filled with greetings cards, the words became too much. She resented them. Stupid words that make you feel and do stupid things. 'Congratulations! IT'S A GIRL!'

Jean thought she was going to choke to death on her tears – they just heaved through her chest like bags of heavy groceries. She swiped the cards off and sat down next to the baby, sitting in its carrier, facing the TV. Jean was holding a small white pillow with the words 'Trish' stitched in it. It wouldn't feel a thing, she told herself. And neither would she. The silence of the whole thing would make it easier.

Her fingers trembled as she slowly brought the pillow closer to baby Trish's face, then the theme song for the weather came on the TV. Trish let out a gurgling laugh. Jean froze. If someone walked into the room there would have been no way possible of explaining what she was doing in such a position. It looked like she was about to smother her child because that's what was actually going on. She dropped the pillow. She couldn't believe she had gone so far. But it would just be another trauma queuing, taxiing up behind her psyche. She thought it would make it easier. It was her that never got any sleep; it was her that had to change Trish in the middle of the night, staggering out of bed, right in the vortex of her hangover (the curse of morning-into-afternoon drinking: the night-time hangover and the failure of sleep); it was her that had to fend off prying strangers' fingers; it was her that understood just because you have a baby, you don't automatically feel love for it: how can you feel love for something when you've only ever felt love once in your whole life, and that was standing in a playground when you're fifteen years old, just skinny little Jean from Murray Street?

Now there was a different kind of black cloud hanging over her. One, much less dense than the last, but deceptively more destructive: Guilt.

This one didn't make her outwardly depressed. Instead she learned to hide what she was feeling, burying it deep down inside her, ready to explode one evening as she watched East-

Enders, poor Tiff getting killed off. That was when all the stored up years of guilt came sweeping back to flip her life upside down again. If she was such a good mother she would have known where Trish was that day. She would have raised her to cross the road properly. But she never did. She was too busy smoking cigarettes and sitting at that goddamn kitchen table twitching her leg, spilling gin on the goddamn lino. She passed the best years of Trish's life at that table, looking through to the living room. Her entire life was marked by what she heard Trish watching on TV as she grew up, the sudden rise in volume as the adverts came on. She drank faster whenever she thought of Trish one day looking her in the eye and telling her, I know what you were going to do to me that day.

A feeling compelled her to get up off the sofa and show her daughter just how much she loved her. How much she had always really loved her; she was going to do it right away. Just after this drink. Just after I've defrosted something for dinner. Just after just after just after...

She was tired of Bill trying to convince her to explain herself. Why did she have to explain anything she did anymore? No one would understand because no one knew what she had been going through. Her libido was nil and yet that seemed all like Bill wanted to tap in to: Jean lay there with no expression as they had I-Don't-Really-Love-You Sex. The worst kind. He humped away vacantly, picturing all the women he had wanted to fuck that day – the only way he could get hard for a few minutes.

For two years he humped away vacantly. For two years Jean waited for EastEnders to come on. Trish was growing up fast and her love for her started to grow. She couldn't believe what she had been like through the pregnancy with her. She was going to have another kid, and show everyone how much love she had to give – she could love, not just one, but two kids! But the more she thought about it the more she couldn't face another pregnancy. She heard about post-natal depression on This Morning with Richard and Judy one day and she couldn't wait for Bill to come home from work. It was a revelation for her, finally what she had had been given a name. It was no longer just in her head. She went to the doctor who confirmed she had post-natal depression, but also Mrs Burns, what are these marks on your arms? Are these from a razor blade? Did you do these yourself, Mrs Burns?

Christ. If she knew there'd be so many fucking questions she'd never have gone.

Bill called it hokum and said to lay off the gin for a

while. Night and day she pestered him, though, that she was ready for another. Only this time they would have to adopt. If she got pregnant, she'd have to stop drinking. So they adopted Maggie from her teenage mother who was never heard from again. It's for the best, the people who wore navy suits, chewed the end of biro pens, had greasy hair and worked in the hospital, said as they signed the papers.

Jean rewarded herself with a little drink every day that she was a good mother to Trish and Maggie. She deserved it, she thought.

Now watching the rain coming down, Jean took another swig from the bottle of gin. She was being a good mother, she said. She would maintain the loving memorial Trish's family and friends had built for her on the corner of Murray Street. As long as I don't let anyone take this memorial away, then I've been a good mother. The day went on and on and the rain became unrelenting. The bottle of gin was nearly done and Jean fell into a deep sleep.

She was back in school. Her and her friends were round the back of the PE block smoking cigarettes. They flicked the butts at the first years as they went past, the stupid geeks with their perfect uniforms. They've even got blazers. One said to Jean, 'Just cos your parents can't afford them,' then laughed with all of her friends before running away.

Jean stepped forward and tried to flick her fag at them like the others had but got it horribly wrong, the butt hitting Kathy F in the face. She lunged for Jean, the stupid cunt, and they scrapped like wild animals. The others joined in. 'Skinny little Jean from Murray Street's a tart!' they sang.

A crowd gathered round the fight and cheered the girls on. Then a boy stepped forward and broke them up, much to the annoyance of everyone else, enjoying the scrap. The girls walked off, fucking bored now.

The boy asked, 'You alright? It's Jean isn't it?'

She was mesmerised. His hair was slicked back, and his face so strong and masculine thanks to extraordinary cheekbones. He was holding a mucky football under his arm – he doesn't even care if he gets his shirt messed up! - and it was the sexiest thing skinny Jean from Murray Street had ever seen. 'Yeah, that's me,' she whimpered as he dropped the ball to take her hand. Time seemed to stop for Jean, his smile spreading wide. Then as quickly as he found her, he let her go and ran back to the pitches. She didn't even find out his name, but she waited by the school gates every day in case she saw him; he never appeared.

There didn't seem to be any explanation, except maybe that he was off sick. Once, Trish was off primary school for a whole month and a half with whooping cough. It had been nearly a month since she had seen him, so Jean kept waiting at the gates for six more weeks, just in case that was what her hero had. But soon after she moved schools and never saw him again. She was so upset she refused to come out her room for a week, lying in bed, and during this time discovered masturbation by mistake.

Then one night, her parents away out for a chippie - as she lay on the sofa cursing the world for making her so unhappy - a black and white film came on with an American actor playing someone called Rick. He was so dashing, but most of all he looked just like her hero. Of course Rick was older than him, but the sculpture of the face was just like how his would turn out, she could see him growing old, turning in to Rick. And that brooding morality of doing the right thing no matter what the cost didn't hurt. So chivalrous. Jean couldn't take her eyes from the screen even after the credits rolled. She was spellbound, and from then on her hero's name was etched into her brain forever. Rick Blaine. The man in the white dinner jacket.

A policeman rapped on the driver's window. 'Can you roll down your window, please?'

Jean was drunk. 'What's the matter?'

The policeman took a good look around inside the car, recoiling from the smell of stale alcohol, and fags. 'Are you alright in there?'

'I'm fine. Why?'

'You're going to have to move your car.'

'I'm not on a yellow line.'

The policeman paused, then repeated. 'You're going to have to move your car.'

'I don't have to do anything,' Jean said, her foot kicking the empty gin bottle on the floor.

The policeman clocked it. 'Have you been doing some drinking today?'

'I've not been driving. Just leave me alone. You can't arrest someone for living in a car.'

'That's right, madam. But my colleague reported this car in a disturbance here last week. You've been here in this car since last week?'

'S'right.'

He paused again. 'Do you have somewhere you can go?'

'Officer, I can't see the flowers very well from in the car here. How do they look? They don't look brown or wilting, do they?' Her eyelids were fighting to stay up, both with different levels of effort and success.

The policeman looked at the pathetic sight of the bunches tied crudely to the railing with moulding-green string. The pounding rain and wind had left them in tatters. The bears were filthy, after cars splashed the dirt and rainwater all over them. 'They look ... ok, I suppose. I don't really know much about flowers.'

'They've got to stay nice and bright. And flowering, like my Trish.'

The policeman now realised who Jean was and couldn't help looking pitifully at her. 'And you're sure you're alright, Mrs Burns?'

Jean rolled the window up.

12
The Polonaise

Maggie was due to receive a certificate at her school's inaugural end of term Award Ceremony, in recognition for her work in English and Music classes over the term. All year she had been striving to write as many short stories as she could to impress Miss Gray, her doting teacher. She encouraged Maggie to write whatever she thought she could manage, but never expected her to be quite so precocious. Throughout the year she had already read and wrote essays on The English Patient, A Room with a View, and Empire of the Sun.

As for the music class, Maggie's prize was more down to rather pitied practices by herself during lunchtimes, after the chaplain stopped letting her hide in the Oratory Room.

Miss Gray worried about her like she was her own child, always asking how things were at home. 'Beautiful,' Maggie said, dropping the 't', with a smile. She was pleased with herself. She had been practicing that smile in front the mirror before going to bed.

With Bill at the workshop and Jean stuck in Murray Street, Maggie invited Bertrand as her 'relative/guardian – delete as appropriate' to attend. What she had really wanted, though, was Bill and Jean there to see her collect her certificate, so they would realise she wasn't useless. They were both too busy.

In a way, having Bertrand there was better for Maggie. He would understand the meaning of the piano piece she had been asked to play. In fact it was him that recommended The Polonaise by Chopin. She had been practicing every lunchtime and after school on many occasions to make sure she was ready. No matter how hard she tried though, her long skinny fingers, which should have been perfect for a pianist, just couldn't get the fingering correct the whole way through. She worried that under the pressure she would crack and slip ugly, nasty phrasing in and ruin her chance to shine. Plus, the only reason Maggie was allowed to play the piano was because no one else could, but the headmaster was determined someone would perform at the piano to impress the council representatives who were there to see how well he had improved the school, if at all, from the dingy backwater slum it had been for years. The school was still a tip, but if he could raise the profile with some classy performances, then maybe they would up his funding for the next few years. Either way, it was down to Maggie to perform.

Backstage, Maggie rehearsed the movement of every finger, drumming her fingers along a tabletop, her tartan blanket covering her head.

'What are you doing, Maggie?' Mr Quinn asked, peering round the side of the hooded figure. 'Maggie? Is that you under there?'

'Yes, sir. I'm just practicing.'

'Do you know what you're doing out there now?'

'I think so.'

'Just do a good job. We've all got a lot riding on today. Not least a new roof. And cook wants a new grill.'

The last roof caved in with the weight of a heavy rainfall, falling in the middle of one of Maggie's maths classes with Mr Wilson.

She stood up, the blanket still over her head and peaked out behind the backstage curtain, at the hundreds and hundreds of faces dressed in perfect uniform for once, and rows and rows of parents sitting at the front. She whisked the blanket back over her head. Maggie hadn't thought about what the auditorium would look like full. With all the seats taken it seemed larger by a hundred-fold. All the faces were staring to the front. She desperately wanted to see Bertrand's face before she began but she couldn't make him out.

Mr Quinn tapped the microphone to check it was on, like the rank amateur he was. Feedback rang out along with a few titters in the front row, then he said, 'Thank you governor Wilkins for that inspiring speech.' He waited for the audience to clap, but they didn't. 'OK then ... without further ado, to start our ceremony please welcome our school's lead pianist, Maggie Burns!'

Maggie stepped out from behind the curtain - the blanket wrapped over her head - and strode across the stage, for what seemed like miles. Mr Quinn looked on from side stage, cursing and swearing at his deputy heads to do something. The crowd murmured, unsure of what was going on, then a solitary person clapped her as she dropped the blanket down to her shoulders. She smiled to herself, picturing Bertrand clapping away, somewhere out there.

She tucked the bench in, took a deep breath, pressing the left pedal down, and began the opening keys. The first few bars came out perfectly, right in time, then the blanket fell from her shoulders and a sudden fear shot through her body, a feeling of nakedness. She lost where she was, making her finger twitch, hitting entirely the wrong key. 'Shit,' she cursed aloud, unaware of what she was doing.

Backstage, Mr Quinn held his head in his hands.

Maggie wanted the ground to swallow her up right there. It was the sack race in primary school all over again. After a few leaps, it was clear she wasn't going to win. She felt the crowd were all shouting against her, with none of her family there to cheer her on. She gave up and turned the sack round, up over her head and started saying nursery rhymes to herself. Her teacher had to forcibly remove the sack from her, and even then she pulled her t-shirt over her head instead.

Maggie kept looking out the corner of her eye at the blanket lying on the ground, more and more mistakes following. 'Shit,' she said again with each duff key she hit. 'Shit ... Fuck ... Shit ... Fuck!' They could almost handle the Shits but not the Fucks. Her fingers just wouldn't fall true, and her annoyance grew louder. 'Shit ... Fuck ... Fuck! ... Fuck!'

The crowd started to mumble amongst themselves.

She coloured the air with obscenity after obscenity with each stray key. She was on the verge of tears and about to stop all together, when she heard a hearty laugh and applause from someone in the crowd. Maggie looked out into the crowd but could only see indistinct faces as she tried to concentrate and get the piece back on track. It seemed the more she swore, the more he applauded.

Mr Quinn ran onstage, offering the palm of his hand to the audience in apology for Maggie's performance.

She stood up, still trying to play, welcoming the mistakes: 'Fuck! Shit! Fuck! Fuck! Fuckpiss!' as Quinn prised her away from the piano. She banged the keyboard with her fist, shouting a final 'Shit!' in unison.

There was complete silence. Then Bertrand stood up and applauded as hard and loud as he could.

'Bravo! Bravo, Maggie! Encore, encore,' he shouted encouraging the rest of the audience, but they remained unmoved.

Maggie smiled at him as she wrapped the blanket back over her head again, and walked backstage, where Mr Quinn was sitting on the floor smoking a cigarette in defeat
'Was that OK, Mr Quinn?' Maggie asked, touching his shoulder.

He exhaled. 'I knew it was a mistake. They told me you couldn't play it...'

The rest of the ceremony went off without a hitch. Maggie collected her certificate to the complete indifference of the crowd.

Bertrand met her afterwards in the playground with all the other parents and walked her home.

'That has simply made my day,' Bertrand beamed.

'Air raid sirens have been welcomed more warmly,' Maggie replied, holding her blanket, throwing her scarf round her neck. 'Falling bombs have been better received.' She never did get round to giving it to Bertrand.

Bertrand sat down on the hillside next to the football pitches – the fourth year's match seemed incidental they were scrapping and fighting so much, the ball rolling away as fists were flung – and gave Maggie a Thermos cup of hot tea from his Marks and Spencer's 'Bag for Life'. 'So have you uncovered anything in the letters, Maggie?'

She shook her head, standing over him. 'There's nothing I can see. I'm sorry, Bertrand. I looked so hard. The last letter had Rose stuck on the island waiting for you to come.'

'What was the date of that one?'

'7th July 1943. I don't know what to do. Bill was right. I'm too emotional. Too stupid.'

'Don't be upset, Maggie. I tried for many years to find her, and I didn't get anywhere. And I had more than just letters to go on. Maybe if you had my contacts from all those years ago. Most of them have passed on by now.'

Maggie could see it was getting to him. He had given up. She could see it in the way his neck craned forward, as if trying to make himself smaller so the world wouldn't notice him. 'I'm sorry, Bertrand. I guess I'm just not smart enough to work it all out.'

'You shouldn't say things like that, Maggie. People make the mistake of underestimating you. I don't.'

'Bertrand, where were you? Didn't you ever make it to the island?'

He spoke to himself, 'Don't be upset. There's nothing to be upset or sad about. Don't be upset...'

She looked down at Bertrand's papers she was holding, titled "What Regret Means" and "Thoughts on the Colonel", shuffling through them as he spoke.

'I never made it to that island. It's not that I didn't love her. I did. Everything was ready for me to go: my bag packed; a boat organised to sail first thing in the morning. I was at home, on our family croft. It was late. It must have been four or five in the morning. I had been climbing Ben Kenneth again. It was horrible without her. When I came back I found Colonel Pinter home on leave from service. My mother had lied to him that I signed up. She only wanted to protect me. Needless to say, he found out. A man in his position is privy to information and of course it was easy to find the truth.'

'Colonel Pinter? This was your father?'

He laughed to himself. 'He wasn't my father. Funny, I never thought anything about calling him by his title. He demanded it, at home, and especially in public. Even 'sir' wasn't good enough. His rank was to be respected. Anyway, my mother and him were sat at the kitchen table, all my writing about Rose lying in a pile in front of them. Including a letter I had written to Rose, promising my imminent arrival. The Colonel must have intercepted it. He hadn't been home an hour and he had been searching through my things. He hadn't even taken his uniform off, or his medals from the other war. Being a man, and thus, overly proud. He would always say it was "his family", sticking his chest out proudly and raising his chin. I hadn't seen him for almost a year and a half, yet he never looked at me when I came through the back door, still in my dressing gown with my father's old walking stick and bunnet. He threw the writing paper at me and asked me why I was wasting my time with words when there was a war on.

'I told him words are all you have left after love. There's nothing else to feel. You see, Rose showed me so many beautiful things. I had never noticed them before she came along. Everything seemed so dry. So predictable. The rigours of a small island were draining. I just felt so compelled to document all the beauty that I felt inside. If only for myself, for a document of the times. Otherwise what good was it? Even if no one ever read it, it didn't matter. Sometimes you forget the way you felt at a particular moment: a person's scent, if they held your hand a certain way, a change in their normal laughter...'

Maggie looked down at Bertrand's persistent grip, holding on for dear life. He wasn't used to telling this story.

'...or the breeze of someone walking quickly past you. I notice that a lot. Rose used to slow down when she was walking past old people. Old people like me now. She didn't want them to feel like they were part of a forgotten past, when things were much slower. When steam trains came along people were getting run over. They simply didn't think it was possible for something to reach them so fast. That's what words were for me before my ... spell. A great big walloping steam train, ready to trample over everything you desired. Never satisfied to stay rooted on a page, or one of these computer televisions. If you can remember one thing, remember this: words can breathe, they have a pulse, they understand you, they always listen.

'But Colonel Pinter was adamant: there was no future to

be had in words. That wasn't a profession. That was no way to live your life. Now fighting a war - that was a way to live. I told him that I could build entire lives out of nothing more than words. Whole worlds can spring up. But it didn't matter to him. He demanded I tell him where the island was that Rose and the others were hiding on. That it was useless to hold out. That he was stronger than I was, and my defeat was inevitable. I refused, thinking about what Rose would do in the situation. I knew she would rather see me alone on an island, than face their retribution. The Colonel ordered me to sign up for the army the next day at the recruitment office in North Uist. He said I was one of the lucky ones, that only his authority would stop me from being punished further. I fell to my knees and begged him not to do it. He slapped me across the face and told me to stop being emotional. There was no room for such ignominious frailties in this world, he said. I told him it was the greatest thing in this world, to feel. Even if you feel like you've lost. My nose was streaming as I yelled at him, Then I'll write in the attic for the rest of my life whatever it takes I'll always have her and you can't take away my mind and I love her and you hate me for seeing things you'll never see and I pity you and your sad life and my life has a love in it and it makes me stronger than anything you've ever fired or tougher than any forest track you've run. He slapped me again and asked me if I still felt the same way. I told him I did. He slapped me again, twice this time. My mother tried to stop him and he slapped her as well. She ran upstairs holding her face, while he beat me further.

'So the Colonel kept at me, until the sun rose, constantly screaming after every punch, "So can you still feel something?" Each time I replied, "There's nothing you can do..." which only angered him more. What else could I say?'

Maggie finished her tea and placed the cup down in the uncut grass and folded her arms. Ready for a story. 'Then what happened?'

13
Cherry Tree Estate (a hospital of sorts)

Bertrand was in a haze when he awoke, his face and body swollen and tender from the constant beating throughout the night, and the next day, and the day after that from the Colonel. It hurt to move, it hurt to lie still in bed; it hurt to look in the mirror.

The Colonel was already shouting about something downstairs, the abuse muffled by a series of closed doors leading to Bertrand's room. Such uncertainty about the nature of the Colonel's abuse set him on edge, clasping the bed sheets with curled, white-knuckled fingers. He stared across the room with huge, watering eyes as images of Rose flicked rapidly through his head, like flashcards handled by some hectic magician flicking through a deck. He screamed into his pillow as one by one he felt them fading. It wasn't that he couldn't remember what she looked like, she was just getting further away. He could only picture small fractions of her at a time. He was losing her synergy, that fulsome glory of all-of-her-at-once.

He staggered towards the curtains and hauled them aside with disdain. The air had a cinematic grain to it as the wind whooped and hollered around the croft, searching in vain for tree branches to blow around, but there was only wispy, sparse grass, the maddening emptiness and hollowness of the space, tiny buttercups pinging resiliently back and forth. Bertrand felt it weigh heavily on him, feeling so stuck in all this space, watching mad Bruce hopping and barking and lashing around at the gale, tethered to the old cattle shed, nowhere to go, Bertrand longing not to feel like this anymore. It was too painful to think of Rose on that island. It felt very clear to him all that was left now.

He watched Colin making his way towards the croft in his cart and postman's pony, turning into the driveway for the Colonel's mail. There wasn't much time to think.

He took the only thing to hand - a packet of matches from the landing table - and wrote as many words as he could fit: 'I love you. I can't make it. You would understand. x', stretching around both sides of the box, taking up every inch of available space, scoring the 'x' on the strike patch with his fingernail. His hand trembled as he wrote, the skinny letters huddled together like starving prisoners against a wall. He dashed downstairs, leaping three and four stairs at a time, then quickly slowed outside the kitchen door, steadying his breath as if to appear composed. His heart was throbbing and felt misshapen, at some new angle in his chest. The Colonel stood in the centre of the room, drinking from a mug of hot water. 'Bloody rationing,' he grimaced after a mouthful. 'Can't even get a decent cup of tea these days.'

On the table were all of Bertrand's letters to Rose, the poetry she had inspired him to write, the thinly veiled stories about their love with silly pseudonyms like Violet and Bertie, a couple so in love they attached themselves by a length of rope, tying it around each other's waists so they would never be apart. Bertrand knew how much Rose would love that story, and indeed, all the others. It didn't look like she would ever read them. The Colonel held one handful of the letters, and with the other prodded the coals burning in the stove.

He threw in the letters in much smaller handfuls than he could have, pausing between throws to gauge the anguish in Bertrand's face, to see how much of a man he was taking it like. Even with his back to him, the Colonel could shove Bertrand off with one arm. His baton arm. Bertrand had never felt so weak. It reminded him of those dreams when you can't run no matter how hard you try. He couldn't even raise one more hopeful 'please' as the Colonel balled up the last page, it disappearing into his enormous fist.

The Colonel unlocked the kitchen door with a key from his pocket (as he had locked all the doors in his house to stop Bertrand from escaping), Colin bringing a rush of wind from the outside with him, which whistled through the house, setting off a chain of slammed doors. He took a second to appraise the situation, the look of terror in Bertrand's eyes telling him that something was wrong.

Hiding the matchbox in his palm Bertrand shook Colin's hand, sliding the matchbox into it, mouthing 'Help' whilst his back was to the Colonel. Bertrand nodded at what was in Colin's palm. 'I hope you're well,' Bertrand croaked.

The Colonel eyed him suspiciously, rising from the open stove door, the last of Bertrand's writings turning orange and then black inside the pit: gone forever.

'Not too bad,' Colin said, before clearing his throat, desperately trying to appraise the situation. 'My wife, though. She's been waiting on a letter. She's starting to get worried it might not arrive.'

The Colonel snarled, 'I know. No damn order around here anymore. Just look at the state of the crofts with the women running them. No order. It's unreal.'

Colin waited for Bertrand to give him some kind of code for what he was going to do, but with the Colonel watching them now, Bertrand could only stand there and smile. No one had ever forced a smile so much against their will. His body tensed all the way down to his feet to get those lips stretched apart.

Colin lay down some mail on the table, next to the Colonel's whisky. They were letters from Rose from the island.

The Colonel stepped in front of Bertrand and scooped the letters up. 'That will be all, Colin. Thank you.'

Colin paused in the open doorway - the wind dancing around Bertrand's ankles, below where his pyjamas stopped – his face etched with a 'what can I do?' helplessness.

'Good morning for a smoke, Colin. Get the air about you, eh?' Bertrand suggested, eyeing the matchbox in Colin's hand. It was unclear whether he had understood or not.

The door slamming shut stole all the air from Bertrand's lungs. He knew there was no way he could make it to the island. Not then. Not ever. If love had made him strong before, then he needed it soon. He wouldn't let himself be taken. Not like this. He had done what he could, to give Rose a final note of his love. A goodbye.

He ran upstairs and closed his bedroom door, not planning to leave until he had committed to memory all that had been lost. But without paper the memories came and went, repeating lines to himself, then another image would come into his head, overriding the previous one. He rolled about on top of his bed covers, trying to think of nothing, to empty the carnival in his head, but every time he got close Rose's face would pop back in, the pressure of a rushed embrace, Rose kissing his neck when he dipped his head to hug her.

On the second night of his incarceration, the Colonel sat outside Bertrand's room, lecturing him quietly about the life of the mind, and how there were other, more fulfilling ways. Bertrand had never seen him sitting on a floor before, and he struggled to picture it.

The Colonel explained, 'You see, boy, it's just no good. It will never be enough. This girl; eventually she'll want to find a real man.' He paused, calculating if this alone was enough to convince Bertrand. There was no way the Colonel was going to bed knowing he hadn't broken him. And whilst in uniform. He went on, speaking softer now: 'I imagine you're upset at me for throwing away all that guff you wrote. I felt sorry for you, reading some of it. You think you know love? Do you think you've really felt it? It doesn't exist, Bertrand. It's just an illusion. You think love is binary: you either have it or you don't, but it doesn't work like that. You think those words are love? Those dirty stories, rutting in boat houses, what.' The word "love" came out the Colonel's mouth in an uneasy way. He could never really commit to the strength of that first syllable.

Bertrand marched back and forth between his bed and the opposite wall, clasping his hands over his ears hard enough to hear the seashell effect inside. Still the Colonel's words came droning on under the door. Bertrand cried to himself, 'Get me out of this head, I don't want to be here anymore, **GET ME OUT OF THIS MIND-'**

The Colonel could hear his crying, but that only spurred him on, speaking faster and louder, getting to his feet, prodding the door with an outstretched finger. 'Telling stories, saying it aloud, feeling things, all these things are just in your head. You really think LOVE will save you? It only makes you weak ... you can't go into battle weak, sunshine, let me tell you that. Love isn't real! It's just another bit of your sordid imagination. Nobody's coming for you, boy...'

This chiding went on for several hours, the Colonel knocking on the door every few minutes to keep Bertrand awake - each time it sent a little electric shock through his body, making his legs jolt. It was too much. Bertrand realised for all his proclamations of love, he could only really do it from the distance between a pair of eyes and a piece of paper. He couldn't stop seeing it, the distance between his thoughts and the things he loved, the girl he loved. He couldn't find it anymore.

Rose turning in slow motion to him on the machair, wind blowing her hair sideways, her left cheek so suddenly exposed over her shoulder. The surety of love lifting up through her skin.

Bertrand was choked. 'Why can I only tell you how I feel after you've gone? All I ever did before was kiss you.' He placed a wooden chair in the centre of the room. He pulled down his curtains from their hooks, which let the moon stream in across his floor, serving as a spotlight for his final act of defiance. It was the curtains that blocked out the outside world, that place that was cruel and violent and irrational and loveless.

He just kept thinking about how he would never hold her again. All those tiny little touches he had taken for granted. All those summers, all those winters. 'It's night now,' he said, the curtains tied around his neck to the ceiling beam. He

rocked the chair away from under his feet.
Rose's face on the machair in close-up now.

Rose's face.
Rose's mouth.
Her...

White.

The Colonel burst in seconds later (hearing the snap of the fallen chair and Bertrand's ensuing gurgles), taking the weight from Bertrand's gently swinging body hanging from the beam across his bedroom ceiling from the calves and pushing him up, like a cabre tosser, Bertrand's face numb and blue, his whole body stiff like timber with effort.

He always knew, in a way, that he would try his hand at suicide. It spoke to him. That desire to finally, once and for all, get away. To stop having to feel like this all the time. To make it all stop. And once you failed the world wasn't yours anymore. It was everyone else's. Those people who did want to be here. The world was theirs.

'Cherry Tree Estates' the sign said. A smiling nurse and a smiling doctor exchanged notes beside Bertrand in the backseat of the Morgan, driving slowly down through the long avenue, cherry trees lining their path. Bertrand's eyes fluttered open, still drowsy from the dosing the Uist doctor had given him. It's far too green and there are too many trees for me to still be on Uist, he realised. He had never seen green like it, in fact.

Painful amounts of green everywhere. Everything spoke of lushness and vitality, mocking him with how alive they were.

The car pulled up outside the hospital doors where two hefty orderlies with saucepan faces accompanied a smiling doctor. Bertrand would never see him without it, as if he had always just been given some good news. Everyone was so happy there. No melancholy here, as the doctor said.

The orderlies took an arm each of Bertrand, marching him down an anaesthetised corridor. The entire building seemed made of corridors, those long, endless corridors of wellness. Everything was contained there, in sealed rooms and bottles, the surfaces all shining and reflecting.

'You don't have to hold me like that,' Bertrand argued, trying to shrug himself free. 'What is this place?'

The doctor followed behind. 'Are you causing trouble already, Mr Mantis? You're here to get well, after all. Aren't you?'

'Yes,' he mumbled. The orderlies led him inside a small room, with a single bed, a bedside cabinet with a lamp on it (the cord disappeared into a hole in the wall), and a window with wire mesh across it. The view looked out to a small wooded area, ripe with summer foliage, and even more dazzling colours than the driveway.

'There's no melancholy here, Mr Mantis,' the doctor said again.

'Right,' Bertrand agreed. 'What is this place? Is this a hospital?'

The doctor's head leaned from side to side. 'It's a hospital ... of sorts. A place for you to get better. They haven't been looking after you in the other place. But we have some good ideas, some very modern ideas to help you.'

Bertrand felt a long growth on his face, and he seemed to have acquired a boniness around his cheeks he couldn't really remember. There was a pile of letters and drawings and poems and stories on the bed, the weight of which caused the mattress to dip. He picked one of the drawings up and mouthed, 'Rose.'

The doctor stood disconcertingly still, staring Bertrand down. He pointed at the bed. 'Your, uh, your mother forwarded those here. You've been a busy boy the last few years.'

Bertrand realised he couldn't remember anything since the Colonel pulled him down from his bedroom beam. He began to cry. 'What year is this?'

The doctor stopped, his hand on the doorframe holding him back. 'You've been in the hospital on Uist for a little while. It's 1949.'

'You're not speaking German.'

He patted the frame happily. 'Get some rest. You've had a long journey.'

The rest never got started, as an entourage of doctors and orderlies, and strangers in the background scribbling urgent notes on his behaviour, crowded around him over his bed. He felt them watching when he slept.

He drifted in and out of consciousness until evening, the medication wearing off, as he sifted through the weighty correspondence he had written: letters to himself in the third person, inanimate objects called Bertrand, and all kinds of poetry and detailing of thoughts from different periods in time, even years when he wasn't born. Every page brought the potential for new horrors. He remembered waking up in the Uist hospital, a full ward to himself, strapped to his bed, the Colonel sitting bedside, arms folded. Such memories cartwheeled from the back of Bertrand's brain to the front. His first weeks in Cherry Tree brought a constant sense of dread; that at any moment a truly terrible memory would seize him and become a horrible truth. One night it came to him: the island. As the realisation hit, his stomach turned and he closed his eyes in despair. What had happened to them all?

The doctors came to see him in the evening. It became a timepiece for him, the unmistakeable brisk clack of footsteps down the hall counting off the seconds, the sideways glances from the window on his door, checking it was safe to enter. Bertrand went after Prentice, his neighbour through the wall. He was foolish enough to try and fight them. Always causing trouble. They held Bertrand gently down on his bed and put a strait jacket on him. There was no good faith in Cherry Tree Estates.

'There's no need to be afraid, Mr Mantis,' the doctor promised.

But he was perfectly calm. 'I know, doctor. I can't do anything to help them. It's too late.'

'Thaaat's right, Mr Mantis. Too late to help you.'

They walked him through many white double doors, falling away to the side like dominoes, until they reached an open-plan reception area, other patients sitting in heaps bordering the room. Some cackled inanely, some drooled down their overalls, while some stared at the white walls, their pupils hopping about, alive with hallucinations. These people are mad, Bertrand thought.

The orderlies took off his strait jacket.

The nurse came out, syringe at the ready in case of any

trouble. 'We're ready for you, Mr Mantis.'

Bertrand was the only one that would walk serenely into the room, without orderlies to force him. 'I know it's useless to fight back. You can do whatever you want to me. It doesn't matter anymore.'

The machine with all the dials started to whir as he helped the orderlies fix the straps around his ankles, then offered them his wrists.

They applied the mask, which stopped him biting his tongue off.

'That's right, Mr Mantis. We're going to make you better. With a little help from Mr Benjamin Franklin here, we'll get you back to normal. Seeing normal things. Get you better.'

He closed his eyes as the machine cranked, then he slurred through the mask, 'If only you could see what I do.'

Later in the Relaxing Room, Bertrand noticed a newspaper on the snooker table. Not that there was ever any snooker played on it. It was far too dangerous to have snooker cues and heavy snooker balls lying around with all of these melancholy people.

The date on the front page read, 19th August 1951. Another two years slip by without her. Another box of pictures of her face. He was making a charcoal drawing of her made out of tiny love hearts when a young man Titus, even younger than him, sat down beside him. 'Any news, soldier?' the man asked, chewing his thumbnail hungrily.

Bertrand put down his pencil and writing pad. 'About what?'

'The Gerries. We'll have em fixed soon. Wait and you'll see. Just wait till they let me back on the front line. Back in the trenches with Georgie, that's where I need to be.' Then he wandered off, still muttering to himself.

Bertrand started writing "Thoughts About Being Locked In A Cage And Told Every Day That You Are Free".

Madness was never discussed in Cherry Tree Estates. It was quite ironic that so many people should be in an asylum, seeing as no one was mad. It was an interminable Mobius strip: to even suggest that someone might be mad, was looked on as a characteristic of madness itself, and justified your being in an asylum.

Take young shell-shocked Titus. He had been sanctioned after one of his friends, Georgie, on the front line shot himself, hysterical from 'melancholy', according to an army report. In fact, Bertrand's was called the melancholy ward. And there must have been a lot of melancholy about then. From ruined businessmen, to tortured painters, to crofters' sons.

After a few months of shocks, Bertrand couldn't remember a lot. Only of Rose. He thought about her night and day, and how little difference it would make if she were here. He couldn't imagine being able to hold her as tightly as he wanted, or to kiss her as hungrily as he needed, or for as long. It would never be enough. He wanted the ability for memory, as islanders called it Ionndrainn: a longing for that which can no longer be remembered. Eventually, that is all love is: a series of memories.

Anything short of completely consuming her whole would never be enough. And now all he wanted was for them, all those normal people, to destroy him once and for all. Not to forget her, just to keep those notions of love somehow repairing him, to a minimum. That's why he helped them shock him. For Bertrand, this was all there was now: acceptance of his solitude.

But then he didn't know what had happened to his mother? To the Colonel that had him committed on grounds of 'irrational behaviour' and expressing 'mad thoughts which he sought to keep secret through writing'? 'Attempted to hang himself, due to melancholy'. This melancholy stuff was pretty dangerous, no?

'He is clearly delusional,' the Colonel had argued. 'Look at this, talking about seeing burning boats whilst in his dressing gown on top of Ben Kenneth. Mad as a loon! He'll have to go the mainland. They can't do anything more for him here.'

The doctors agreed (once their modest fee had cleared, of course). 'Naturally, Colonel. These writings are quite clearly the work of melancholy. Technically, we call it Eidetic Delusions. An unnatural vividness in mental images that the patient believes are actually visible, often with great detail. Even a cursory look at his writing suggests a deeply serious case. But we have very exciting technology that is proving very adept at limiting such unnaturally vivid thoughts and behaviour. No sane man can see such things. And the pictures of this girl he's been drawing in the past few weeks since the melancholy began, we're not even sure that she exists.'

14
An Investigation Of Sorts

Maggie put down the piece of paper titled “Cherry Tree Estates – a hospital of sorts” on the long grass. Bertrand sighed as the boys playing football swore profusely at each other, using the bad ‘C’ word, then took it in turns to shout abuse at Maggie and Bertrand up on the hill overlooking the red blaze pitches:

‘It’s skinny little Maggie from Hunterhill!’ But they soon got bored of that and left the football to chat up Lianne G and her sister, each pushing prams along like they were still children pushing dollies around. ‘And I get a hunner pound a week. It’s fuckin minted, no...’ Lianne spat.

The boys were sad. Lianne’s tits were ruined.

Maggie was crying, wetting Bertrand’s letters in her hands. ‘That’s why you couldn’t radio the island, then. It must have been horrible in there.’

‘There were ... unpleasant times. But the thought of getting out and seeing Rose again. That was enough to keep me alive. I wrote so much about her when I was in there. At points I thought that the whole world was part of some elaborate construction so I could find things to write about. All little scenes playing out in front of me. People doing absurd things, sad things, amazing things, saying ridiculous things to each other, just for me. That was where most of these were composed.’ He pulled out one from Maggie’s satchel entitled: “Feelings about – The Sparks That Flew Off The Machine One Day”.

‘They strapped me down on the table as usual, and attached the rubber mouth piece to stop me swallowing my tongue, savouring the taste again. But there was a problem today. All the nurses were crowded around the machine, and I thought, “If Rose is still alive then make the machine spark”. And right enough, the metal clamps that applied the electricity spewed sparks high into the air like a Catherine Wheel. It was almost uncontrollable. I smiled to myself. I knew she was there in the room. When they fixed their machine, I welcomed the clamps, because it meant Rose firing her way through the nerves in my body. We were always looking for ways to be one entity; we invented hundreds. I called them *“Ways That Rose And I Can Always Be One”*.

‘The machine starts and the nauseating voltage flew around my body. I can see the sparks racing between blood vessels, through my veins, and deep into the centre of my heart, where they gather together, forming an unstoppable ball of light, constantly turning over on itself. I have seen what a soul looks like tonight. And I am so peaceful. Because I know that nothing can ever take it away from me. They have tried to shock it out of me, but it has only made me stronger. They give me pills in the hope of altering my brain patterns, to change the way thoughts flow between the different parts of my brain, so that I can no longer see her, and all the other things she makes me see. But it only strengthens my imagination. They think her love has made me go mad. Or melancholic. They wish my imagination would cease, but I say no more! will you dilute my thoughts, to see what they want me to. I just don't want people to be so joyless! If this is mad, then let it hold my hand and take me to the maddest places I can imagine. I am not afraid anymore.'

The sun had gone down now and the boys were finished playing football and fighting and chatting up Lianne and her stinking sister. 'Neivver of em have got decent tits now' one of them said. 'She gets a hunner pound a week, but! I'm gonnae speak to ma bird about a wean...'

Maggie looked up from Bertrand's letters and noticed his face - it was like watching television in the early evening, and not realising how dark the room had become. She could only see the outline of his face in the darkness.

They started to walk home, Bertrand holding Maggie close, as passing gangs of Neds drinking cider taunted her in her red coat and leather satchel. 'Hold me closer, Bertrand,' she said. They walked the deserted streets of Bertrand's estate, the streetlights flickering on as they reached his house. Maggie sat down on the kerb, looking up at the dark empty houses surrounding Bertrand's. He had never really found his way out of Cherry Tree Estates, geography aside. Bertrand groaned as he sat next to her, the pair of them pulling their feet in as a boy racer sped past, abusing the lack of traffic in the street, his stereo pumping out obnoxious dance music with lyrics sung by a girl, pleading with some boy to 'just give it to me. Yeah.' The 'yeah' was so dead sounding, and the girl in the passenger seat was so vacant looking, so happy with her fella and his motor. Maggie hung her head in sudden depression, as if trying to make herself smaller so the world wouldn't notice her. This really is not my world, she thought to herself.

'So when did you get out?' Maggie whimpered, as the car's wheeze of gear changes and coughing exhaust faded into the swollen belly of the estate. 'Did you ever see the Colonel again?'

'The Colonel died only a few days after going back to the front lines. My mother not even a week later. The doctor told me a matter of weeks after my arrival at Cherry Tree Estates. Like a coward, though, he waited until after one of the evening "invigoration sessions". The doctors were so scared, thinking I wouldn't be able to handle the sadness. If only they had known what I felt like without Rose, they wouldn't have bothered to waken me up in the morning.'

'When did you get out?' Maggie sat poised with her pen and notepad.

'Sometime around '55.'

'1955! You were in that place for nearly five years?'

'They said I was rehabilitated. That I was ready to rejoin society, nice and healthy. In normal thoughts again. In reality, they only kept me there as long as the Colonel's pension could afford to. If he was a General I might still be in there.'

'Then what did you do when you got out?'

'I moved to a village south of Oban – just to get away from the Estates – taking a job as a printer for a local newspaper. One day I was setting the pages, when I looked closer at the typeface: it was an obituary for Joseph Angus.'

Maggie's pen halted. 'Joseph, from the island.'

Bertrand took a deep breath. 'There were so many Anguses on that island, I wasn't sure at first. So I made some phone calls. Lindsay had died when I was still in Cherry Tree. I got the Caledonian MacBrayne ferry back to Uist for the funeral, in the hope she would be there. But no one knew a thing. She had vanished off the face of the earth. I even paid a fisherman to take me to the island where they were. It was turned into a weather monitoring station for a few years, but it's gone now. I'm ashamed to say I gave up over ten years ago. Scared that even if I did find her she would have married someone else. I couldn't live with such a thought. So I lived in blissful ignorance, convincing myself I had done all I could. Now I'm not so sure.' He held his hand in the other, as if contained his fears.

'Didn't you have any visitors in Cherry Tree?'

'They wouldn't allow visitors at Cherry Tree. At least none I knew about. If I had any they were kept behind a two-way mirror. You see, they couldn't have normal people coming in to mix with the crazy people like me. Imagine if all my mad thoughts got out into the real world! They couldn't have that. Infecting all the sane people. What if everyone ended up like me?'

Maggie reached for his hands. 'But don't you see? If you

don't know if anyone visited you, then maybe Rose did come to see you. And maybe, just maybe, if she did, she might still be alive.'

The car came racing back down the street. The girl woohoo'd out the window at Maggie then chucked her fag at her.

'I wish I was on that fucking island,' Maggie said, watching the car slam the brake lights on, then rip away again.

27th June 2006

Pythagoras number +2
Busy day on Saturday. Bertrand and me are going to check the visitor log at Cherry Tree Estates. I've no idea what we're going to find. I've no idea where Cherry Tree Estates is.
Last English class of term got cancelled so I took the rest of the day off to work on my writing. I've still got a few letters to read.

15
Wilting

30th July 1943

Dear Bertrand

So this is really how it will end. I imagine you are going mad wherever you are, my love. It's the not knowing that really hurts. The not knowing if I will hear your voice again. Remember how I said I would sit on the fence all day long waiting for you to arrive, and I would say your name to myself. It comforted me. Surely everyone needs what we have had. It is a lifeblood to me.

I grow weary of reminiscing now, which is sad when you have no future. All of time hurts now. Every second. Is it bad that I just want my life to be over? Joseph hardly leaves the old animal shed now. His eyes have glassed over completely now. He walks around the cottage in circles, muttering to himself about Lindsay and how she never speaks since seeing the bodies in the sea. My body grows weary with each circuit he makes: he's always there in my peripheral vision, regardless of how hard I try not to look. He's worn a path in to the ground. I stare down at this paper, counting to myself the seconds it should have taken for him to be out of sight of the window. But time and time again, there he is. If only they were as strong as us, then there might have been a chance for this to work.

I suppose there's no point in casting blame, considering the circumstances. Not now. I've decided to swim for the shore this afternoon, so this is the last time I will write from this stupid room, with its stupid window, where stupid Joseph is prancing round again, kicking his feet through the vegetable garden he spent so long perfecting. I actually sit here laughing aloud about all this. That we can be so foolish to think that it is us that decides who to love, and when, and how much, and when it should end, and...

We are in control of nothing here. Least of all fate. Let someone else decide such matters. I have no interest anymore. I thought that we could build something magnificent and beautiful here, but yet again man's stupidity has gotten in the way again. If only you had made it here, Bertrand, you could have showed them what it was to be joyful, and filled with life. They would have run away, horrified at themselves for thinking they knew what it meant. They would sprint to the pier and leap off the edge, swimming faster than any boat, desperate to get to shore, to yell, **I HAVE NEVER SEEN ANYONE SO IN LOVE AS BERTRAND MANTIS! WE SHOULD ALL JUST GIVE UP, HE LOVES ROSE MCDONALD SO MUCH. NO ONE ELSE SHOULD WASTE THEIR TIME IN ATTEMPTING IT.**

But you never did make it. So no one will swim to the shore and shout the above.

Joseph thinks we have enough food without Colin's aid, to last only another few weeks. Lindsay stays in bed all day long, wrapped up tightly in blankets. She refuses to come out unless there is a boat to take us all home. She's had enough.

A raven has appeared overhead when I go out walking. It seems to sing directly at me, and I'm sure I flies straight back to Uist every day. It's madness, how close we are to everything. Nothing is far away now.

The one thing that could save us would be a U-boat running aground and we can steal their supplies. Ironic, isn't it. We wanted so badly to get away, to disappear, and now all I want is to be found.

Your ever wilting

Rose

3rd August 1943

Dear Bertrand,

What I would give to read another matchbox of yours. Or perhaps the sole of a shoe. Or maybe a piece of paper tied to a rock that you've thrown from France, or Holland, or wherever the hell you are.

If you are dead, Bertrand, I think I will be joining you sooner rather than later. It's easier than trying to stay alive.

Rose

16
Dear Diary

28th June 2006

A boy was playing football outside his house when I was walking home. I haven't seen him before. He smiled at me and I blushed. It's nearly the summer holidays!
Pythagoras number +3

Still 28th June 2006

Jean still hasn't come home yet. I asked Bill if she was going to live in the car for the rest of her life. He said probably.
The boy playing football yesterday was walking down the street holding some girl's hand. She was dead pretty and I hate how I'm not.
Pythagoras number +2

17
The Optimistic

Maggie awoke with the letter from Rose still in her hand, and the torch light still on, her hand sweaty from holding it under the blanket all night. Maybe it was the unusual quiet around the house that unsettled her. It had been like that for the past few weeks, especially since Jean had taken to living in the car beside Murray Street.

She badly wanted to hear some sullen complaining from the bedroom next door:

'Maggie, where's my hairdryer? Well, you had it last, you bitch! What?! Mum, she started it, she lost my hairdryer...'
'Jean, didn't you buy any milk? How am I supposed to have cereal in the morning without any milk? ... Why couldn't I buy some myself? Because it's your JOB!'

The hustle and bustle of family arguments had pinged between the rooms - now everything had lapsed into comatose in the Burns' house since Trish's funeral. It was up to Maggie now. I'm the woman of the house, she giggled to herself. She could laugh at all the stupid things Bill would say to Jean because Bill's thick as shit. It's what happens when you listen to football managers and illiterate pundits on Sky Sports all the time.

Bill would sit there complaining about the new 'buttons' while Jean did the washing up. 'Jean, where's the old remote?'

'It was broke, so I bought a new one at Asda's.'

'But I liked the old one. I could feel my way around it without having to look at the buttons. I don't know where anything is on this. Look. I HIT THIS, and it should be Teletext, instead it puts the sound off. Then if I want to TURN THE VOLUME UP, it changes the fucking channel. It's no good! I need to look at this one. It's like trying to find a needle in a pin.'

'Haystack. And that was the best one they had.'

'I don't want the best one. I want the old one. How much did this piece of shit cost?'

'£10.'

'£10? Right, right hold on. So you spent £10 on a new remote that doesn't even work? Well, if that's not shooting yourself in the head...'

'Foot. Does it not work? I'll bring it back if it's not working.'

'No, that's not the ... the buttons work, right. It's just no GOOD. Take it back tomorrow when you're out at the shops.'

'But I'm not going shopping tomorrow.'

'Does the pope shit in the woods?'

There was a long pause from the kitchen.

Bill was adamant, 'You'll take it back tomorrow.'

Jean stared down at the floor as she opened a new bottle of gin. Good old Jean. She knew how to have a quiet life.

Maggie was roused from all the pages on the living room floor by a knock on the door. She looked through the peephole. She twitched back. It was the cute boy playing football in the street from the other day, and not a dead pretty girl in sight. Maggie patted down her frizzy hair in the mirror, the boy's tasty outline in the frosted glass of the front door just inches away. She took a breath and opened the door as casually as possible.

The boy looked surprisingly sheepish without his football. 'Aye ... my ball. It went into your garden.'

Strange, Maggie thought. He's not wearing his Celtic strip like he normally does. 'Aren't you supposed to be at school today?' she asked.

'Aren't you?' The boy grinned at his quick thinking, taking an obvious look at Maggie's bare legs.

Maggie blushed and pretended to have an itch on her cheek.

'I was wondering if you could take me around the back to get it.'

Maggie smiled. 'Course I can. I'll need to unlock the gate.' She tried to seductively slide her feet into her pair of manky Reeboks like they were Cinderella's glass slippers. Maggie had seen a programme on Channel Five about body language, and how 'casually' touching someone can let them know you fancy them. So on the way out the door she reached for his arm, trying to lead him round, but as soon as she made contact he jerked his arm away. Maggie tried to keep smiling.

Still, she noticed a definite spark between them. Something Maggie was prone to see quite a lot of. When she walked around the streets, she would see sparks the same way that people see auras. People holding hands and swinging them together: they sparked the most, walking about like there was a welder's torch between them. Then other times people would be holding hands and there was nothing at all. No spark. Not even a flicker. Their faces were so joyless and resigned. She hated seeing that. Oh Maggie understood real love, alright.

She opened the gate, and as soon as it swung shut, she realised there was no football in the garden.

'I thought you said-'

The boy pushed her up against the gate and wrestled his tongue against hers. He had never broken his VL (virgin lips) and now that he had, he decided it was great. Tastes like one big thick strawberry lace, he thought as he fumbled with her denim shorts.

Maggie wasn't so sure about him. She could tell by his desperation he was inexperienced. Then she realised it was a little bit like the film that came on Channel Five after the body language programme (which - now that she thought about it – had a lot of sex in it). A woman was so passionately in love with a strange man that they gave in to their base instincts and screwed up against a wall. The woman was overcome with passion, excited at the mutual spontaneity. Maggie tried to fit her body into all the same positions, recreating that celluloid moment, kissing him back and opening his trousers. She pulled back to inspect for evidence of sparks but saw none.

'So you love me, right?' she asked tentatively, his zipper between her fingers.

The boy couldn't help laughing.

She came down off her tiptoes and adjusted her shorts. 'Don't come back. You can kick your ball into someone else's garden next time.'

Maggie went for a walk to have a look at the sparks between different people. Just because she saw no spark with the football boy didn't stop her from hoping there would be one in the future. Maggie's romanticism was never outdone by her optimism.

It never failed to amaze Maggie how many times there were people that created a spark and didn't know it. So often she would see a man on one side of the street minding his own business and a woman on the other. The two wouldn't so much as make eye contact, but the spark leapt across the road, right over the traffic, connecting with the other person. And other times she would see a spark about to happen and the pair were about to realise it, maybe in the queue in a shop, or passing each other getting on a bus, when someone would come between them. A clumsy shop assistant dropping a tin of beans, or an old woman taking too long getting off a bus, could jeopardise two people's entire lives, even fate itself - but then it couldn't have been fate if it was meant to happen, Maggie thought. Then she would counter herself and think, but what if we all stayed at home and never left our houses. Would our other sparkee just show up at the door? Maybe that's what drove

Maggie to open the door to football boy in the first place. Maggie just couldn't say no because ... what if...?

However, Maggie had also seen sparks come together in the most inopportune moments. Outside the changing rooms in Topshop, a boyfriend would be moping about outside, waiting for his girl. When a young, weekend assistant drops a hanger and boy meets girl's eyes at ground level. Sparks are flying all over the place, uncontrollable sparks! What colour extinguisher is for electrical fires again? Someone call the fire brigade! The tills are going mad, spewing out love hearts not receipts; the security gates beeping out love songs in binary beeps. Only a few millimetres of curtain away is his girlfriend who thinks they will be together forever, admiring her growing chest in the mirror.

Maggie was crossing the road? To get to the other side - Maggie laughed to herself - when a huge spark leapt over her head from the woman drinking a cup of coffee to the man in a suit and carrying a briefcase, his shirt collar accidentally flared out over his jacket lapels, making him look like a 70s throwback. He was in such a hurry he didn't notice any of it happening. But Maggie saw it and knew what she had to do.

She threw herself out in a heap on the middle of the road, pretending to faint whilst crossing. A car horn blared and the two sparkees turned to look at the commotion. They each ran over to help her. Maggie peaked through a half-closed eye and saw the sparks flying back and forth like a roving Van De Graaff generator she had seen in science class.

The woman asked, distantly, 'Are you OK? Let me get you up. Are you OK?' looking at the man the whole time. The space between his eyes was a vice, and she was locked in.

He smiled, staring back in disbelief at the woman's beauty. Aching at the shape of her legs beneath her long skirt. 'Yes, of course. Are you OK?'

They helped her to the other side of the pavement and Maggie opened her eyes. She wiped her forehead, and said, 'You know, I feel fine now. Thanks anyway.'

The pair were so giddily lost in each other's dilating pupils (Maggie read that it happens when we see something we like the look of) they barely noticed Maggie.

The woman fixed the man's shirt collar when Maggie suddenly sprang up and ran away, laughing manically to herself, overcome with joy. It worked! She was seeing them everywhere now. Bertrand was right.

Maggie kept running, until she found herself at the top of Murray Street. She realised where she was and her giddiness was wiped away.

Jean's vigil had passed the three week mark, the flowers not just slouched between the railings but weeping now, the teddy bears arms raised up as if looking for some passing stranger to take them away. It was no longer a touching tribute by a loving mother in a desperate attempt to keep someone alive, it was like a hurricane had randomly blown the contents of a deprived child's bedroom and a cheap florist's against a railing, items tattered and turned over.

The rain had seeped down underneath the cellophane wrapping of the cards on the flowers, reducing them to a sloppy ink-blotted mess, sadness indecipherable from love, hearts indistinguishable from crucifixes. The sign of what constituted love had been hopelessly confused. Was this a celebration of the opening of the 'Fags and Mags' across the road or a memorial? Love had become terribly unclear.

Maggie held her hand out at the car window, her motion casting a shadow where there had been light over Jean's sleeping body.

Jean opened her eyes, her woozy feet colliding with many empty bottles of Asda gin. 'Maggie,' she said, not out of recognition, but in trying to remember who she was.

She opened the passenger door for her and Maggie climbed in. Jean's eyes were sad, sunken and hollow; a brown crescent moon lying on its back underneath each one.

'What are you still doing here? Come home,' Maggie pleaded.

'Not until I'm a good mother.' Her voice was a shell of her old cutting, raspy shriek.

Maggie gave her the answer she thought she wanted to hear. 'You are a good mother.'

Jean felt Maggie's cheek, which reminded her of the way Bertrand would sometimes do it, when she said something that charmed him. Charming, yes. True, no.

'Why didn't we call you something pretty, like after a flower?' Jean pondered. 'Like Lily.'

'Or Rose?'

'Aye. Rose is a nice name.'

'Bill says Maggie sounds like an old woman's name, so no one will like me until I'm seventy.'

Jean laughed, which turned into a cough. She opened the glove box and took a fag from it. 'Do you want one?'

'No.'

She smirked with disappointment. 'Don't even know if

my daughter smokes.'

Maggie rested her head against the door window. She had never been described by Jean like that before. Maggie was always ... Maggie. It was all she was. 'It wouldn't be your fault if I did. Kids these days, huh?'

'Yep. Kids these days. Drinking and yelling. You probably won't believe me, but I used to be one myself when I was your age.'

Maggie laughed, 'No? Really?'

'I'm going to try harder, Maggie.'

Maggie considered the prospects, like kicking Bill out, and have Bertrand move into Trish's old room, so he wouldn't be so lonely. He could help around the house, so Jean could get a job at Asda on the tills, just like she always wanted. Maggie was always so impressed with how they managed to stop the conveyor belt right before your things spill over the end. She always reached for them, each time it seemed more inevitable than the last, that there was absolutely no way they were going to stop in time. But they would. And the way they handled large wads of notes. There was no way they could count money that quick. Sucking in air as they counted them aloud: OnetwothreefourfivesixseveneightnineTENELEVEN-TWELVE...

'So what are your plans, then?' Maggie asked.

'Rick says that we can get out of here. Together. He has tickets for Lisbon, then from there he can take us to America. We can all settle down. He can open up another bar, I can get a waitressing job, and you can go to a nice school, one where the roof doesn't fall in when it rains too hard...'

Maggie wasn't listening. She looked out across the street. No sparks anywhere. I need to go and see Bertrand.

Jean broke off and threw the driver's door open. Some council sanitation workers were starting to pull the flowers down. She threw her cigarette at their feet and pushed them back. It seemed they were prepared for the situation, as they didn't seem surprised to see a woman come flying out of a parked car wearing her bed clothes in the middle of the afternoon, to protect some dead flowers and filthy cuddly toys sitting by the roadside.

'Missus, just take it easy, eh?' one of them said. The other – new looking - stayed far back from her. Maggie got out as well, standing next to Jean.

'These are my daughter's things. You can't just take this away. It's private property.'

'Look, I'm just doing my job. My boss says there's some

dead flowers on a railing. Go take them off when you're doing Murray Street today. So I say "fine". Look, the flowers are dead, missus. The toys are filthy. It's starting to look a mess.'

'Do you know what will happen if I don't look after this place.'

The man lit a fag. 'What?'

Jean paused. 'You don't want to know.'

The man sighed in exasperation. 'Mikey, give us a hand here, eh.'

Jean slapped his hands, and Maggie sat down in front of the railing. She looked at one of the cards, the only one that had survived the rain. The one that only she knew she had written for Trish. Maggie wanted it to stay there.

The man who was doing all the talking gave up. The two walked off with their litter pickers slung over their shoulders, cowboys on the New Frontier of Filth.

Jean fixed what she could, but the struggle had broken more of the flower stems. Maggie tried to pick her up and get her back in the car, but she couldn't. Lifting a sad person is impossible. Maggie remembered Bertrand had told her that. In fact, it was one of the first things he told her. That when someone is sad they take on the problems of the world. Everything is incredibly heavy. And they suddenly worry more about whether someone loves them. Or as Bertrand wrote in 'To be in love with words (but not the way I use them)':

'Sometimes I have something I want to describe. Something I haven't noticed about the world before. Now, my pen and paper is laid out in front of me. I know what I want to write about, and why, but when I try to move the pen, it is impossible. The more you try to move it, the harder it becomes. The pen is fighting back at you! It won't let you! And sometimes I find myself screaming at the pen in my hand, 'why won't you leave me alone?!' But it never listens when you shout at it. Never ever ever ever ever ever ever ever. You got that? When does it listen if you shout at it? Never ever ever ever ever ever ever. No, Bertrand! It's never ever ever ever ever ever ever ever.'

Maggie would nod to herself, having memorised it.

'Something is stopping you from writing. And you know why? Because you don't understand it yet. You don't understand what you're trying to write. And someone else knows this and stops you from writing, to keep you making a fool of yourself. This is the same reason you should never try and lift a sad person.'

Maggie took her hands out from under Jean's arms. 'Mum, I think it's time you came home. I don't care what Bill says, you can't stay here forever.'

Jean walked back to the driver's side. 'It's alright. Rick will be here any time.'

Maggie sat by the Cenotaph in the town square for over an hour and didn't see a single spark. Out of pure boredom she decided to make the sun fall, then rise again in quick succession. Then she made the moon come up at the same time as the sun, and made an eclipse. Maggie laughed to herself that no one else noticed it. She got bored with that, though, so instead made the sun jump in front of the moon and vice versa. She turned the moon blue, and put a smiley face on the sun, but it just spun itself around, flipping the smile upside down. And the moon got tired of Maggie's games and refused to come out and play anymore. So Maggie yelled at the sky, 'Well, I'm not playing either, then!' much to the dismay of the passers-by.

A sign at the doors to St Mary's of the Immaculate Heart said 'Open 9-5' which made Maggie imagine Jesus standing bored behind a till, waiting for knocking-off time.

'D'you want a bag for that luv? That'll be £2.35. Nah, that's only £2.25 you've given us. Ta ra, Maggie. Peace be with you.'

Maggie cracked the door open the tiniest amount she could, when an old lady threw it all the way open from inside. Maggie jumped back letting the lady past. She tiptoed inside and took a seat near the back, next to a row of wooden cubicles, each with a red light above it. It was only Maggie, and a solitary nun sitting in the front row. Maggie thought it would be nice to go and sit with her because she looked lonely. Which surprised her, because Maggie was always told by Chaplain Charlie at school that God was always with you. Then why do you need to keep praying for him to hear you then?

The nun was kneeling and had her head bowed, which meant her prayers would get to God faster than if she were just sitting. Kneeling meant that you really, really meant what you were asking.

Maggie crossed herself, but got her hands confused, and so gestured a 'sorry, I forgot' towards the altar. The nun sat at the very end of the row, and every few seconds Maggie slid down another few feet, and another few feet, until she was sat right next to the nun. 'Hello,' she said rather loudly, then covered her mouth, trying to take the volume back.

The nun smiled.

She lowered her voice and kneeled down. 'I hope I'm not disturbing you.'

'No, that's OK.'

Maggie paused.

'Are you wanting to talk about something?' The nun had a calm voice. Maggie was used to hearing anxious, hurried, stressful voices, always shouting or annoyed about something. Just ... just ... FUCK! The nun sounded like she could dismantle any theological argument with sheer calmness alone.

'I don't know.' Maggie took a second to think. 'Is your voice so peaceful because you know you are going to heaven?'

'No one knows they are going to heaven. You just have to try very hard, and be good. Have you been a good girl?'

'I don't know. I suppose if I don't know that's not a very good sign.'

'Well ... not normally. But there's always time to be a better person.'

'Is that why you're here? You haven't been good lately? By the way, can I call you, Sister?'

'Of course you can call me sister.'

'Good. Cos my real sister didn't like me calling her that. She's dead now.'

'Oh, I'm sorry to hear that.' The nun held her gaze longer this time.

Maggie felt the nun's smile was truly genuine. A real smile always looked easier, the lips sliding back with ease, unlike a politician's grimace.

The nun said, 'To answer your other question, it's really not for me to say. I don't think I've done anything wrong, though.'

'But, hypothetically, Sister.' Maggie relished saying it, got her money's worth from it. 'Say for instance you sit here and pray all day, and always say rosaries and you get into heaven. That's fine, you deserve it. But what if I don't really do anything horrible, you know, I try to be as nice a person as possible, and try to find beauty in the world, and I don't pray every day, but I still get into heaven? That's not very fair on you is it?'

The nun looked like it was the first time she had really had to think hard about a question from a girl of Maggie's age. 'If God deemed you worthy to get to heaven, then I would be happy, too. I must say, though, I'm not sure I get your point.'

'I suppose I'm just asking, how can you be sure whether what you're doing is enough. What if you can just get away with being cruel and mean all your life?'

'I doubt very much that God allows that.'

'Then why is that the way the world is, Sister? What if

heaven is the same? And even when we die it is horrible and useless, and the bad people get away with anything? Then why don't we just go about being horrible and mean and driving cars down streets really fast with horrible music with a really ugly girlfriend in the passenger seat and have kids every other week cos you want a new Burberry jacket and if you ever want anything you can just take it, and if you don't like your daughter you can just shout at her anytime you want, and boys can use you and throw you away whenever they feel like it?'

Maggie looked behind her. One of the doors on the wooden boxes at the back opened up and the red light went off as a man came out.

The nun said, rising, 'I'm sorry, it's my turn for confession.'

Maggie got to her feet too. 'But I thought you said you haven't done anything wrong? Does that mean God is always angry with you no matter what you do?'

The nun's patience was now shot to hell. 'Just try ... and be thankful. Now I'm sorry, I really must go, young lady.'

When Maggie left, she was terrified of doing anything wrong, sure that as soon as she put a foot wrong, a bolt of lightning would be tossed down from a cloud on to her head. A car roared past, blaring loud dance music, just the kind she always heard on the estate. The passenger dangled out his window, shouting obnoxious things to a blonde woman who looked very nice and was harming no one. Maggie was about to shout at the car, but fearing the lightening from above, instead said to the sky, 'I am thankful for all the people you have made, God. Truly made in your own image, as Chaplain Charlie said.'

Maggie ignored the smelly football boy as she walked past. Look at him trying to do keepie-ups to impress me. He looks horrible and sweaty. I never really liked him anyway. Then Maggie mumbled to herself, 'I take back what I said earlier, God. You're a bastard, a real tit, and when I get to heaven I'll tell you to your face. I hope it's really cold up there.' Then she muttered under her breath, 'Stupid cunt.'

Bill was sat watching Sky Sports News, clutching the remote in his hand as if someone might jump up behind him at any second and snatch it away.

Maggie walked through to the kitchen.

'I hope you're going to make dinner,' he said, still staring at the TV. 'I'm famished.'

'What would you like?'

'What is there?'

'I don't know!'

'You mean you haven't been to the shops? What have you been doing all day?'

There were already four empty cans of lager next to his feet. Maggie stood in the doorway unsure whether to say.

Bill tutted and reached into his trousers, digging out a tenner. 'Here. Suppose you better go down the chippy.'

Maggie reached for the note, then Bill pulled it back.

'And don't go faffing around with large chips. Small'll do you fine.' He shouted after her, 'And make mine a jumbo sausage!'

18
County

Someone had been fly-tipping in Bertrand's garden overnight, meaning Maggie could no longer plot a route through the labyrinth of old tyres, busted washing machines and other garbage; she had to scramble over it. No matter how cold it got, Bertrand always left the kitchen window open for her.

She didn't need to climb through, though. The back door was smashed in. Bertrand sat at the kitchen table, looking through to the living room, where the television used to sit, its stand bearing the shape of its dust imprint. The wall behind looked terribly naked without it.

'Bertrand,' she said. 'Where's your television gone?' She walked down the hall, feeling a breeze coming from the front door. It blew towards her as she held her hand out to close it over, sealing up a wind tunnel between it and the kitchen window, making the house seem like it had exhaled all the breath out of itself. She looked into the living room on the way back, Bertrand's papers in disarray, but as if they had been brushed past, worked around, rather than rifled through.

Maggie hugged herself in the kitchen doorway, inspecting Bertrand's hunched demeanour, blowing hot air into his gloved hands. 'Some kids broke in, didn't they?' she said.

Bertrand aimed his speech down at the tabletop; miserable, cold, and hopeless. 'What's on the agenda first? Are we going to go and shout at the skinheads again? Or maybe sit in a church and talk to a nun?'

Maggie pulled out a brush and pan from under the sink and swept up the broken glass around Bertrand's feet. 'No, no. It's straight to Cherry Tree Estates.'

He raised his head up slowly, eyes straining as they met the outside light over Maggie's shoulder. 'So where is it?'

'Where's what?'

'Cherry Tree Estates?'

'Bertrand, I've got no idea. You mean to tell me you don't know where the asylum is that you spent five years in?'

'It's on the edge of town, I remember that. Out past the west end. No. Past the east end. Or maybe it was the south side. I ... I can't remember because...'

Maggie flicked the broken glass out the window and dumped herself into a chair beside him. 'Bertrand. You know everything I know.'

'I know.'

*

The main room of Central Library: helpless students desperately trying to escape the vapid excesses of Paisley University's union; lost looking old people tracing their genealogy; and unemployed/unemployable people reading the free newspapers and abusing the patience of the staff with requests for obscure or out-of-print true crime books with titles like, The Monster Next Door – An All-American Murder or Murdering Mothers – They Loved Their Children ... TO DEATH!.

Maggie insisted on hopping on her left foot to the inquiry desk in the reference room. The librarian glowered at her as she made her way across the room, squeaking the floorboards with each hop. Bertrand trailed behind.

'Hello!' Maggie said far too loudly.

The librarian said nothing.

'We're looking for some information, please.'

He looked back down at his Observer Sudoku puzzle, and said, 'Computers are over there,' pointing to a row of black Dells.

Bertrand looked worriedly at the machines. 'Do you know how to use these things?'

'Sure, we use them all the time at school,' Maggie said, pulling a chair out for him.

'Does this seat go any higher?' he asked, pressing the lever under the seat, sending his seat careering down to the floor like an express lift.

Maggie spluttered a laugh, followed by a snort, much to the librarian's annoyance. She pulled up a Google search page and typed in 'Cherry Tree Estates'.

'Search results 25 of 1,351
1. Cherry Tree Estates – ***For the best the Peak District has to offer in family holidays***
2. Cherry Tree estate agents of Blackburn
3. Save Ye Olde Cherry Tree! ***The annual Tour de Tendring charity cycle race will see the 10-strong field ... including a team from Barton Industrial Estates...***
4. Cherry Tree Hotel and B&B, Eastbourne, Sussex, England. ***Behind Chesters Estates***
5. Mary Poppins in Cherry Tree Lane by PL Travers. ***Explore all the locations interactively with Fabulousfiction.com'***

'I don't suppose any of these make any sense to you, do they?'

'That's a nice name.' Bertrand squinted. 'Who is Mary

Poppins?'

Maggie clicked the 'local' icon and pressed 'ENTER'. 'She's a bit like you, really, Bertrand.'

The results decreased to five.

Bertrand pointed at one entry reading 'Local Heritage' entry. 'What is this?'

'Local Heritage – Because this wasn't always such a big town!'

Maggie clicked on a screen-size icon of the old Anchor Mill leading to an index of redundant landmarks of the town, all with the same cheesy monikers about how successful the town was: torn down poets' houses (now drug rehab clinics), and the old hanging square (now a regional Scottish Socialists' Party HQ). Maggie was just about to close the page when Bertrand halted her.

'No, wait. I recognise that,' he said - an old school surrounded by hedgerows and an array of multicoloured flowers and shrubs. The colours were so vibrant in comparison to the other locations. Bertrand touched the image on the screen like one might a familiar mole on the skin, running the fingertip back over and over. He was certain. 'That's it.'

'But that's County. That's where Dee-dee is.'

'That's where I was, Maggie. I couldn't mistake it for anywhere else.'

Maggie clicked on the image and a page of history of the hospital unravelled. 'Look at all this: County Hospital (or Cherry Tree Estates as it was called up to 1982) has been the town's only fully operational mental hospital for over 50 years now. Thanks to the town's economic expansion, County Hospital is now larger than ever! For the most advanced treatment of paranoid schizophrenics, it is consistently voted the best in the region.' At the bottom of the page was a picture of the Mayor, the phrase, 'Progress. At any cost!' underneath.

Maggie took the address down in one of her sizeable notepads. She took the pad over to the librarian – still puzzling with his Sudoku – placing it in front of him, open at a page with the words 'ROSE MCDONALD 80 YEARS OLD?' filling the entire A4 page. 'I need to find this woman,' she announced, lowering her voice as Bertrand approached. 'To see if she's still alive. It's for the old man, you understand.'

The librarian sighed and shook his head. 'So you're looking for a Rose McDonald in Scotland who is around eighty-years-old, to help an old man?'

'That's right!'

'The phone books are over there,' he said, pointing to a

row of enormous yellow volumes – at least thirty, each as big as a volume of the Encyclopaedia Britannica - then looked back down at his Sudoku.

He can't be that good, Maggie thought. He's using a pencil with an eraser at the end. She turned her head to get a better view of his puzzle. After a moment the librarian looked up, staring across the room, waiting for her to leave. She jabbed at some of the empty boxes, her dirty, chewed fingernail standing out against the whiteness of the page. 'You want a four there, then a twelve there, and a six and seven here,' Maggie assured him.

The librarian paused to check Maggie's calculations, then scrunched the puzzle up in a ball. Outwitted by skinny little Maggie from Hunterhill.

'Come on, Bertrand,' Maggie said, taking his hand. 'We're not wasting our time with phone books. I've tried all those numbers already. If you don't believe me, I'll show you Bill's phone bill at the end of the month. We've got someone to go and see.'

After some confusion about how many tickets Maggie should be buying on the bus, it took them through the smoggy industrial estates, and past the Mercedes and Mondeo estates (the latter just for the weekends, naturally) of Lincoln Fields. Then the grey gave way for the green of golf courses, and the land became more heavily forested. The last stop was across the road from County. If you didn't know what you were looking for it was easy to assume there was nothing there at all hidden behind the tall trees leading to the winding driveway. Only a discreet intercom next to a rather vague sign saying 'County' on it, suggested something beyond the high spiked gates and perimeter fence wrapped in hedging.

Maggie could see Bertrand was unnerved by its apparent innocence. 'Was it like this when you came here?'

'It's exactly like the picture on the computer. It hasn't changed at all.'

Maggie walked towards the intercom, and Bertrand reached out to her.

'Maggie,' he cautioned her. 'Maybe we shouldn't.'

She felt the weight of all of his years on her young shoulders. With a smile, she took his finger and used it to hit the intercom.

A flash of static then a put-upon voice enquired, 'Visiting or dropping off?'

Maggie stammered, 'Em ... visiting. Dee-dee Russell.'

She shrugged at Bertrand as the gates slowly opened, leading them down the driveway Bertrand had described before. She could smell the colours, taste the petals. She missed real flowers. It was something she noticed at the funeral. In the staleness of the suburbs, she rarely got a glimpse of something so full of life. The people sure smelled, but they definitely weren't as alive. Nothing grows in towns. It reminded her of the book London Fields she had seen Mrs Gray reading once. Maggie liked the title: how did towns and buildings become the thing? They just became, didn't they? Why cities? Why that?

'I don't remember it taking this long,' Bertrand huffed, marching up the long avenue, a light sweat forming on his forehead, his nasal passages clogging with the greenery.

'You had a nice car to drive you, that's why.'

Bertrand reminisced about the smell of the tarmac after a rain storm; how the heat of the sun on the wet road unlocked its molten scent. That was the true smell of Maggie's town.

A nurse was waiting for them at the front door when they arrived, leading them through two reinforced double doors. 'One signature is enough,' the nurse indicated to Maggie about to fill in Bertrand's name in the visitor's log.

Maggie couldn't help but wonder if Rose had been told the same thing many moons ago, coming to see Bertrand.

The nurse walked them down the corridor towards Dee-dee's wing. 'And it's Miss Russell, isn't it? She hasn't had a visitor for months. Well, she had a day release a short while ago, but she didn't make it the whole day.'

Maggie looked back and saw Bertrand trailing behind, eyes wandering up and down and across the walls and ceiling, as the memories flooded back. Maggie knew where from: 'Diary: Cherry Tree Estates pt9': 'There's a place in front of the matron's window where Jackson tried to drown himself with a cup of water, tipping it over his head then rolling about on the floor, digging his face into the tiny puddle. And there's a door I used to talk to; it was the only reflective surface that was mine (you couldn't have mirrors in the rooms. Too afraid the guests would try to smash them and use the glass). I was fascinated by how my lips moved. My entire face was a miracle and I realised that such a thing as 'ugly' was an impossibility.'

The nurse stopped outside the matron's office. 'If you just take a seat, I'll be out in a minute.'

Maggie noted the code the nurse typed into the panel next to the door handle. '3251JL. 3251JL,' she repeated over and over in her head. She whispered, 'Bertrand remember this: 3251JL,' and looked for her notepad and pen. 'OK, go.'

Bertrand's face was completely vacant. 'Em...'

Maggie rolled her eyes. '325 ... 1 ... JL? I think that was it.'

'Sorry, Maggie,' he croaked, looking at the floor. Just a stupid senile old man that can't even remember a ... a...

Maggie took a seat on one of the leather seats lined up in a row against a window. 'Look, they've taken the wire mesh off.'

He didn't bother looking. He was staring through the white double doors that led into the ward; memories sliding back, like being reintroduced to an old morning dream you thought lost forever. An old lady pushed the doors open, which Maggie noticed and shimmied about in her seat as she approached - the old leather sticking to the skin behind her knees. She felt grubby, thinking about how many other backs-of-people's-knees (what do you call that bit?) had been there.

The old lady took a seat next to her, although there were plenty others to pick from. Maggie felt vulnerable and looked to Bertrand to come and help, but he was wandering towards the ward doors some yards away, in a nostalgic stupor.

The old woman smelled of stale hospital soap: clean, yes, but caused a certain layer of skin to ferment and flake in such dry, anaesthetic air. She opened and closed her mouth, as if tasting invisible food. The dry chewing noise made Maggie's skin crawl.

The old lady glowed. 'It's good of you to come and see me.'

'I'm sorry. We're actually here to see someone else. Maybe we'll see you on the way out.'

The old lady tried to reach Maggie's hand, but she pulled away quickly, without drawing too much attention, trying to dampen the rejection. The lady thought about trying again then clasped her hands together, satisfied with merely sitting there with someone who wasn't mad or talking to themselves.

The nurse came out the office and Maggie sprang out her seat.

'OK, that's us,' the nurse said. 'I see you've already met Brenda. Let me show you where Dee-dee is.'

Bertrand widened his eyes at Maggie who shook her head, dismissively. 'We'll do it later,' she whispered.

The nurse turned round with a hesitant glance. 'Have ... you been here before?'

Maggie saw Bertrand raise his finger but Maggie interjected, 'No, we haven't been here before. I'm Dee-dee's cousin. Not real, though. I'm adopted, so I'm not real family. I hope that's ok.'

The nurse led them to the ward lined with beds, almost all of them with a body sat on the end of them, shoulders hunched, waiting for nothing. The pattern on the floor seemed designed to evoke bafflement; a swirling pattern of inky lines and dots that never started, never finished. When the others saw Maggie approaching they cascaded down a vast emotional range in just a few seconds, like a tsunami crashing through them - first the fear, then the hope of safety, then the disappointment as they passed on their way to the end of the room to Dee-dee's bed. She was sitting cross-legged on top of the sheets, flipping through her newspaper.

The nurse touched Dee-dee on the shoulder after she failed to respond to their presence. 'Dee-dee, there's someone here to see you.'

Dee-dee looked at Maggie and jumped up to hug her. 'Maggie, you've finally come!' She taunted the nurse, 'See, I knew today was a special one.'

The nurse smiled like a mother, with pursed lips, somewhere between charmed and disappointed to have raised a show-off.

Bertrand stood awkwardly at the end of the bed, shuffling his feet, looking around at the other patients like someone was tapping him on alternate shoulders.

Maggie said, sitting down gingerly beside Dee-dee, 'Look, I really can't stay long because there's something else I'm here to do. First I need to ask you a question.'

'How much does he love me?'

Maggie hesitated to disappoint her. 'Em, no, something else. Do you know where they might keep the old visitor's logbooks?'

'I don't know anything about that. There's a basement, so I'd imagine all the old stuff is down there. I'm not allowed down there, though. He says I shouldn't go down there.' She noticed something going on behind Maggie. Dee-dee shouted across the room to a bed with its curtains drawn around it, a constant groaning sound emanating. 'Hey, Kilpatrick! Keep it down over there. Some of us have company.' She returned to Maggie. 'I'm sorry; it's old Kilpatrick, giving himself a chug again. Can't help it, poor bastard. They had to switch his curtains to wipe-down ones. You should have seen-'

Bertrand edged down the bed towards Maggie and nudged her.

'We're looking for someone,' she blurted out.

'Oh. If you're looking for someone, you can check my

missing person's page, here.' She laid out the paper at the Classifieds. 'Or maybe you want to buy a grand piano. Says here it needs tuning but it's in good condition apparently. Or maybe a keyboard, or a Premier drum kit? Or a Golden Retriever, or a Scotty? Or how about taking a trip to Co-op?'

Maggie tried to interject, 'That's alright, Dee-dee. We need to be-'

'They've got Jacob's cream crackers, only 15 1/2p, or a bottle of White Horse whisky for £6.25. That's quite dear, even for the old days, isn't it? Where is he? He's got to be in here somewhere...' Dee-dee started running off at breakneck speed through more lists of Co-op shopping items, local news stories, and horse racing odds of the day, turning the pages quicker and quicker.

Maggie touched Bertrand on the back, and nodded down the hall where a nurse was handing out medication from a hostess trolley, working her way towards the ward exit.

Dee-dee was still talking through the contents as fast as her mouth would allow her to - 'Did you know St Mirren drew one each with Partick Thistle, after McDougall scored a goal in the last two minutes? Isn't that incredible? And winning a game was only worth two points back then. Oh where is he?'

Maggie saw the nurse getting closer to turning the corner of the room. 'What's on TV tonight, then?' she asked, patting Dee-dee on the hand and slowly rising from her seat.

Bertrand was pacing slowly around the ward, hands held respectfully behind his back.

Dee-dee hummed for a second. 'On BBC One at 7.20, is Blake's Seven. "When Avon is captured and Vila discovers the silo containing Scorpio is impossible to open, things look bad for the Liberator's survivors." Then from 9 to 10 on STV is East of Eden. "The final episode of John Steinbeck's best-selling novel about the conflict between two brothers."' Dee-dee laughed to herself. The kind of manic laugh most people only feel comfortable enough to do by themselves normally. She had no fear in letting it all out. One of the reasons she ended up in County.

The nurse turned the corner and Maggie stepped forward away from the bed, but Dee-dee grabbed her arm.

'Wait,' she said. 'It's not here.'

Maggie looked at the paper. 'What's not?'

'The "Intimations".'

'What, what is it? What's gone?'

'A bit of the day. A bit of my day, it's not here. Pages twelve and thirteen.' She turned to the centre pages and showed Maggie the inside staples. 'You can see it there,' Dee-dee whimpered. 'The page has been ripped out. Who would do such a thing? My day. Someone is trying to destroy my day. It was so beautiful. It was so perfect! And I was so close to finding him. Maybe that's why. They obviously don't want me to find him. I mean, what if he's on page twelve? Or page thirteen?!' She shook Maggie by the shoulders and her voice raised enough for the nurse to come running down the aisle.

Maggie's heart sank, sensing her chance was gone.

Dee-dee begged her, 'You've got to find my pages. You've got to. Look, they're coming to sedate me. Seduce me with that medicine. You've got to take your medicine - they say that, don't they? Be a good girl and take your medicine-'

The nurse rubbed a solution on Dee-dee's arm and readied a syringe. 'It's ok, Dee-dee. We'll calm you down.'

'Yes, that's right, calm me down. Bring me back down again, nurse, Sister. Maggie had a sister didn't you, Maggie? She was a nice sister, bit of a cunt sometimes, but a sister nonetheless, Sister. You can be a bit of a cunt too, can't you, Sister? Ha! Haha!'

Maggie stood back away from the bed, colliding into Bertrand who wasn't watching what was happening.

The nurse pressed down on the syringe. 'There we go.' She turned to Maggie. 'I think it's maybe best if you go. Dee-dee seems a bit energetic this afternoon.'

Dee-dee's eyes were closing already. 'Yes, I'm done for now. No more talking today. I'll be falling asleep soon. Putting me to sleep. Put me out of my misery, once and for all. No more numbing. Thumbing the pages, thumbing the missing pages. The missing pages make me numb. I'm helpless without it, aren't I, nurse, Sister, mother, lover, fucker, fuck her, fuck me, love me, my lover...?'

The nurse tried to push Dee-dee the last few inches down on her bed, but she suddenly fought back. Some more nurses and doctors came running down the ward, the other patients shaking their beds and cheering and clapping.

Maggie backed away and said, 'Dee-dee, I'm gonna find that page for you. Don't worry.'

Dee-dee cried out as another syringe was plunged into the yellowing skin on her arm. 'Isn't this day perfect?' she howled.

Bertrand had edged back against the far wall, convinced the doctors were coming for him. He slid along the wall, hands flat against it, feeling his way out.

The doctors hurriedly shut the curtains around the bed

to quieten the other patients. Maggie grabbed Bertrand's hand, and they made a dash for the lower level door. A man with stubble and Eraserhead-hair was sat up on his bed, staring at them. Maggie put her finger to her lips and smiled as she took out her notepad. The man put his finger to his lips and smiled back.

She pressed the code into the panel and the handle gloriously gave way. They fell through into a dark staircase. The door slammed behind them and then it was silent.

Bertrand leaned back against the door, holding his chest. 'I thought only 'Anna Karenina' could make my heart beat like that.'

At the bottom of the stairs was a long, dimly lit corridor, the sound of water slowly dripping in the distance.

Maggie led the way. Every few yards was a blank door with a blanked out window. 'What do you suppose is in there, Bertrand?'

'ECT machines.'

'What makes you so sure?'

'They used to take me to that one down there,' he said, looking at the ground as he pointed to a door as anonymous as the others.

They stopped outside and Maggie tried the door. It was locked, and there was no panel for entering a code this time. It was straight out of "Diary: Cherry Tree Estates pt13": 'They would leave us in there afterwards to gather ourselves; for the red on our temples to die down; to let our limbs stop spasming.'

Bertrand stepped forward slowly, as if about to be grabbed at any time and returned to his room. It was like being led through a familiar dream, or nightmare, walking around unrestrained. 'It's so different now,' he said.

Maggie took his hand again and led him down to the end of the corridor, to the last door, 'Archive'. The door let out a puff of air as she opened it.

'Like it has its own little atmosphere in there,' Bertrand said. 'Quickly, Maggie, they might find us.'

A small window at outside's ground level let in a thick shaft of light in the dingy, spider-webbed room. Filing cabinets lined each wall, each with a year on it. The one closest to them said '2004'.

Maggie took the torch from her bag and ran to the far end of the room and shouted to Bertrand, 'It starts at 1909!' She ran in and out of the cabinets that towered over her. She shouted out the years as her torchlight passed over each card in front of the cabinets, '1940, 41, 42. Here it is, Bertrand! 1943! I can't reach.' She rolled the cabinet ladders along and bolted up the steps. Out of her peripheral vision she could see Bertrand ducking back and forth from behind the cabinet, terrified of getting caught. His fear was making her nervous, her hands skiffling through the letter 'M's, and quicker and quicker through the 'MCs' and the 'MACs' and the 'MAs'. And there it was – 'Bertrand Mantis'.

Maggie shone her torch down on him. From so close-up the light seeped in to every crevice of his face.

'What have you found, Maggie?' he asked, covering his eyes.

'I've got your file. It's got everything. Look,' she said, climbing down. They scanned the pages together, both their hands quivering.

'My medicine dosage, my food menu, voltage applied, and for how long. Is there a visitor sheet?'

'Wait a minute,' Maggie said, bolting back up the ladder again. She stuck her head all the way in, her body nearly tipping all the way over, muffling her voice. 'Maybe there's a record for the time period, not for each patient. Sorry ... guest.' Bertrand was still dancing about like a wee boy trying to hold in a pee. 'Come on, Maggie they could be here any second.' She tipped herself back and let out a triumphant, 'Here it is!' She dropped a large leather volume on the floor, which sent a cloud of dust up through the shafts of light from the window. 'Do you recognise that?' she asked.

Bertrand stared in awe at it, raising his palm at it like it had heat.

Maggie shuffled through her bag and read aloud, 'Cherry Tree Estates pt14: "It had red leather on the front. God, it was burned on my brain. It was my bible. The most sacred book in the building, lying just beyond our grasp, between the double doors and the real world."'
Maggie flicked through the pages, but each was almost fifty lines long and filled with names, sometimes in eligible handwriting. 'We'll need to take it with us,' she said, struggling to fit the enormous book in her bag.

Bertrand looked around. 'Does that mean we can get out of here now?'

Maggie paused. 'I just want to check something.'

'I don't want to stay here anymore. Let's go; we've got the book. I'm sure we'll find what we need.'

'Just hang on,' she panted, mouthing the years as she raced around the cabinets. '1978, 79, 80 ... 1981.' She opened the bottom drawer and pulled out the visitor's log.

'Maggie, what are you doing? What's going on?'

'Just wait.' She rushed through the pages as fast as she could, past June, July, August, September, and stopping at October. She looked down all the entries for 4th October 1981. There was no mention of Rose's name, or anyone else that aroused interest.

She shut the book and replaced it.

Bertrand asked, 'What was it, Maggie?'

'Just a hunch.'

She pulled out each book from 1943 to 1955 and opened them out on the floor, checking each 4th October entry.

Her torch stopped over the 4th October for 1950.

Bertrand didn't know whether to be scared or excited.

'Maggie? ... What is it? What have you found?'

She could only shake her head at him in amazement. 'I never thought it would actually work.' She picked up the book, and showed the page to Bertrand.

'What is it, then?' he asked. 'Is it Rose?'

She shined the torch on the entry and pointed. '4th October,' she said.

There in perfect, flowing cursive was the name of Ichibod Mantis.

Bertrand stumbled backwards into a cabinet. He covered his mouth. 'My father,' he said.

'It must have been your father that sent me that note. He must want us to find him. The year, 1981. It's not a year at all. It must be something else. Look. It's a patient number. You were listed here as patient number 1981, Bertrand Mantis.'

Bertrand took a seat on the bottom rung of the ladder, talking as much to himself as to Maggie. "Thoughts on my father": 'He disappeared when I was only a boy. I couldn't even tell you what he looks like. He was in all the newspapers. "Sir Ichibod Mantis missing".'

'Sir? He was a knight? He hasn't signed his name with "Sir".'

He didn't know what to say.

'You never told me. So we've both got parents that abandoned us.'

'It wasn't that simple,' he said. 'He never wanted rid of me. On the contrary, mother took me away from him. I set out to find him but Colonel Pinter stopped me before I got on the ferry. He was in hiding around the Cairngorm Mountains. Last I heard was what was in the papers: he had a mansion and a huge acreage somewhere out there.' Bertrand sniffed. 'He must be ... 101 years old now. I don't understand how he found you.'

'I don't know, I don't know.' Maggie scraped her hair back with violent sweeps, trying to think. 'For all we know Rose's name is in one of these books, she's still alive, and desperate to find you. Now he gets so close to you with this note ... I think there can only be one possible explanation.'

'Which is?'

'Maybe Ichibod knows where Rose is. And-'

'If we find him we find her.'

The pair froze, locked in semi-hunched positions, as if they were quieter than standing straight. There was a girl's muffled yelling coming from down the corridor, the kicks and scuffs of her feet on the linoleum floor echoing against the empty walls. Then a door slammed shut further away and it was quiet again.

Bertrand took Maggie's arm. 'Come on. We should get out of here.'

Maggie put all the books, 1943 to 1955 in her bag. The weight of the volumes pulling her back, something like the weight of the past.

19
Mister E

Maggie was on her knees rummaging through Trish's chest of drawers; an entire orphanage of clothes building to an anthill around Maggie's legs. All Maggie had could fit into a tiny MFI wardrobe with a broken door, not like Trish's immaculate IKEA drawer set, where she could subdivide her clothes into season and fabric. Maggie had one pile on her bedroom floor, as if she were always ready to go on holiday (the Burns never used suit-cases when taking their holidays – they always drove to their holidays – they never left the UK mainland). Her wardrobe was now a Bertrand Archive and a Maggie Imaginarium of scribbled paper, half-thoughts, and short stories; elaborate family trees for the characters she invented. Bertrand's history was proving quite a more difficult task, though. This was reality she was dealing with.

Bill ambled past the room, beer bottle hanging miser-ably, like a dead flower basket, between fore and middle finger. He stopped at the door, and for a second he considered asking what she was doing. But he just didn't care.

'Will I get you another bottle of beer?' Maggie asked.

It was a non-sequitur to Bill. 'No, no,' he whined, falling back a step. 'I can get it. Not completely useless, you know.'

Maggie could hear the shuffle and thump of him tripping on the carpeted steps going downstairs. He quickly sought to reassure the living room, hands out to insist on calm, 'No, it's alright, I'm just a little drunk. No damage done.' Then he would snigger to himself.

The presence of such casual drunkenness, and the possibility of some explosion in Bill's mood, left Maggie with a constant sense of unease sitting in her room. Every sudden noise or shout from under her floorboards made her freeze, eyes wide with listening, waiting for an indication of what rage was coming this time. She had drawn it once as upstairs (the safety of her closed door, and sanctity of imagination) being Heaven, the staircase (with its outlook through the staircase spindles and through the glass living room door, had a full view of any emotional Bill-carnage, but far enough back to feel safe, and help-less to intervene) as Purgatory, and the living room and kitchen (the blast of heat from the open oven after dinner) as Hell.

In amongst the condoms and empty fag packets (where Maggie found a small lump of cannabis resin, which she pocketed) was Trish's book: a diary and phonebook rolled into one. The Vatican thinks it knows how to preserve secret books? No they don't. They never knew about Trish's. Regardless of how Maggie put it back in exactly the right place, and even left the drawer slightly ajar as she had found it, Trish would come back from Shack B's – her nineteen-year-old DJ boyfriend - and know she had been in there.

She found Dee-dee's name, and underneath was Raymond E's – that's Mister E to his friends and users - with a little cannabis plant logo beside it.

Maggie noted the address down in her notepad. 'Raymond E. 24 Rowan Street.'

Mr E was the saviour of school pupils from Maggie's estate. They were his best clients. Want some sedatives or relaxants for maths class? Sure, no problem. Nothing was ever a problem for Mr E, provided you paid your tick on time. Otherwise that would brutally piss him off.

Rowan Street looked like a microcosm of what would happen to planet earth fifty years after the end of humanity. Plants were overgrown and stretched up the sides of houses, the grass in the front gardens rising, swallowing up heaps of plastic-moulded toys left to rot and grow mouldy in the rain and sun, grass springing out from the gutters like hair in an old man's ears.

Suddenly a child sprang up from the plantation in a front lawn, the grass as tall as he was. He had been dressed for an entirely different climate and season, evidence of curtains not being drawn in his house until well after midday. He was shivering in the drizzle and breeze in his little shorts and sailor-striped t-shirt, grimed with three days' worth of muck and toil. Maggie shrieked inside, the way she would do in the cinema, managing to not show any outward judder, but inside. Inside...

The boy ran inside, the grass springing back from his movement, unseen beneath the undergrowth.

Next door was twenty-four which was even worse. A run-down-looking semi-detached with a psoriatic flaked Artex exterior. The building heaved with dryness; an enormous concrete lung filled with smoke. Inside it was its own little universe of glass jars, bongs and scales, where people only talked in ounces and druggie film references.

She knocked on the door. Bertrand would have to sit this one out. If he saw what was going on inside he would have been thankful.

The door opened with the chain – industrial thickness - still on and a voice spoke out from the darkness, 'What do you want? Today's my day off. If you're here for anything less than an eighth I'm going to be brutally pissed off...'

Maggie thought, wow, even dealers take a day off. Makes sense, I suppose. She said, 'I've come to speak about Dee-dee. I went to see her-'

'How old are you?'

She considered lying but knew her pause would give her away. 'Fourteen.'

'Half a mile down the road on the left.'

'What?'

'That's where the newsagent's is. I don't sell sweeties.'

Maggie nearly stamped her foot. 'I've come about Dee-dee.'

He was growing impatient. 'What about Dee-dee? What do you want?'

'I'm Maggie. Dee-dee's cousin. She asked me to find something for her, and I thought you might have it.'

'Oh-ohoh,' he said impressed. 'So you're the infamous Maggie. I can't get anything in for her. I've told her that. They know my face, and I'm not going back to youth detention for her. I already lost Suzy J cos of it. Poor bitch is still in there.'

Suzy J, fuck yeah. Maggie suddenly felt all nostalgic for those stolen afternoons shoplifting in Claire's Accessories with her, running home to play dress-up. 'No, it's not drugs, it's her newspaper. She thinks you might have a missing page she needs.' Maggie reached into her bag and produced the weed she had taken from Trish's fag packet as some gesture of goodwill. She held it out through the door. A bony, white hand reached out into the light and quickly snatched it.

He sniffed it then sighed. 'You better come in then.' He understood. Maggie was alright. At least she wasn't a junkie. Junkies are all bastards, always making excuses. Always got stories. So full of shit.

The door shut and the chain came off. A boy of no more than sixteen stood at the door in a pair of white y-fronts (bones keeping them up, not meat), drinking from a glass bottle of milk the same colour as his skin. A bare light bulb swung gently above his head, making Maggie think of a police interrogation room.

'Sorry I'm not dressed. It's my day off.'

'I can dig it,' she said, nodding.

He shuffled forward like a sleepwalker as he showed her through to the living room, thick with smoke from joints and incense. The curtains weren't just shut, they were physically taped to the sides of the walls, blocking out all possible daylight. It could have been midnight or midday. A cabinet full of Special Edition and Director's Cut DVDs lined the skirting board, along with some Doors and Velvet Underground vinyl. Some home-made bongs fashioned from Irn Bru bottles sat on the table next to some lit tea candles that gave the room a sense of grace it didn't deserve. Nearly every inch of it was taken up with some kind of drug paraphernalia.

He gestured to them, 'It's kind of an expansion thing I've got going. Diversifying my business. It's what they want, isn't it.'

Maggie wasn't sure who 'they' were. 'That's very smart of you,' she said, sitting down on the three-seater opposite Mr E's recliner. She tried to avert her eyes from the hardcore pornography running muted on the TV, which the two boys next to her were transfixed by, in a bored sort of way.

Mr E showed no signs of discomfort. It was like watching Neighbours when your granny came round.

'Wow,' Maggie said. 'They must really love each other.'

Mr E laughed dismissively, 'Yeah, that's love alright.'

He put his feet up and started building a joint with the weed Maggie gave him.

'Nice stuff, this,' he said, crumbling it into the papers. 'So what's this about her newspaper? Something's missing? I'm telling you, that fucking thing has done nothing but brutally piss me off since she got it. I don't even know where.'

'It is kind of strange.'

'Yeah, well. I do what I can for her, you know. I mean, I feel kind of responsible, her being in there and all. There wasn't a day that went by she wasn't up here rolling, smoking. I told her to cut it down, but she didn't give a fuck. You ever tried telling a stoner they've got a problem? Like telling young folks not fucking is the best form of contraception. They just won't hack it.'

Mr E talked about teenagers like he wasn't one himself, and could now counsel his peers with the wisdom of experience. But then everyone seemed like Mr E; in a few years, there would be no more children. They would just sprout from the womb, the nurse would jack a fag in to the little tyke's mouth, then they would jump straight in to tracksuits, hanging around on street corners asking for gear.

'Don't waste your time,' he warned her. 'Weed kills your ambition. Look at me. But someone had to take over the family business. Got to keep all these clowns numb from the outside.

Might as well be me seeing as I kinda am one of them. Don't blame them, neither.' He laughed ironically, and went into a sombre, soporific tirade, his voice never angry. Just sad and hopeless. 'And they call us mad. Try living in the real world, s'what I say. Prancing round shopping centres, yelling at your weans, yelling at your sorry ass man, yelling at the woman at the Post Office, and it's always buy buy buy as much shit as you can get for the least amount, and at night strap yourself into the sofa and plug into your TV-'

'Yeah,' Mr E's colleagues agreed, headthrusting.

Maggie's heart was already soaring with something like love for Mr E.

'-shouting at people you don't know on talent shows cos it makes you feel better about your pathetic, empty life, and they never realised they haven't lived a day in their life: they've just settled. Given up. They think they know love? They look under the Ls in the index of their Argos catalogue. It's not there. And they don't know what to do about it.' He screwed his forefinger at his temple. 'And they call us mad?' He leaned forward towards Maggie. 'See I know what it's all about: fuck reality.'

The boys beside Maggie low-fived on the sofa, their hands moving terribly slowly, smoke creeping out their mouths, croaking, 'Yeah, man...'

Maggie adjusted in her seat as she low-fived the boy beside her (who hadn't really clocked Maggie's presence until then), a nagging feeling in her stomach, wondering what it would be like to kiss Mr E.

Mr E sat back. 'Then me and Dee-dee started seeing each other. That was my mistake. At first I thought it was just for the weed. But after like a week she kept talking about how in love she was and she couldn't take it and all this. Fuckin hell, then one day she left here, cops found her running up and down the high street screaming that Jesus and the apostles were running after her, trying to kill her.' He did a low-key impression of Dee-dee, '"Dirty fuckin Pharisees", she kept shouting. Fuck me, I didn't know what to do. She came here and stayed for a while and she was like fuckin Marlon Brando for the first three months, sat right where you are now, tanking that fuckin green, mumbling to herself, "The horror. The horror." Fuckin crazy. I kept trying to get her to back off, but she wouldn't let go. Then one day she ran out and her family stuck her up there. Last I saw of her since.'

Maggie thought she knew exactly what Mr E was talking about. 'She went insane with love then? Or loneliness.'

'Same difference. I says to her, "If only you stopped smoking the grass then", who knows, she might have been alright. But she needed the numbing too much. "Too much noise outside," she says. We were going to go live out in the country where it's nice and peaceful, like. But I couldn't score people out in the sticks. Still, I guess she got her wish now, hasn't she. Out there on the edge of town, away from everything, that big old building out in the fields. I think she's better off there.'

Mr E offered Maggie the joint, and she thought it would be rude not to toke. With one long puff she felt her body shrink up inside itself, like a ball of cling film, eventually, slowly expanding back out again, her brain trying to fill the empty air.

'S'good stuff,' she bleated, speaking as she breathed inwards.

'Yeah, girl.'

'So ... do you ... know where this ... paper is ... then?'

'It was for her own good. It was the Obits page. I didn't want her getting any ideas, know what I mean. Got one of my dames to sneak it out a few days ago. Hell, I'm not going up there. Her seeing me ain't a good idea.'

'When do you think she'll get out?'

'Hard to say. I don't think she'd make it. Not in the real world. She's too far gone. If things got to her before, well ... they'll be even more worse now. You can imagine.'

Maggie's stomach turned to candyfloss, flipping her hopes and fears in to one another. She knew it wasn't the joint: it was a realisation hitting home about something, something she had just said: Insane with loneliness.

The hours frittered away with Mr E playing some movies. Before Maggie realised what the time was, they had sat through The Shining, and now the final sequence of Apocalypse Now played out. Brando's voice echoing, 'The horror ... the horror ... the ... horror.'

'I'll tell you a story about that line-'

A knock at the door stopped Mr E in his tracks.

Maggie put the ashtray holding the joint down on the table. Mr E wasn't worried, though, getting up slowly, stopping half-way for another puff. They could just fucking wait.

Maggie heard the door unchain.

Mr E's voice grew audible. '...it's my fuckin day off, man! I told you last week. Don't come here on my fuckin day off ... Right, you're just brutally pissing me off now...'

He stormed through to the living room (as violently as his condition allowed him) and Maggie stood up, like he was royalty. 'Fuckin junkies, man...'

'Maybe I should go,' she said. 'You know ... and it's late and...' her voice seemed to echo around the room, bouncing around in her head.

Mr E was sifting through drawers next to his recliner for a phone number. 'Yeah, I think that would be best. If this fucker thinks he's got anymore more tick with me...'

'Thanks anyway, then.'

Maggie hurried down the hall, her hands out to the sides, springing herself from wall to wall, dodging broken remote-controlled cars, old Argos catalogues, and a long parade of empty milk bottles leading like a runway to the front door. She squeezed past the man at the door, who was looking over at his BMW, his hands turning invisible knots. It was dark out now, and the light from the hall light bulb cast her shadow down the whole length of the garden slabs. 'He's just getting something for me,' the man snapped at Maggie.

'Good for you, man,' she replied.

The parked BMW was attracting some attention from the local kids playing on the street with sticks and rocks.

When Maggie got home, Bill was waiting for her. He could barely speak he was so drunk, slouched halfway down the couch, his neck where his lower back should have been.

'What time d'you call this? I've been sitting here waiting for dinner.' He hadn't the energy to make it to the chippie, having been round at Charlotte's all afternoon, his morning beers segueing into a premature hangover, which he proceeded to fuck away.

Maggie dropped her bag on the hall floor, standing still for a moment, the momentum of her walking suddenly catching up with her and rushing from the back of her head over the top. She giggled to herself.

With the memory of Charlotte still fresh in his mind and his fingers, he shouted at Maggie, **'PAUL NEXT DOOR SAID HE SEEN WITH YOU WITH THAT CLOWN FROM DOWN THE ROAD, THE ONE WITH THE CELTIC TOP. POOR WEE BASTARD'S PROBABLY TURNED QUEER NOW HAHA...'**

Maggie peered into the living room, unshaken. 'You've wet yourself, Bill.' Then she trudged upstairs with her bag.

Dear Diary

3rd July 2005

Some facts: If I can find a link between Ichibod Mantis and Rose McDonald, that means:

a) She will have told Ichibod the story of how Bertrand and her conspired to run away from the war by hiding on that island

AND

b) If there is no record of Rose being alive, maybe it's because she has been living on Ichibod's estate

I read thirty pages of the logbook for today (nothing found. Again.) And I started a new story. I might call it, 'Inside my head – the only place that isn't completely and utterly cruel and mean'. Bertrand will like it, so that's all that matters, really.

20
The Life of Sir Ichibod Mantis

Sir Ichibod Mantis returned from his usual morning walk around Lochnagar - his own private loch at the foot of Ben Macdui - the smell of freshly cut timber in the air. Life was simple for this knight of the realm. Rise around six, breakfast at half past, then his walk for two hours would see him return for his lunch which was always sitting with a metal cover over it on the table in the back garden. Only it was difficult to define where Sir Ichibod's garden began. The whole estate amassed over one hundred and four acres of woodland, water and mountain. Since the Twenties he had been living in isolation, far from the public eye since his rise to prominence.

He had been one of the most famous aristocrats in Britain, with land ownership all around the world, particularly in Kenya, where he ran the largest safaris on the Masai Mara. Fame arrived after a very public fling with Princess Veronica of Sweden. Their subsequent engagement saw them thrust into the limelight of the London society scene. Hobnobbers, philanderers and scene-makers everywhere wanted a piece of them. Each night they would have invitations for the most fashionable parties and launches, and charity fundraisers. But then the bottom fell out.

Sir Ichibod's hell-raising drinking and partying saw him fall out of favour with the Swedish Royal family, who had watched their only daughter and heir to the throne reduced to a laughing stock back home, pictured by their native press falling out of taxis in Covent Garden, and thrown out of the Proms at the Albert Hall for drunkenness, Ichibod loudly berating the conductor for his timing of Schubert in the middle of the piece. 'Too damn fast, you fucking savage!' he called from his private box.

The Princess was forced to call off their engagement and Ichibod became a running joke for the press. His boozy nights became a weekly event for photographers. Then suddenly it all stopped and Sir Ichibod Mantis disappeared off the face of the earth - or so it seemed. Editors across the land demanded he was found as their circulations plummeted. Money in six figures were mentioned for news of his whereabouts.

But they never found him, and Sir Ichibod holed himself up on his grand estate to share with no one for the rest of his life, as far as he was concerned. He never wanted to see anyone or speak to anyone ever again. He only spoke to his team of butlers, cooks, and gardeners by telephone, intercom, or even sometimes, letter. He made up his own personal stamps, and arranged a private delivery system between the very grand staff houses and his own mansion, the centrepiece of the estate: Veronica Hall, named after his spurned Princess.

Sometimes he would lock himself up in one of his many bedrooms, sealing the curtains to the wall, to block every last drop of sunlight out. He had locks put on the door, and when his servants called, they would only hear his wimpish voice speaking from the dark.

One day a butler called on him about trespassers on his upper-third of the mountain. He ignored the report and passed a letter under the door, the envelope sealed with candle wax.

'I never want to hear of the madness of the outside world again,' he wrote in the letter, which was to be circulated to all his staff. 'Let them roam free. I don't believe in imperialism any more than I believe in this ridiculous knighthood of mine, bequeathed to me by incestuous Germanic thieves. I wish only to live in my head for the rest of my life.'

The pain of having his son taken from him after the Princess Veronica affair (the courts deeming him an unsuitable father) had caught up with him in more harmful ways. He had developed a morphine habit which had come to twist his mind so rapidly he would incur fantastical visions and hallucinations, normally whilst on his morning walks.

For over a year he thought the Loch Ness monster was, in fact, living in Lochnagar in front of his very own Veronica Hall. He would stand in the loch for hours, in pouring rain or driving snow, trousers rolled up to his knees, smoking a pipe, staring out across the water. 'Where are you Nessie? I've got a fresh sleeve for you here,' he'd shout.

If he had turned round he would have seen the butlers stood at the window, shaking their heads at the mad fool.

Some months later he could be found on top of a twenty-foot high platform he had his staff make for him, throwing hoops up in the air. He believed there were a group of five elephants – part of a travelling circus – living in his garden. He demanded the animals be kept entertained.

'They are finer specimens than any human. These creatures have souls,' he said.

For as long as Sir Ichibod was prepared to pay them, the house staff were happy to indulge his madness, living like kings in a utopia.

Madness had long run in his family, and it seemed the

morphine had pushed him over the edge.

'OK,' he'd say. 'See that the elephants are washed down, and the acrobats have a good dinner.'

The head butler bowed gracefully as usual. 'Yes, sir.'

Ichibod chose a bedroom for the night at random (all twenty of them were dressed and prepared with clean sheets, dropper and needle at each bedside, in case he wanted to swap rooms in the middle of the night, something he was prone to do in his jagged state after his morphine hit). Every room had its curtains securely taped to the walls, all to make sure that absolutely no daylight would enter the house. That was very clear; a sackable offence if not carried out. Ichibod lived in this dark exile for years, preparing the needle in his bedclothes, wrapping his leather belt around his arm, and tightening it until the veins bulged.

The relief of the plunger lowering was always life-affirming. That was the release; the thing that truly gave him peace.

He would sit in a huge purple leather chair, resting his feet on a matching footstool, and feel the night fall away. Images danced before him in the darkness, speaking to him in dulcet tones as he slowly drifted to sleep.

Years passed, and his addiction had grown to horrendous measures. Then one morning he awoke with a letter skidding under the door along the polished wooden floor, finishing right at his feet.

It was addressed to 'The Estate of Sir Ichibod Mantis'. How it had reached him was anyone's guess. The only forwarded mail Ichibod received was from his many business associates that handled his global assets. The back of the envelope told him as much. It had been forwarded from several other addresses, firstly from the 'M'eudail Hotel' (from the Gaelic, meaning beloved or soulmate) on South Uist which he owned. It was the first property Ichibod ever bought, and was named in deference to the Gaelic phrase he would purr to baby Bertrand in his arms, lightly touching his tiny chin, 'M'eudail, m'eudail'. He had never felt as much love for anything as he did when he used that word. Then to his mines in South Africa, to car factories in Denver, to textiles in India, then to his art gallery in Paris, then to Veronica Hall, forwarded by one of his most discreet accountants.

He broke the candle wax seal and opened the crisp paper, headed with the title **'IN THE EVENT OF MY PREDECEASING MY FATHER'**. The handwriting had the melancholic majesty of a delicate artist, someone who understood love.

There was heart in its crossed Ts, and yearning in its low-sweeping Ys.
It read:

10th June 1943

'Dear Father,

That is the first time I have written such words directly for yourself. Too bad it is to deliver my final wishes, as I don't think I will be able to hold on much longer. The ECT has been more rigorous of late – much more than the first three days - and the doctors grow impatient with my lack of progress. What can I do? I refuse to bow to their antics. They will not remove my thoughts of her. Or memories of my bed sheet I slung over the ceiling beam to deliver me from despair. I failed.

I can't bring myself to tell you where I am. They won't allow me any visitors for the initial months anyway. They can't risk my madness affecting others on the outside.

To assure you, sir, I feel no grudge about your leaving. It wasn't your making, and mother told me you desired to stay here with me (I write 'here' as if I am still on Uist). What I ask is for you to carry out some tasks on my behalf.

My fiancé, Rose, and I, planned to run away from the war by taking refuge on Anderson's Island. Only I have failed to reach her and worry about her wellbeing. Could you arrange her and her companions' safe return, but ONLY if they will be safeguarded from South Uist. They will surely be severely punished for their actions.

To conclude – I wish to state on record, on paper, in sacred word, that although I have never really known you or spoken to you about all the beauty of this world, but having heard mother's stories about how hard you battled for me, I feel as I am so close to death now, that I can finally say with absolute conviction, that I love you. I love you, father. And now I have loved enough.

Could you also please furnish Rose with all my writings, which are kept in my bedside cabinet next to my bed.

Your ever loving son, *Bertrand Mantis*'

Ichibod dropped the letter and sobbed his bloody guts out, too stricken to move for hours, crawling along, pounding the polished wooden floor with his fists, his nose streaming, his vision unclear in glaucoma'd grief. I have loved enough. He had never been prouder. He kicked over the side table where his needle and morphine sat, and ran around every room, tearing all the curtains away from the window; blankets of white light pouring into the room, revealing walls and walls of leather-bound books. The staff came running out their quarters as word spread that Ichibod was coming outside. The butler walking towards Ichibod's bedroom dropped the tray with his breakfast of omelette and coffee.

'Are you OK, sir?' he asked, wondering if he had taken a hit too many.

He marched past him, clutching the letter. 'Get me a phone line to South Uist coastguard and ready my plane at the Garten military base.'

The butler gazed around the room. He had never seen it in natural light before. Every inch suddenly lit up and alive, the house was being exhumed.

'My son mentions madness in this letter. I want a list of every sanatorium in Scotland with a contact address.'

The butler looked around him for his support staff. He hadn't been given so many jobs to do for years.

'Well come on, man, chop chop!' Ichibod yelled, clapping his hands. 'We've a busy day ahead.'

21
Names, names, names

Maggie's eyes were exhausted from reading the endless blue ink scrawled in the visitor logbooks. When she wasn't reading she was writing; she found the hours slipped away that bit quicker the more she immersed herself in the written word. Her universe sprung to life, and the vibrancy of existence was so strong, so cataclysmic, she vowed never to leave it.

Every day was a thousand new names. James McKee, Billy Brown, Andrew Young, Mr and Mrs Long John Silver (written in childish spaced-out letters), a man named simply Max, twins Roberta and Robert Sullivan, the Paddington family...

After a while her head felt like it switched to the BBC intermission picture of the girl sat in front of the blackboard, a game of knots and crosses behind her. Where had she gone? Did the BBC kill her off? Did she ever win that bloody game? The colour band skewed and distorted every few seconds, images flashing epileptically in and out of her brain. Then her head would be filled with nothing. Completely empty, and she felt like she had drifted outside her own body. She was but a passenger now, her bones feeling light and adrift, untethered.

Her concentration couldn't maintain after more than forty pages of reading. Her mind wandered to thoughts like, 'what would happen if I tore out a page from the newspaper archive at the library. Would all the news from that day be forever unknown? Would time travellers that happened to be in that day, be stuck in a black hole forever?' 'Although time travel is impossible right now, surely it won't always be impossible? So that means there must be time travellers walking amongst us at points. I wonder who they are.' Also, 'what would happen to the world if the letter 'e' disappeared? Like that book A Void by Georges Perec that Miss Gray showed me after class that one time. It was really rubbish. The world needs the letter 'e'. Surely?'

She thought:

The sun wouldn't burn –
that much was obvious.
No light would fill the days,
and humanity would think,
'Why? The sun cannot fail!'
But it has. And it

was us that did it.
Now the stars follow,
dying in thousands.
Can't nations stand tall,
bringing about magic
for all? What I would risk
for that fantasy of yours.
It isn't a solitary wish.

Maggie put down her notepad and pen and vowed to stop wasting time. But she couldn't bring herself to close the logbooks. She was still ten pages short of her target, but there was a chance that if she kept reading in her state, that she might miss Rose's name all together. Then she would have to go back and start all over again. And then she found what she needed. That grain, that seed. Hope.

She had to find Bertrand immediately. She packed up all of Rose's letters and everything else of Bertrand's in to her backpack. There was nothing else to be gleaned from them. The last letter she read ended with Rose talking about coming to the end of her life, despite her tender years. Maggie thought how cruel it was for someone to die so young. She couldn't help but think of Trish, and replaying the accident in her mind. That piece of paper going up in the air that piece of paper going up in the air that piece of paper going ... She wondered if she should have been playing around with that torrid line of self-pity, IT WAS ALL MY FAULT! IT WAS ALL MY FAULT! But that never occurred to her. It was quite obvious it wasn't her fault. She hated when films and books dragged that old emotive carcass out the drawer. There must be some other line of questioning when an accident happens. Why did no one ever blame God for giving us free will, and the freedom to run out into roads without looking first? Huh? Why not blame him?

The rain had been coming down in one giant smeared sheet upon Maggie; feeling no gaps between the drops.

Trish and her had been arguing all that morning. They should have been at school, but neither Jean nor Bill were around to make them go. Jean was out at Asda, and Bill was at work, leaving the two free to skip classes.

Maggie remembered Trish yelling at her to leave her alone: 'Shack's coming over, and I don't want you hanging around, flirting with him. You always do that. Why can't you just find someone of your own? You're such a manky wee slapper.'

'I can't go to school today. Jenny Spanner's gonna be at PE class, and they always laugh at my skinny legs when I'm getting changed. I hate her. She's a stupid boot.'

A car blasted its horn at Maggie as she nearly stepped out in front of the traffic. The rain teeming down now, the sky's own sadness, weeping for something. Maybe for me, she thought.

Maggie took off her backpack and hugged it, trying to keep the rain from soaking through the lining and ruining all of Bertrand's precious letters. She quickened her pace, jogging at first as the football boy and his mates stood under the roof of the old shopping arcade ('To Let' boards stuck on every window) shouting abuse at her, making her build to a run.

'There she goes. Skinny little Maggie from Hunterhill's a tart!' they sang in chorus.

She started to yell out, 'Bertrand, Bertrand,' although she was still a good two streets away from his house.

The streets grew quieter as she reached the abandoned end of Hunterhill, more and more windows covered with plywood. She stopped running and sat on the edge of the pavement to gather her breath. She didn't want to alarm him. Her face was dripping, the cold bringing out the first blemishes of teenage spots on her forehead - the one reason she never looked at her face when she got out the shower. She enjoyed a cold shower, like they were a test of sorts that she had to prevail - she had to be able to take the pain of the freezing water. Stepping out from behind the curtain in to a soft towel, that was her favourite moment. At that point no one could stop her. The freezing water had been her sworn enemy; a collective enemy of everyone that made her feel such melancholy. Then she would see herself in the mirror...

She climbed over the tyres in Bertrand's garden, slipping on one and striking her face. Being rubber it shouldn't have hurt as much as it did, but the thud had really sunk in to her cheek bone, right where Bill had smacked her one, earlier that morning. There was a brief pause for the pain to sink in and to feel the frustration of the pouring rain, then she yelled out. She punched her thigh, just to let out the anger. Feeling the numbness, she did it again, convinced if she kept at it, it would make her feel better. The pain slowly crept up.

She punched her leg again. And punched it, and punched it, and punched it, the ache building in her hands, until she sat down, giving in to her tears. 'Bertrand, where are you?' she cried out.

She yelled and yelled for him but there was no answer.

He should have been there, cradling her like a father, her head fitting perfectly into the space between his chin and chest, the rain soaking through his cream shirt, then through his vest, clinging to his sagging old man pecs.

She cried some more then kicked the broken kitchen door open, ready to leave, when she heard him talking to himself in the living room. She crept in, standing in the kitchen doorway, her hair strung down her forehead from the rain in thick strands. She inched forward into the living room, dripping in to the box marked, 'The only things that make me happy in the morning now she's gone'. She took pages out from it and started to read aloud to herself, still half-sobbing.

'"I was watching the weather this morning. It makes me happy, watching the presenters when I'm still waking up. They're so chirpy and happy and enthusiastic about this thing that hardly anyone cares about. Except golfers and people wanting to dry their washing.'

'It's true. They make me feel so happy, it's a great way to start the day. The way they find a link between the last news item and the first part of the weather report.'

'I watched the news this morning. The last story before I left, was a dour-looking policeman with a moustache in the TV studio saying, 'Terror was still a threat'. Then they cut to the weatherman who was smiling really wide, and said, 'I'll tell you what else is a threat: this great big band of low pressure coming our way! The heavens are surely going to open over Scotland".'

Maggie knew Bertrand was laughing. But she no longer knew who was speaking. Herself or Bertrand.

'"But I was looking forward to it. I thought it was such a nice thing to hear. 'The heavens are opening'. I ran outside and told the postman to go home and get all his family and friends round to stand in his garden, because the heavens were going to open. He didn't even care. I couldn't understand why he wouldn't be excited. Then this afternoon, the heavens really did open, and it was a horrible surprise. Not like I imagined at all.'

'I wouldn't be too concerned about the heavens opening. I'm not holding my breath that it would be anything special. There's nothing up there that you can't find down here. I'll bet God hates it up there, that's why he makes things so hard for us all. He's just jealous that he's losing. Sure, all those people in suits and politicians, they're all losing. All those people killing other people, they're losing. But not us. God can never beat us. Do you know why?"'

Maggie shook her head, as she flicked forward to the end

of the page marked, 'What will happen when the heavens open'.

'Because he can't take us out of our heads. No one can.'

Maggie nodded and put the 'What will happen when the heavens open' papers down.

'So ... have you found anything in that visitor's book, yet?' he asked.

'No! No, I haven't found anything, yet. I'm just stupid, skinny little Maggie from Hunterhill!'

Bertrand held his arms out to hold her. She fell abruptly into him, pushing his chair back a few inches.

'I thought my father was dead, you know.'

Maggie squinted. 'What do you mean?'

'When I was in Cherry Tree, I wrote to my father. The electric convulsive therapy was rough. It was only my second week there. In hindsight I feel foolish for entertaining such thoughts, so I never said. But at the time, I was more than prepared. I swear I thought I was dying and there was nothing I could do. It didn't matter how young I was. But I wrote to him, a letter begging him to get Rose from the island, to get her to safety without her having to go back to South Uist. I dread to think what would have happened to her there. Whether it be from her own thoughts, or the actions of others.

'I left instructions for my writings to be given to Rose. And I told him it didn't matter that I couldn't remember having met him, or what he looked like, because he fought for me; he never gave up on me, until the courts told him to. I dread to think what it did to him, as immodest as that sounds.'

'Not at all. It's understandable. Ichibod's lucky to have you as a son. I don't understand how he found me, and not you, though.'

'It's something I think about long and hard into the night.'

Maggie pursed her lips. 'I can feel that we're so close to the truth now. It's not far away.'

Bertrand sat beside her on the sofa, the cover with more holes in it than fabric. Stains from food eaten years ago, crusted deep inside like the nicotine-stained fingertips of men sat at bus stops reading Racing Form.

'Bertrand, I have to tell you something.' She pulled out one of the leather binders and opened at a yellowing page. She touched his hand, waiting for his attention. 'Bertrand. Look, look at this! It's Ichibod's name.'

He didn't budge. 'Yes, Maggie, we know that already.'

'No, there's more. Look here. At a later date.'

She flipped the book around and pointed to the entry at

22nd May 1952.

He read it out. 'Ichibod Mantis. That's what I said. We know that.'

'Look at the next entry.'

Bertrand peered at the small writing, then his eyes widened. 'Rose ... McDonald. They're at the same ... the same...'

'The same date, the same time! 22nd May, 1952.'

'That means...'

'They were signing in to see you. They were there together!'

Maggie was overjoyed as she documented the occurrence in her pad, like she had the whole journey, grinning at how she was bringing them together. She could really find love out of nothing!

Bertrand hugged Maggie as tight as he could. 'Oh Maggie, that means he got my letter. He rescued her; he got her off the island. Thanks to my letter.'

Maggie wriggled out of Bertrand's embrace. 'But what do we do now?'

'I don't know. What do you think?'

Maggie chewed her pen, then raised her finger, as an idea came. 'Where did you say that estate of Ichibod's was?'

22
Bill's Tics

Charlotte and Bill had been together for most of the day, taking half hour breaks for Charlotte to have a shower after each act, blow-drying her hair after each fuck, and reapplying touches of her makeup. Bill didn't mind, as it gave him a chance to watch the Top Gear reruns on UK Gold on the bed. God, how he wished he was Jeremy Clarkson.

Charlotte was used to Bill's tics – she had one of her own, like always shutting her eyes when they screwed. Bill didn't care about that, though. He had heard people talk at great length about how beautiful someone's eyes were. Bill never felt anything when looking into someone's eyes, or got 'lost in them'. Eyes were for looking and that was it. What more could you really expect from eyes? Eyes! That's what they are. That's all they are.

He could feel his legs growing weak, he couldn't maintain much longer. He banged away harder than he ever had.

'Shut up!' he kept yelling as Charlotte groaned.

As Bill's agitation grew, the more it seemed directed at himself, or at least some internal dialogue going on inside him.

'I'M THE MAN OF THE FAMILY,' he yelled as he came, before rolling quickly off Charlotte, and slid his boxers back on, his erection yet to decrease.

He sat on the edge of the bed, stared intently up at the ceiling, ignoring Charlotte's attempts to caress his back. Noticing his lack of response, she slowly slid her hand further down, creeping around his stomach and under the waistband of his boxers. She stared at his brick wall of a back, looking for some indication he wanted more.

WHAT'S SHE DOING NOW? I WISH SHE'D LEAVE ME IN FUCKING PEACE. ALWAYS WANTING MORE. IT'S NEVER ENOUGH...

GIE HER A BIT AH ROUGH, SON. IF THAT'S WHIT SHE WANTS, THEN GIE IT TAE HER.

...I'M NOT GOING TO HIT HER. NOT YET, ANYWAY...

YOU ALWAYS WERE A SISSY. I SAID TO YER MAW ONCE, HE'S A FUCKIN SISSY, THAT BOY, BILL. HE WANTS TEACHING IN HOW TO BE A MAN. WHO'S GONNAE BE THE MAN AH THE FAMILY EFTER AH'M GONE? BILL? HA HA HA HA!

...I AM THE MAN OF THE FAMILY...

YER NOTHING, SON.

Charlotte was rubbing harder now in long motions. Bill closed his eyes in anguish and pushed himself up onto his feet.

Charlotte smelled herself and thought about taking another shower. She looked down at the carpet and tutted. She got out of bed and started picking up a trail of Bill's sock lint leading to the bed. It seemed so easy to her, to present everything just so: neat and tidy, clean lines and polished surfaces. She didn't understand why everyone else didn't do the same. Presentation could do so much. She was the elegant swan on the stream, kicking away frantically underneath.

She wiped her hands. 'There. I can relax now.'

Everything about Charlotte irked Bill now. He wanted her to bend her legs at a more acute angle when they fucked. He wanted her to lean down when he did her from behind. He wanted to sweep her hair off his shoulder when it tickled him. He didn't want her to come into the shower, then touch his face and kiss him. His back was not meant for kissing. But these things happened anyway.

'I don't want to do this anymore,' Charlotte revealed quickly and got out the shower.

Bill went after her to try and pull her back in. 'Don't be stupid!'

'I don't want to do this anymore,' she repeated starkly. 'And now you're dripping all over the carpet.'

GIE HER A SLAP FER ME, SON.

'NO!' he yelled.

'This situation depends on me. I say when we stop!'

RIGHT, NOW SHE'S REALLY ASKIN FER IT. IF THAT'S NO ASKIN FER IT, I DON'T KNOW WHIT IS.

Bill threw down the wet towel on the floor. 'There. What you going to do about that?'

Charlotte stepped forward and slapped him.

Bill pulled his fist back ready to punch her, his hand trembling, ready to let the springs in his shoulder and elbow go.

GO ON, SON. NOW'S YER CHANCE!

But he couldn't do it. Charlotte jumped forward and kissed him, digging her nails into his back. This was what she needed. A real man. Finally!

Her moaning and groaning covered up the keys turning in the front door, and the slow, depressed footsteps coming up the stairs. Henry opened the bedroom door and didn't really react to the sight of his wife kissing another man, both freshly shower-wet. He put his briefcase down, gently, like it contained unwrapped glass inside, and he cleared his throat.

Charlotte whipped around and grabbed at the bed sheets to cover herself. Bill laughed to himself how she was covering herself from her own husband. He decided not to point this out, though.

'Henry?' she barked accusingly at him. 'You're not supposed to be here. Why are you not at work? You're supposed to be at work!'

Henry's mouth dried up, his speech indistinct even to himself. 'I'm ... I'm sorry.' His and Bill's eyes met. Henry wondered if this would end in his being beaten up. 'You know it's bad for the shower to leave the immersion on like that.' He went downstairs, leaving his briefcase standing on the bedroom floor.

'Fuck,' Charlotte said to herself as she put her clothes on over her wet body. 'Come on, you,' she directed Bill, 'get out of here.'

SHE'S GOT SOME MOUTH ON HER, THIS ONE, AH'LL TELL YE.

YEAH. I'VE BEEN SHOWING HER HOW TO USE IT.

HA HA HA HA HA! GOOD FOR YOU. THAT'S MA BOY. THAT'S MA SON. *THE MAN AH THE FAMILY.*

Bill dried himself and slid on his oil-stained overalls much slower than what he wanted to, just to annoy Charlotte, just because it wasn't what she wanted.

Charlotte stood soaking into her clothes, leaning over the kitchen table as Henry boiled the kettle.

'Would you like a cup?' he asked her.

'No.'

'What about him?'

'His name is Bill.'

'I know. He told me when I booked the car in two weeks ago.'

'Don't take that tone with me.'

'Sorry.'

'Stop apologising.'

'Sorry,' he said again, dropping his cup, spilling the coffee beans all over the counter.

'Henry, look at the mess you're making.' Charlotte swept them up in her hand. 'And don't slam those cups. They're Royal Doulton.'

'Is there anything I could have done differently?' he asked, staring out the window at the neighbour's garden, balking at how, at such a moment, he could be wondering: How does he get his hedge so level? Mental note: ask Fred how he gets his hedge so level. Some kind of special spirit level? He shook himself back to attention.

Charlotte wanted to be clear on this point. 'No. You'll always be you, and there are things I need that you can't give me.'

'Why did you marry me?'

Charlotte huffed, trying to move as much as possible; opening and closing cupboards for unneeded cups, and running the tap then stopping it, running orbits around Henry's satellite presence, left in no-man's land between fridge and breakfast bar, open space. Stillness was an enemy at times like these. 'Don't be so stupid, Henry. It made sense at the time. We're perfect.'

'Clearly we're not.'

'But no one else knows. So what does it matter?'

'Is it over? With ... Bill.'

'Of course it is. I have no emotional investment in this.'

Bill appeared at the kitchen door, hands stuffed wrist-deep in his pockets. He had heard every word since coming down the stairs, and – strangely - hearing from Charlotte's mouth to someone else that it was over, made the whole thing seem more final. He didn't like hearing her say it. I have no emotional investment in this. Only posh folk talk like that.

Charlotte looked at Henry. 'Henry!'

'What is it?'

'Are you not even going to offer Bill a ride home?'

Henry out down his coffee. 'Sorry. Bill would you like a ride home?'

23
Another Obscure Request

Maggie skipped happily down the street to Bertrand's. She didn't care about the other kids laughing and pointing at her for skipping at her age. She didn't even hear them. But that skipping petered out as she approached Bertrand's street, the air filled with the noise of machinery; of tractors moving, and bulldozers pummelling; falling bricks and crumbling mortar. Maggie rounded the corner to see the houses at the end of the road being demolished, a row of concrete barriers erected only a few houses down from Bertrand's to stop anyone getting past. WORKS ACCESS ONLY the numerous signs said.

Some workmen walked around just beyond them. Maggie tried to get their attention but they couldn't hear her over the noise. She wanted to ask them to keep it down, for Bertrand and her had a lot to discuss, but they would just have to make the best of things.

Maggie made her way round to the back of his house, being careful not to fall on anything as the light drizzle had made the tyres, and everything else, extra slippery. Maggie looked at the boarded up kitchen window and door. She stood for a moment like a cat presented with a physical obstacle, and walked to the front of the house.

She knocked on the front door for so long she had to swap hands every other minute. 'Bertrand, Bertrand,' she called out, looking up hopefully to the first floor windows. 'Come on, we don't have time for this!'

She resorted to throwing bigger and bigger stones at the bedroom window until she ran out. She paced around the garden, trying to rationalise it. He was an old man after all, and it wouldn't be the first time Bertrand hadn't heard Maggie's voice. Sometimes it was like Maggie simply wasn't there.

'I can't get in, Bertrand, cos you've boarded up the back window and door.'

Still no answer. There was a padlock on the front door.

Maggie walked away, looking back at the house every so often, in case there was a slight twitch from the curtains. But there was nothing. She rounded the corner, and, feeling the house move definitively out of view, kicked at invisible objects.

A feeling of nausea crept around her stomach as she wandered the empty streets to the library.

When she got there she found the storm doors shut over. She was too early, by almost an hour, so she climbed the fifty or so steps and sat on the top one, dropping her backpack down between her feet. It wasn't so bad - it meant she could sit with the visitor's log and look over all the times that Ichibod and Rose had come to see Bertrand over the years from 1952: roughly twice a month up to mid-1955. Yes, that makes sense, she thought. Bertrand told me he got out sometime in 1955.

Maggie waved to each person that walked past as she waited. Some waved back, some didn't. A postman crossed and re-crossed the street, because he was new to the job and kept missing the even numbered addresses. Maggie thought he was looking for some polite human interaction, not just the blank shut doors he did business with.

'Do you like being a postie?' she shouted out to him in a childish high pitch.

'Naw, it's fucking shite,' he replied without looking at her.

The only people he would really get close to in his mornings were the people that had to sign for packages too big to fit through their letterboxes, or recorded delivery items. They would be dressed in their nightclothes, bleary-eyed (Maggie laughed, some with drool marks on the corners of their mouths) and scared to get too close to them because their breath smelled so bad. Maggie wondered if the real test of how much you love a person is if you can kiss them first thing in the morning – and not just a wimpy closed-mouth peck on the lips, but a full-on kiss with tongues rolling around. That was definitive proof, you can endure that stale taste you love so much, just because it's part of that person you love.

Then Maggie realised none of the fifteen boys she had been in love with that year had stayed long enough for her to find out.

There was movement behind the storm doors, keys turning and finally they opened. The librarian – the one who had toiled with the Sudoku puzzle – stood over her. His head dropped and he sighed as he recognised her. 'Oh Christ. What now?'

She raced in front of him into the reference section and waited at his desk. He sat down wearily. Maggie looked at the 'How To Win at Sudoku' book sitting on his desk. The man quickly put it away in the drawer.

'What'll it be?' he asked, grimacing as he put on his name badge – 'Jon'.

'Are you OK?'

'I'm hungover. Do you know what that means?'

'Yeah. It's what happens after you've had sex with someone.'

'Well that's not quite-' He shook his head as if to say, no, I'm not having this conversation this morning. 'Please, just tell me you're not going to have me running around for 19th Century newspapers again are you?'

'No. But how about some from the 20th?'

'What are you looking for?'

Maggie flipped through her notepad. 'I need all the articles you have on Sir Ichibod Mantis, from the Forties to the present day.'

The man was trying to type faster on the computer than he was capable of. Maggie noticed him making a lot of mistakes, banging the delete button after each flurry of keys.

'Do you know the 'h' is missing from your name.'

The man stared at the screen and took a long blink. 'No. It's not.'

'Sorry. I guess you get that a lot.'

'No. You're the only person that's ever mentioned it.'

He got up and disappeared behind the rows of archaic shelves, collecting all the relevant material. Ten minutes later he lay down a huge stack of leather bound newspapers.

'Everything from 1942 to present day. But you're going to have to find the articles yourself, because they're only hardcopies and not everything is subcategorised.'

'Alright. Thank you,' Maggie said graciously, opening the first volume: The Daily Telegraph, 3rd June 1942. One of the two headlines on the front page, -'Aristocrat to wed Swedish Royal Beauty.'

The morning wore on, the unemployed slowly filtering in to read the free papers. Maggie noticed a correlation between the earliness of the day and the more obscure the requests: 'I'm looking for information about a horse that ran in the 60s called Sparky,' 'I need to view the minutes of the last Council meeting that was written in ink. Not typed, mind. Ink.' 'Now I'm in a bit of a hurry, so I need you to find me a book on how to get people to change their wills.'

What Maggie really hated was that she would be thought of as just another Obscure Request. Another blank face with a stupid question. Jon hadn't even asked her her name.

Maggie was amazed at Ichibod's notoriety, and for how long. He maintained stories on the front page for some six years, until sleaze in politics started getting more headlines. By the late Forties, Ichibod had been reduced to leering 'remember him?' stories coupled with photos of him lying in some street in Chelsea in the early hours; speculations of mental breakdown and suicide attempts abound - the sort of behaviour of 'mad' people. It hadn't been long before the society pages got tired of chasing a ghost that never gave them solid stories, so he faded into complete obscurity.

It had taken a little over four hours to reach the end of the entries for The Daily Telegraph - who were more inclined to carry stories on Ichibod back then – going up to November 1981.

Maggie moved on to The Times, and early afternoon turned into early evening. She thought, I should ask Jo(h)n what time they're open till tonight, but he was gone for the day now. The lady that had taken his place was doing a crossword at the desk.

Maggie asked, 'What time are you open till tonight?'

The lady was tapping her pencil on the page, confused by something. She suddenly remembered herself and looked up with the smile of a grandmother. 'Sorry, my love, 8pm.'

'OK.' Maggie turned her head to see the clue, mumbling to herself, 'Inclination, ten letters...'

The lady stared at the page, flicking her pencil back and forth like an out of control pendulum.

Maggie shut her eyes, pausing to think. 'Yep,' she was sure, feigning hesitation. 'It's em ...'proclivity', you want there, not 'partiality', otherwise '23 Across', which should be 'acrimonious', won't go.'

The lady froze, working out if the combinations worked; she stopped flicking her pencil and changed the word. Suddenly it made sense. 'Th-thank you, dear.'

Maggie's vision started going the same way it had after the Cherry Tree Estates' visitor's logbook. The problem was exacerbated this time, as she didn't know exactly what she was looking for. A hint at the whereabouts of Ichibod's estate could have been included in even the most trivial article, so she had to be aware at all times, never skipping a page or seemingly inconsequential paragraph.

The unemployeds were now back for the Evening Times. Maggie hated how they asked for them in such a challenging manner – forgetting it was a gratuity they were asking for.

One of them brashly hauled out a chair next to Maggie, and sat down. His anorak kept ruffling, the only sound in the room. Maggie tried to concentrate, but with every slight movement her eyes glazed over the page. She was now simply staring at the page, out of focus, waiting for the next rustle to come, and when it did, she jumped to her feet and yelled, 'Can't you just buy a fucking paper and leave me alone? They're only 30p across the street, you stupid bum!'

The lady at the desk spun her chair round, so she could laugh without anyone seeing her. The man flung his chair back, striking the chair behind, and stormed out. Everyone looked at Maggie.

She pulled her chair in and said quietly, 'I'm sorry about that. Some people are awfully rude. My friend Bertrand – he's my only friend in the whole world – he would have done the same thing.'

The light outside was dimming, and Maggie's hope of finding what she was looking for before closing seemed increasingly unlikely. She read with great sadness as the true extent of his breakdown following the end of his relationship with Princess Veronica unravelled. The Princess had turned to bulimia and cutting herself, fleeing banquets in the Royal chambers to purge herself and break open discreet passages of skin (inside of the legs was best. Only lovers would see there. And if they didn't understand why she did it, she didn't want them as lovers anyway. It was a whole system of savagery she had with lovers after Bertrand). They loved to speculate on madness. Reading the stories in chronological order only heightened Maggie's emotions to it, life becoming linear again. Ichibod had been so desperately abandoned, no one wanting to know him now that he had no link to royalty. Ichibod's extravagance had the glimmer of a broken man, drinking and doping himself to death to escape the outside world.

Then an idea came to her. She skipped forward to The Herald, dated 4th October 1981. Nothing on the front page, or the opening inside pages. Then as she kept turning, she reached the 'Classifieds' pages. 'Grand piano for quick sale. Requires tuning but is in good condition.' 'Golden Retriever for sale. £45 ONO', then over the page was an ad for the Co-op and some familiar offers. 'Jacob's cream crackers, only 15 1/2p. A bottle of White Horse whisky for £6.25'; familiar to her like the feeling of your own bed, only to find it warm from a stranger sleeping in it during the day. She knew now who had sent her the note '4th October. 1981. Read me.' Things were starting to make sense to Maggie.

Fighting off a growing feeling of faintness, she flicked through her notepad, with all the names and dates she had been collecting. She imagined Trish feeling the same just before she died; car headlights catching her eyes, helpless to do anything but wait for it to hit and sweep her off her feet. She had a tiny moment to realise what her life had been for and where she might be going. Trish only had time to think of a single word or image. She must have thought of something. How can one word or image sum up an entire life? Maggie knew what hers would be. She saw a heart, not a Valentine's Day heart, but a proper biological heart, drained of sentiment and smooth curves. It was a charcoal drawing of her heart, easily smudged by rain, and frequently ruined by the grubby fingerprints of strangers. That's what she wanted to see.

Maggie put the binder down on the lady's enquiry desk, the paper turned to the back pages.

'Are you alright?'

Maggie stated, 'Did you know St Mirren drew with Partick Thistle on 4th October 1981?'

Her smile was as sincere as several hours ago. The kind that made Maggie want to forgive everyone in the world. 'No, I didn't know that.'

Maggie closed the binder over as the lady checked the others back in. When her back was turned, Maggie sneaked the one binder she didn't have time to look through, into her bag. She had a feeling there was still more to be found out about Sir Ichibod Mantis yet.

Dear Diary

5th July 2005
I'm on the bus and I've just found another letter from Rose.

20th August 1943

Dear Bertrand,
FUCK! FUCK! FUCK! FUCK! FUCK! FUCK! FUCK! FUCK!
FUCK! FUCK! FUCK! FUCK! FUCK! FUCK! FUCK! FUCK!
FUCK! FUCK! FUCK! FUCK! FUCK! FUCK! FUCK! FUCK!
FUCK! FUCK! FUCK! FUCK! FUCK! FUCK! FUCK! FUCK!
FUCK! FUCK! SHIT! FUCK!
FUCK!

That's it. That's all it says. It's really sad.
There's a really cute boy sitting across from me. I'm giggling now. He's wondering what I'm giggling about. He thinks I'm crazy. Look at him, with his floppy hair. He has no idea that I'm writing about how cute he is. And he'll never know. Know what I think?

FUCK! FUCK! FUCK! FUCK! FUCK! FUCK! FUCK! FUCK!
FUCK! FUCK! FUCK! FUCK! FUCK! FUCK! FUCK! FUCK!
FUCK! FUCK! FUCK! FUCK! FUCK! FUCK! FUCK! FUCK!
FUCK! FUCK! FUCK! FUCK! FUCK! FUCK! FUCK! FUCK!
FUCK! FUCK! SHIT! FUCK!
FUCK!

24
The (w)hole of my heart

When Maggie arrived home, she was met with the strangest sight: Bill getting out of a Mercedes, the man from the hotel from Trish's reception driving him. He got out with two bags from Haddows, clanging all the way up to the front door.

Bill didn't see her, so Maggie hid behind the hedgerow then sneaked into the back garden. She sat on the bench below the living room window as drizzle started to fall. After a few minutes her skin was greasy from the rain, and she reminded herself not to look at her reflection in the mirror when she went inside. But she didn't want to go in just yet. Bill was drinking like a man possessed, gulping down bottles of beer like water.

As soon as one was finished he lunged feverishly for the bottle opener, scared that for one second he might not be intoxicating himself, and therefore giving Charlotte's words – I have no emotional investment in this – a chance to reappear. It was all he had heard in his head the whole ride home in Henry's car. Every question Henry asked could be answered with the same response.

'So where do you work?'

I have no emotional investment in this.

'Are you ... em ... married, then?'

I have no emotional investment in this.

'Do you have any kids?'

I have no emotional investment in this.

'I was thinking ... the car's due its MOT soon.

I have no emotional investment in this.

And so it was until they pulled into Hunterhill. Bill could sense Henry's disgust with Charlotte growing, as pathetically placid as he had been about the whole thing. Henry was too used to delegating, to being removed from decision-making, to feel any real emotion about what had been going on with his wife and his mechanic. Maybe Charlotte would tell him what to feel when he got home.

Bill talked up the reconstruction of the neighbourhood, but nothing that could placate his feelings of hopeless inadequacy in the company of such wealth. He could imagine Henry laughing inside, that for even a second he had felt threatened by Bill. OK, so he had screwed his wife - and evidently better than him - but that meant nothing in the Spence circle. Bill knew it was Henry that had the longevity. Henry had the emotional involvement. Henry was the one who actually slept with Charlotte.

He collapsed in the chair, changing to Sky Sports News. With every comment uttered he shouted at the TV: 'THIS GUY DOESN'T KNOW FUCK ALL! GET HIM OFF (he petted himself heavily trying to produce an erection). WHERE'S THAT BRUNETTE WITH THE BIG TITS?'

Maggie sat outside, listening to the one-way quarrel; the occasional empty bottle smashing against the wall or the radiator. She looked up, seeing how long she could let the drizzle fall straight into her eyes.

It was completely dark out now, so she contemplated trying Bertrand again. Wherever he had gone he should have been back.

She locked the back gate, leaving Bill's shouting and banging behind her. When she reached the town centre, she saw David and Lucy, the ones with the spark that had fallen in love because of Maggie. They were walking hand in hand, the hoods on their jackets down, not caring about how soaked they were getting as the rain turned heavier.

Maggie stared on from the other side of the road, arms hanging dead at her side. 'I don't want to be alone anymore,' she told herself. 'It's too hard this way.' As she started to cry the pair smudged into oblivion, and no matter how hard and fast she wiped her eyes, Maggie couldn't see them anymore.

At that time of night - around 9pm, Mr E's peak hours – Maggie noticed the kind of character walking nearby Rowan Street: speed freaks looking for the next buzz; churlish smackheads looking for a come-down (always one talking feverishly, the other repeating 'Aye, aye' at every other noun or adjective); grubby stoners looking for the next high, a lot more relaxed in their addiction, because they never thought of smoking weed as an addiction. The stoners were more inclined to smile at you. Their high was of a different sort, taking them to a place that was calm, generally of their own making (which Maggie liked).

A steady procession vacated Mr E's semi-detached, happiness on their faces from finding a score, or wild desperation to get home and score it.

Maggie knocked on the door. The peephole flapped on the other side. She didn't have an appointment.

The chain came off straight away. Mr E stood drinking his milk, in a fresh pair of y-fronts. And Maggie had thought it was just a day-off thing.

'Maggie,' he proclaimed. 'What you doing here? You after something?'

'Not really.' She noticed his pleasant expression drifting. 'Actually, yeah. I could do with a smoke.'

He smiled. 'Come on in then. There's some people here, but they're too fucked to annoy you.'

Mr E shut the door, making sure the chain was back on. He couldn't have any twisted freaks just walking the hell in. Goddamn, that brutally pissed him off.

'Maggie, this is the Marky twins: Marky G, Marky P; Mr Mr, and Stevie D.'

She looked at their sorry faces, eyes wiped empty with chemicals. Mr E's homemade bongs stood proudly on the living room table, like trophies at a football club.

'Help yourself.' Mr E encouraged her towards the bong.

Maggie sat down, crossing her legs, and lit the bong with some premium grass inside. She sucked in and blew out.

'It's good shit,' she groaned, but it sounded like a scream in her head.

A DVD of The Big Sleep played on the TV, though the others had lost track of the labyrinthine plot after fifteen minutes.

'Oh, I know someone who loves Humphrey Bogart,' Maggie swooned.

Mr Mr sat up, noticing Maggie. 'Holy shit, someone better call the nursery. One of them's escaped.'

Marky G and P laughed.

Mr E threw a cushion at them. 'Hey, shut the fuck up, you two. Show some respect. Maggie's a guest. You two have been here two days. Isn't your mother wondering where her benefit money's gone?'

Mr Mr 'oohed' at the twins. 'You taking that, boys?'

Marky G got up, real fuckin slow, reaching for the bong. 'No I'm not. So I'm taking this instead.'

Mr Mr put his feet up on the vacant couch, Mr E telling him to take his goddamn shoes off.

'Don't people's ignorance brutally piss you off, Maggie?'

Maggie was completely satiated.

Mr Mr took out his crack pipe from behind the sofa – just to let Maggie know he was hardcore. Maggie hadn't seen one since Pete D's – she was too scared to take some. At least that's what Jenny Spanner had told everyone at school.

Mr Mr's face was ravaged from the stuff. His eyes looked like flat stickers put on to his face, his skin seemed to be weeping off his face, pockmarks forming a slalom run down his cheeks. His complexion told of many chemicals from a young age, far too young to have seen and done all he had. It was as if he was too full of experiences to make room for new ones, and now he was just sailing out to sea a burning wreck, ready to sink.

He pulled out a silk hankie expecting to find a rock. 'Hey, Jambo! I need filling up!'

'Can I get some water, Ray?' Maggie asked.

'Sure. I'll take you through. It's just ... some of the rooms are occupied. It might be a bit dodgy.'

He took her down a pitch black corridor to the kitchen, where a middle-aged man – the one in the suit that was brutally pissing off Mr E before – sat at the table doing lines, while a tall guy of seventeen stood over the sink with a kettle just boiled. He held a small bottle – a mixture of acetone, water and powdered cocaine – over the steam, spewing out the kettle. Then he took a small metal rod and dipped it in the neck of the bottle, a crystal forming around it. He placed the crystal down on the sink's draining board to cool down. Mr Mr appeared, taking the fresh ones off the board and going back to the living room.

'Jambo, can we get in here a sec?' Mr E asked.

He was adamant, 'Your house, man,' and beckoned him over.

Mr E gave Maggie the glass of cold water, which she flushed down in seconds. 'Thirsty, huh?'

Jambo smiled at her, and whispered something to Mr E, who didn't seem impressed with what Jambo had to say.

'Nah, man. She's barely fourteen.'

Maggie interjected, 'I'll be fifteen in October.'

They all went back to the living room; Mr Mr spaced on the couch, the credits rolling on the DVD.

Mr E said, 'Why don't you put some music on, Maggie? Let's see what you dig.'

Maggie crawled along the floor, sliding in one of the ten 'Doors' CDs sitting on the hi-fi. After some gentle guitar licks, Jim Morrison's voice broke in, The End, and everyone shut up.

Mr E, tapped Mr Mr on the leg. 'Told you she was golden.' He took Maggie over to the drinks cabinet and produced a newspaper. Or at least, two pages of it. 'You recognise this?'

Maggie looked at the headline. 'Tragedy of mental patient suicide'.

'I couldn't have Dee-dee reading that shit day after day. It might have struck a chord eventually. I thought you should know, seeing as you've been up seeing her.' Mr E closed the drinks cabinet with the pages he had stolen from Dee-dee locked inside. 'Felt like the least I could do after what I put her through. It's too much responsibility that: being loved by someone. It's not fair in a way.'

Maggie tried to take Mr E's hand but he walked quickly to the other side of the room and rolled a joint as quickly as he could, trying to smoke something before any tears could come.

Mr Mr was sat on the edge of the couch with the crack ready in a sheet of foil. He was smirking, anticipation building as he lit the glass stem, trying not to hurry. Smoking a crack pipe properly is difficult. It's no Irn Bru bottle, anyway.

Jambo said to Maggie, 'So what's it like round your bit, just now? It must be pretty noisy with those bulldozers.'

'What do you mean?'

'Hunterhill. They started tearing down the old houses, haven't they?'

Maggie took a pass of the joint going round the room. 'That's a little bit away from me, all that. I've got a bulldozer of my own at home, anyway.'

Jambo said, 'D'you hear about all that, Ray? Your old man lived down there, didn't he? Before he went in the clink.'

Mr E wasn't in the mood now. 'That's "Mr E" when you're smoking my shit. Apart from Maggie. She knows how to be civilised. And I don't give a shit about my old man or where he used to live.'

Maggie looked around the room, carefully scrutinising each face one by one. Jambo was too old, but it seemed like he had shown some interest back in the kitchen. Mr Mr was too engrossed in his pipe and Maggie couldn't be sure of anything he would have to say. Either of the Markys was just too weird to contemplate. Then her eyes fell on Mr E. He was cute, uninvolved. But poor Dee-dee, she couldn't do that to her. The awful truth dawned on Maggie, that there was no possibility of her falling in love or at least getting pregnant by anyone in the house, unless someone appeared from one of the other rooms and proclaimed their love for her. But that seemed unlikely as they were either already getting laid or shooting up. Not that Mr E sold junk, but hey! his casa, was your casa, and whatever you wanted to bring to his casa...

Her mind wandered to the contents of her bag and what she had found in the library. There was even a second when she considered just throwing her bag in the fireplace and lighting it. Smoke a bowl and forget about the whole thing. She knew if she did, it would probably destroy Bertrand.

Maggie took another pass of the joint, and the music seemed to make more sense to her. 'I went to see Dee-dee ... oh yeah, I told you...'

'Yeah, you did. I sent someone up to see her again. Yesterday. Was all screwy about something. Talking about "finding who she was looking for". I don't know. You can never tie Dee-dee down to specifics.'

'Did she say anything else?'

'Lots of shit, apparently. The usual.'

'But anything more about who she was looking for?'

Mr E took one of the bongs up in his lap. 'What's with all the interest? Don't let Dee-dee pull you in with all her shit. If you listen to Dee-dee you're not listening to her. You're listening to the voices in her head. She's not really there.'

Maggie massaged her temples and grimaced as Mr E's words echoed. She's ... not ... really ... there. She could feel her head shrinking in on itself instead of expanding outwards.

Maggie staggered up and said her goodbyes with weak hugs - arms never really gripping the back - even to Stevie E sitting in the corner watching the TV: he hadn't moved or said a word since Maggie arrived and was now entranced with the blank screen.

Mr E said to her, 'Come back soon, you hear...'

She heard him slide the chain on the door behind her, which sounded like she was being locked out rather than him locking himself in. The rain was even heavier than before.

Maggie knew she had escaped nothing. There was music playing in her head, of burgeoning strings being plucked with increasing urgency as she waited for the last bus of the night, the words 'she's not really there' continuing in her background. Traffic seemed to make the noise of crashing cymbals as they sped past, colliding with large puddles.

Maggie knew it was all out of her hands now. They were bringing down the old estate. Bertrand had disappeared and Jean still wasn't home.

The bus cruised into the lay-by, its engine chugging and spluttering like it couldn't stand being still.

The doors swooshed open and she croaked, 'Just a half to Hunterhill.'

The driver twitched his head towards the seats. 'On you go, luv.'

The bus stayed empty all the way up to Dee-dee's, or County, or Cherry Tree Estates, or whatever the hell it was called. She held onto the binder with painful concentration, thinking about all that had happened to bring her there.

If only Trish hadn't been such a boot and tried to tell on me. If she just kept her stupid mouth shut. I wouldn't have ran after her; I wouldn't have chased her, and she wouldn't have ran out into the road. She should have just left me alone.

She opened the binder and started looking again, seeking out single words: 'Ichibod' 'Mantis' 'South Uist' 'Aristocrat'. The bus suddenly braked pushing Maggie forward a jolt where she was briefly suspended, and then suddenly back. As she hit the seat her eyes rested on the entry for 12th September 2004.

Something about the illumination of the brake lights ahead of the driver's window set her off, telling her it was over, nearly all over. The column started with 'Reclusive aristocrat reappears for-' She read on, and, relieved to have solitude, started to whimper, 'I need help. Someone please help me. I'm so fucking ... so fucking lonely...'

The driver overtook the stalled car in front, the resuming pace encouraging Maggie's tears.

'Mum,' she cried, the answer to a question she had never wanted to ask: What is wrong with me?

She shut her eyes and closed the binder, as if that made the story unreal. She knew what it meant. 'This the last stop, hen,' the bus driver shouted to her, looking via the rear view mirror, becoming only a pair of eyes and a forehead to her.

Maggie gathered up her things, holding the binder close to her chest, and forced a smile.

No one had forced a smile so much against their will.

Maggie stood at the gates of County; a cacophony of music in her head building and building, with bowed strings flowing back and forth from left ear to right, a steady upright bass-pluck in the middle, and crashing cymbals driving her on.

She followed the perimeter fence around the back of the hospital, finding a tree that could bridge her over into the grounds. Like Cherry Tree Estates before it, County teased at how close guests were to the outside, to the real world, where sanity was plentiful, and melancholy was scarce.

The staff quarters were lit up in the west wing, playing host to late-night nurses' card games, the night-watchmen's portable TVs on their collapsible chipboard tables, microwaves glowing and humming with ready meals.

Maggie made her way through the landscaped gardens and tree-bark walkways to the east wing. She raised her face skywards, feeling the moist post-rain night air, then looked back at the footprints she had made through the heavy dew on the grass. Seeing footprints always pleased Maggie: they were void of any meaning; they were of pure travel, of a journey leading somewhere. And hers lead to the French windows of Dee-dee's ward.

She crouched low, seeing a figure sat up in bed through a crack in the curtains. The bed sheets formed a tent over the person's head, the way Maggie read in bed, like a child. She tapped lightly on the window using her fingernails. The sheets came down off their head with a single swipe, sweeping old Kilpatrick's hair back against its grain across his face, sitting cross-legged, his backless smock shoehorned down around his waist.

'Dee-dee,' Maggie whispered, pointing towards her bed.

Old Kilpatrick hissed towards Dee-dee, who had already kicked her bed sheets down. Her smock was oversized, cascading over her feet, which made her look legless, ghostlike when she walked towards the window. She held her newspaper.

Dee-dee slid open the French window the few inches it could go. Her face was in darkness. 'Maggie,' she whispered. 'You've obviously heard the news?'

'No I ... what news?'

She rifled wildly through the pages without even looking at them, then stopped, seemingly at random, and drummed on the page with her finger. Dee-dee moved closer to the glass, the moonlight now illuminating her face. Her eyes were crimson with tears.

'How could I ever sleep again? He says he loves me. He's coming to get me.'

'Who loves you, Dee-dee?'

'It's what I've been looking for all this time. I can tell you don't believe me. But it's true.' She passed The Herald through the window to Maggie. 'Don't you see?'

Maggie scanned the page, mostly filled with adverts, except for a tiny article at the bottom. The headline was 'Well done!'. Maggie read the rest out: 'Schoolchildren from Elderslie recently raised £36 for the local senior citizen's welfare club by holding a jumble sale.' She waited for Dee-dee to explain.

'Isn't it incredible? That he would do that for me! He definitely loves me.'

'I ... don't understand-'

'To tell the whole world, to take out an advert telling them how much he loves me.' She snatched the newspaper back and retreated a step into the darkness.

'It's great news, alright,' Maggie said in monotone. 'I'm very happy for you, Dee-dee. But I need to speak to you about something.'

Dee-dee had spun around and was waltzing around the ward with the newspaper held to her chest. She was allowing her voice to raise, prompting groans and grunts and thrown pillows from her fellow residents.

Maggie tried to call her back before a nurse heard the noise. 'Dee-dee! It's about the note.'

She kept on dancing.

'The note you put in my coat pocket, after Trish's funeral.'

Dee-dee froze in the middle of the room, her back to Maggie.

'It was probably when you knocked our chairs over. It's ok, I know why you wrote it now.'

Dee-dee slowly came back towards the window, the newspaper now loose in her arms.

Maggie continued, 'I saw the paper in the library today. Your paper. I recognised the 'Classifieds'. Because how could anyone else have something to do with 4th October 1981. The same day as your newspaper matching the note. It was quite a day.'

'There was a grand piano for a quick sale,' Dee-dee added glumly, letting the newspaper drop at her feet. 'Needs tuning but is in good condition.'

'That's right,' Maggie said solemnly, as if she had broken a child's toy.

'Have you ever been in love, Maggie?'

'I suppose. A couple of times. Maybe.'

Dee-dee smiled ironically. 'Then you haven't been in love. It ... destroys you, when it goes away. Once, your life had a reason, a reason that trumped every other pain you could imagine. Every strife that came your way, you could always say, "well, at least I have a love in my life". But when it goes away...'

Maggie reached through the window, but could only graze Dee-dee's blackened fingertips. She had seen the way Oprah Winfrey held crying mothers' hands on her TV show as they explained how their children died, or their husband left them, or how an operation had left them unable to feel love. But Oprah's touch seemed like such a comfort. And the mothers loved Oprah for doing it. It wasn't fair: Maggie had just as much love to give as Oprah Winfrey, but who knew. 'Love isn't for people like us, Dee-dee. That's for other people. We just ... let others practice on us.'

'I know,' said Dee-dee. 'I just wanted to share my day with someone. Because he can never come here. Ray. He thinks it was him that put me here.'

'It was.'

Dee-dee looked down, away from Maggie. 'I didn't want to live in the real world anyway.'

'Do you know if you're mad? I mean, you sit there in bed with all the others around you, nurses down the hall, locked windows.' Maggie leaned in, her voice a kind of pleading. 'How can you tell if you're mad?'

'Other people tell you. But I know this: madness comes firstly with loneliness. Are you lonely, Maggie?'

Maggie looked away.

Farewell, then, love, I barely knew you...

Old Kilpatrick started to groan about the draft, holding onto the bed frame and bounced on it, the metal legs rattling on the linoleum floor. Maggie saw a series of lights go on down a hallway across the garden. Three nurses ambled slowly, crepuscular, towards the noise.

...Let me not fight this solitude, this desolation,
give me her arms, give me words to catch them...

'They'll be here in a minute. I'll need to go,' Maggie said, about to get to her feet.

'Wait. Your friend. Where is he?'

...In my dreams, that's when I miss her most.
Her tender breast, it was my pillow,
and not even God can
lift this devil from me,
it is my nightmare...

'Bertrand? I don't know. Bertrand's disappeared. I can't find him.'

...My dream: a wish I had: to love and be loved...

Maggie continued, 'I can't hear him anymore.'

The sound of turning keys in heavy doors grew closer, a grid of lights turning on outside the ward.

Dee-dee readied the window handle. 'One day he's going to come for me, when the ward lights are down. And he'll take me away from all this-'

'I don't understand-'

...All I ever wanted was to dance
through the corridors of your delicious heart...

The nurses came towards Dee-dee, torch lights leaping around the floor. 'I always knew I was mad.' Dee-dee smiled, stepping back into the darkness, into the arms of the nurses with their sedatives.

...This rusty heart of mine,
that immaculate heart of yours,

I was so scared I'd never find.

Maggie backed away from the window as a torch flashed across her face, making a run for the tree overhanging the fence.

25

15th August 1943

Once my father beat me for talking to myself. Isn't that horrible? Today I talked to the sea, Bertrand. Why was I surprised when it said nothing?

Your ever loving, bright, flowering,

Rose

26
Aroon the roonaboot, and aroon and aroon the roonaboot...

Maggie woke up on the bus stop bench outside County under a cloudy lemonade sky, the sun blazing across her face. She rolled onto her back - her spine slipping pleasingly between two flaking wooden planks – to escape the rapid sunrise, the morning air already thick and arid with heat. She doubted Bill would have noticed her not coming home. There would be no police scrambled from every available estate, their radios crackling with appeals of her name, no descriptions of her starting with 'looks like she has a lot of love to give'; no friendly search-militia trooping its way across town, no one calling out her name in a mass-barbershop group, none of them crying, having to be held up by the person next to them, their arms not weakened with approaching grief, and none of the boys she had ever slept with or kissed or felt up staring solemnly at the ground, thinking about what they had thrown away ... and then a bus pulled up with a hack of its handbrake and a steady black cloud streaming from its exhaust pipe. Maggie wiped her face, the exhaustion of crying morning tears. The driver realised Maggie wasn't getting up, so carried on his way. No. No one was going to come looking for her, Maggie realised.

The estate wouldn't come to life for another hour or so, when the kids fled from their homes, leaving behind some kind of yelling match in the kitchen, and an ever-playing television in the living room, mumbling away in the corner of the room like a crazy uncle.
They sat in rows along tiny fences, their heads all turning at the same pace as any kid who walked past, staring accusingly, a whole bag of insults ready to be launched. The warmer the day got came licence to move further afield, to invite girls out beyond the football pitches and disappear into the long grass for half an hour, or make their way into town and play the puggies 'til lunchtime.

By the time Maggie made her way back into the estate the teenagers were out with their prams, showing off to the younger kids at how great it was to be an adult, to show them what was waiting for them. Heart-shaped pillows dangled from the hoods reading the name of the bastard. Signifiers of how much love was in their lives. Naturally. It was what the outside world recognised as an image of love; to the girls this made their love so real, so authentic. When they shuffled off - one arm crooked to hold a cigarette to their lips, their free hand resting warily on the pram handlebar, still unsure of themselves in their new role as Mother - the younger kids would notice swelling pillows of fat spilling out over their tracksuit bottom waistband as they hobbled off to the shopping centre, and realised that they were still free, that they owned nothing but themselves, and someday, for most of them, that would end.

The tractors and bulldozers slept at the end of Bertrand's street, their digging mouths craned up high, long yawns frozen in the position they were left in the previous night. Workmen stood around in hi-vis vests, smoking cigarettes which they rolled with hardened fingers that had as many cracks as corkwood. A yellow laminated demolition order was stuck on each front door, the last rites of each house. The sun shone on the back of the house, casting the front in a shivery shadow, a silhouette of the house written in dew on the front lawn.

Maggie snapped the sign off Bertrand's door, light moisture on the laminate catapulting on to her face.

'By order of THE COUNCIL, this property will be cleared on 1st August 2005. Any complaints should be made IN WRITING to the appropriate department of THE COUNCIL.'

She dropped the sign on the front doorstep and looked up at the holes where the windows used to be. She knew there was no need to knock frantically on the front door, yelling Bertrand's name, telling him to get out before the wrecking ball started up.

Around the back she walked into the baking sunlight to find the garden free of all the tyres and rubbish and wooden crates. Without it all the grass looked naked and humiliated; bleached shades of white where it had been sun-starved over the years.

In the next garden down a workman noticed Maggie over the fence. 'Hey! What you doing here? This is a demolition site,' he called out, taking his yellow hard hat off to wipe the sweat off his forehead.

Maggie looked at the boarded up back door and window. 'I need to get some things of mine in there.'

The man struggled over the groin-high peaks of the fence to Maggie's side. 'This whole place is coming down the day. What do you need?'

'Some papers. Important papers of a friend of mine.'

'This house has been empty for nearly a year now.'

Maggie marched to the kitchen window and started pulling at the boarding, struggling to get any purchase on it with her tiny hands. 'Please, it's very important.'

The man pulled her back, 'Hey, easy now,' then realised she was crying. He paused, then sighed greyly, 'Come on this way.' He took her back into the cold at the front, then unlocked the padlock on the door. 'You've got five minutes.'

Maggie entered, removing one arm from her backpack. She brushed her hands against the piles of boxes lining the hall as she walked past. 'Hunterhill Young Team' and other gang tags were now sprayed all over the walls beside the staircase. 'Liane S □s Dougie P'. One last image of love.

'And stay away from the windows upstairs,' the man called out, his voice ringing out bassless on the walls.

Maggie slammed the living room door shut, the noise falling straight and dead out into the front garden where the man paced around talking on his mobile phone. At the end of the street the bulldozers were starting up for their first run. Maggie knelt down on the floor, slowly removing the lids of boxes. Taking the first sheet from the top of the pile she read aloud:

'"What regret means: No, I never made it to that island. I've been too scared to say that before, in case it seemed like I didn't love her. But I did. Everything was ready for me to go, my bag packed, a boat organised to sail first thing in the morning..."

Maggie opened the box marked 'Diary: Cherry Tree Estates pt1-14' and read pt9. '"There's a place in front of the matron's window where Jackson tried to drown himself with a cup of water, tipping it over his head then rolling about on the floor"...' She put it down and

Read pt4: '"It had red leather on the front. God, it was burned on my brain. It was my bible. The most sacred book in the building, lying just beyond our grasp, between the double doors and the real world". The real world,' Maggie repeated, like a question. 'I just wanted to find some love in this world, something real.'

Bertrand spoke behind her, 'One afternoon an orderly explained that I was having Eidetic Delusions. When I read something, or hear something, it feels so authentic, so vivid, that I see things that aren't really there. I tried telling them it was love, and if they didn't understand me then they've never felt it. The more I tried to explain, the madder I seemed to them.'

Maggie closed her eyes but her tears still found a way through: they always do. She took out the binder she had stolen from the library.

'The origin of eidetic is eidos. It means the way that societies interpret experience. I always found that word comforting when I was in Cherry Tree Estates. How real is this sentence? Is my love for Rose real, or just a feeling, or just words written down? No, I know love when I feel it.'

Maggie opened the binder to the entry for The Herald of 12th September 2004. 'I tried finding your father, Bertrand. Maybe I should have been looking for you.'

The headline was "Reclusive aristocrat reappears for son's funeral".

'You died last year. Here. By yourself. You never got to Anderson Island, and Rose and your father never found you at Cherry Tree Estates. There's nothing in the logbook. Just a bunch of faceless signatures. But your letter must have got through to Ichibod because it says here he found Rose. He got to the island and brought them back to live with him. Your letter, you words saved them, Bertrand, and you never knew it.' She held the binder up to her chest, as if to contain something. 'They buried you at the foot of Ben Kenneth. Where you first saw love: a burning ship going out to sea. And Rose was there, and I bet everybody cried.'

Maggie flipped over a box lid behind her. 'Thoughts about Rose's first days at school: "That was when I saw her. She had a blue gingham head scarf on, and a long woollen skirt with tasselled fringe. Her long proud neck gaped out from a butterfly collared shirt that she always wore. She stood on the edge of the pier at Lochboisdale watching the ferry until it disappeared, her skirt blowing about in the wind..."'

The man in the hardhat appeared at the living room door, his last footsteps shuffling to an annoyed stop. He said brusquely, 'Right, come on now. I've got twenty houses to bring down today.' He stood and waited for Maggie to pick up what she wanted.

She looked at all the boxes then shook her head. 'Doesn't matter. What I'm looking for isn't here.'

The man stared at her as she walked out the front door, and as he slammed it shut behind him and locked the padlock again, Maggie closed her eyes.

Rose turning in slow motion to him on the machair, wind blowing her hair sideways, her left cheek so suddenly exposed over her shoulder. The surety of love lifting up through her skin.

She looked up at the house one last time: sparrows flying out from Bertrand's bedroom.

Bill awoke on the couch, the sun blazing through the window on to his face. The cheek he had been resting on was sweaty and crushed, all his thoughts spilling to one side of his head during the night. Before he had even opened his eyes, he reached out for the bottle of whisky lying on the floor beside him, SCARED TO DEATH CHARLOTTE'S FACE MIGHT CREEP INTO HIS HEAD AT ANY SECOND. The first sting was what he really liked, that wonderful snap at the back of his throat. It was an endurance test to see how long he could keep swallowing. About seven seconds was the best he could do first thing.

The living room was a wreck, bottles and clothes strewn about the floor, every photo smashed, table lamps (still on) turned over. Something so perverse about a lamp left on all night and rediscovered next morning. Always the sign of a night of great weight.

Sky Sports News had been scrolling all night on low volume, insistent that there be news every second of every day. Bill switched it down to mute. He didn't want to hear their ridiculous voices anymore.

WHERE'S THAT BRUNETTE WITH THE BIG TITS? SHE'S NOT BEEN ON SINCE HALF-SEVEN LAST NIGHT.

He thought about Henry making love to Charlotte in the shower. He wouldn't sit on her bed watching her make herself beautiful for him anymore. There would be no more of the expensive perfume she used, or the silk underwear he would grab at with his big clumsy hands. How he wanted to rip the shit out those things; how he struggled with them, desperately wanting to inflict violence on them, but couldn't, like the taught shrink-wrap on a DVD that begs for scissors instead of fingers.

He kept thinking to himself, I HAVE NO EMOTIONAL INVESTMENT IN THIS, before drowning his insides with more whisky and beer, whisky and beer. Drowning his thoughts. He had gone his entire life without ever understanding what love was.

He picked up the broken photo from his wedding day off the floor, so drunk he didn't notice the cuts it made on his hand. The pair of them looked so dismal.

JUST SHUT UP AND GET ON WI IT, SON.

There was a third left of the whisky. He tipped the bottle up and kept swallowing and swallowing. But he just couldn't get that bite in his throat anymore. He would have to drink some more. He tore open the last bottle of whisky and tipped it straight up. It didn't really feel like anything now. He could keep going like this forever, he thought.

WHIT'S AW THIS WHINING? I'M USED TAE IT FROM THAT TROUBLE-AND-STRIFE AH YOURS, BUT NO MA SON. AND EFTER EVERYTHIN I TELT YOU.

He moved to stand up, pausing half way, back bent, mouth hanging open in a vain effort to release his intoxication. The wedding photo kept on at him, lying there on the floor in pieces; Jean's eyes following him around the room no matter how much he wavered from side to side, anchored on bent knees. A smile crept like a thief across his face as the beautiful brunette came back on the TV, invigorated from a good night's sleep, and through the fog of his vision, Bill moved forward, slowly, to touch the screen, somehow expecting a warm reaction from her. Hidden behind her pixels, the woman talked on, unmoved by Bill. 'If I could have one night with you ... just one night...' he slurred. He sank to his knees, touching the presenter's eyes and lips. Behind him, Jean's eyes continued to follow him from the photo. It was a man's place: to be forgotten by a woman for her children. 'I have nothing,' he complained to the screen. 'Maybe you can be my wife now. Mine doesn't want me. She has her children.' He spat out the final word with disgust. He always knew children would usurp his power one day, and now he could sense women moving away from him, sending him further to the margins where he could only catcall from afar. The TV cut to commercial break and the brunette's face was gone, replaced by a beer advert: all Bill's women moving away.

He sank back on to his heels. I have no emotional investment in this.

Jean awoke with the sun blazing in through the windscreen onto her face. The car had been warming inside all morning, and she was now dehydrated from the heat and the previous night's gin. Her blood felt thick and rubbery in her veins, and her head throbbed in time to the humming of static rush hour cars immediately outside her window. She rubbed the sleep from her eyes and rolled the window down a crack, the heat rushing out, the noises of the real world rushing in. She sniffed the Magic Tree hanging from the rear view mirror, checking through several inhalations before acknowledging it was dead. There was no gin left, but she still had some fags though. That was something.

She got out on stiffened legs and waded through the

traffic filling the T-junction, across to the 'Fags and Mags'.

Benji looked out over the boxes of crisps stacked against the window, watching Jean lose her balance as she approached, her hand gently out to her side, resting on the warm bonnet of a Mondeo to correct herself. He had watched, as Jean had, the quick degeneration of the memorial across the road, how the spaces between the flowers had grown as they wilted and fell from the fence, then were trod into the pavement by pedestrians. The most public of graves. Benji had been the only witness of the entire accident.

...It started with Maggie shrieking 'give it back, give it back' at Trish as the pair ran towards the shop. Trish held a piece of paper above her head like a kite, threatening to let it go onto the road which was greasy with rain. 'Skinny little Maggie's got a boyfriend' yelled Trish towards Jenny Spanner and her crew sitting on the benches by the park a hundred yards down the road. Benji looked out over the boxes of crisps stacked against the window, a worn patch in the lino at his feet from where he did all his public observations, when the shop lulled as it had that day. Trish slowed to a trot, her back to the traffic, making her way towards Jenny Spanner. Trish taunted Maggie, reading aloud in mock-romance, '"That immaculate heart of yours, I was so scared I'd never find."' She whipped around and called after Jenny Spanner, 'Hey Jenny, come look at this...' And with one attempted grab by Maggie, Trish darted across the road. An oncoming red Megane went into a skid. There was something nearly graceful about how Trish's body, facedown, tightly hugged the front of the car, seeming to caress it, her hands going up above her head as if reaching for the window - so it was in a motion of surrender that she died. Benji burst out from his vantage point, knocking over the boxes of salt and vinegar Squares, his hands out at the traffic on the near side to stop to let him across. It was a series of still images that he rushed past: the static Maggie, standing back on the other side of the road, her arms out from her sides, her legs apart, looking like she was about to run but didn't know where to go; the driver sat paralysed in her seat, both hands covering her mouth; Jenny Spanner and her crew stood up on the benches to see what had happened. And then the flurry of motion: Jenny Spanner and her crew running towards the scene; the driver hobbling out, mouth still covered, the realisation that she had just taken a life. The real magnitude of that action bearing down and magnifying exponentially: every breath she took felt like one she had now stolen from the teenage girl lying broken on the road in front of her; cars slammed and screeched to a halt all around, and people their doors open to come and help. So many with mobile phones pressed to their ear, stressing the urgency of the ambulance. 'It's a young girl, see.' When Benji got to Trish's body she was limp as a ragdoll that would be placed at her own memorial a spit away. Benji suddenly felt Maggie standing over his shoulder. 'Is she dead?' she bleated. Benji felt no pulse. 'Yes.' Maggie crouched down and picked up the piece of paper...

'Morning, Jean,' Benji said, not making eye contact. 'Usual?'

Jean pursed her lips at him, barely able to raise her head.

Benji went on tiptoes to check no other customers were around. It was still few hours before ten, when he was legally allowed to sell it. But he had been the only one who had seen the whole incident. He understood why Jean had to do what she was doing. He wasn't going to tell her she shouldn't drink in the morning, that she shouldn't do this to herself, that the world is a beautiful place and there is so much to live for, that the gravity of a person's love is enough to pull you out of anything: but when you're alone. When you're alone.

He rushed the bottle into a brown bag and Jean handed over her £10 note.

'Keep the change,' she said.

Benji called out, almost begging, 'Be well, Jean.'

The day had frittered away to another nothing. The evening rush hour was now filling the road.

Jean sat against the bonnet of the car, smoking her cigarette, looking to strangers who didn't know any better like her car had simply broken down, and she was taking it all very well. Occasionally a driver, paused in the traffic, hung out their window, offering, 'I can call the AA if you need a tow.'

'No, it's alright,' she slurred, throwing her fag into the gutter. 'I'm not going anywhere.'

Benji came out to close up shop for the day, and with the shutters halfway down realised Jean was untying the remaining flowers and filthy teddy bears from the railings. Then she took the pile a little down the road and dumped it all in the bin, the teddies' dirty, furry arms sticking out the lid. The only thing that remained was a note on the ground, fallen from a bouquet of flowers. She picked it up.

She still didn't know who it was from, but she had always suspected it was from that old man, Bertrand, Maggie always talked about. She never had met him. Nor had Bill.

She placed the card on the bar at the bottom of the railing; the only thing left of Trish's memorial. It was time to go home. So she started up her engine and joined the traffic with all the other arms hanging out the windows, feeling the warm night air, sensing home was close.

The Belmont's headlights flashed through the living room window above Bill, sitting on the sofa, with his head in his hands.

Jean ran inside, breathing in the familiar smell of her house, able to take her time with it now. No more counting off the seconds before she became a bad mother, or how long until the world ended.

In the living room Bill was CRYING HIS HEART OUT, but now he heard Jean come home it was time to cut that stupid shit out. He stubbed it all out like the cigarette he squashed down on his arm earlier.

'So you came home then?' he said. 'Have you got nothing to say?'

Jean stood in front of him and said wearily, 'I'm going to ma bed, Bill.'

Bill's father looked down on him from the wall, the only picture remaining intact, the pride growing inside him like the beginnings of a dull orgasm, and he said, quieter than usual, 'I'm the man of this house.'

Maggie sat on the kerb at the end of Bertrand's street, looking down the rows of rubble where the houses had been. A lone car's headlights, Jean driving the Belmont, swung around the roundabout behind her, briefly casting Maggie's shadow down the road, stretching as far as where Bertrand's house was. Maggie looked around but the car was already gone, off towards the bottom of Hunterhill.

Maggie reached into her bag, taking out the piece of paper that had cost Trish her life. She read it to herself, tears bubbling softly somewhere around her forehead before making their way down into her eyes, her mouth. 'Can I ask you something, Bertrand,' she said, dropping the piece of paper down into the cradle of her manky Reeboks. 'If you can't find something real in this world, isn't it ok to pretend?'

Behind her, a boy racer in his Corsa went spinning around the roundabout, his headlights flashing past Maggie each time, aroon and aroon the roonaboot, aroon and aroon the roonaboot, aroon and aroon the roonaboot.

'I won't always feel like this will I, Bertrand?' She asked again, 'Bertrand? My heart is so full up I have no words left.'

From The Herald, 12th September 2004

Reclusive aristocrat reappears for son's funeral

After more than 50 years in hiding, the 101-year-old aristocrat Sir Ichibod Mantis, made a dramatic public appearance on South Uist yesterday, for the funeral of his son Bertrand Mantis, who died in his home in Paisley, aged 80 years old.

Sir Ichibod rose to prominence in the early twenties after a brief engagement to Swedish royal heir, Princess Veronica, which saw the pair the cream of the society press. Following their break up in 1952, Sir Ichibod – a notorious hard drinker and rumoured opium addict – lost custody of his son, prompting his half century exile. Members of his board, Mantis Holdings, declared him a missing person, and after fourteen years was nearly officially declared dead.

Bertrand Mantis was brought up on South Uist, and shortly after the start of World War II was admitted to an asylum at twenty years old, where he remained until 1955. Like his father, little is known about him.

The service was restricted to friends and family of Bertrand Mantis, some of whom Sir Ichibod had to dramatically rescue after they became stranded on tiny Anderson's Island, just off the coast of South Uist, in 1943, thanks, one close friend told me, to a letter sent by Bertrand to his father, telling him they were stuck. Sir Ichibod was never reacquainted with his son.

Press were kept at a distance throughout the day, with a very frail Sir Ichibod refusing to answer questions regarding his sudden reappearance or his son's death. One close friend of Bertrand Mantis, 79-year-old Rose McDonald, who has been living on Sir Ichibod's private estate 'somewhere in the remote Highlands' since her rescue said afterwards, 'It was an emotional day for everyone. Especially Ichibod. We all loved Bertrand very dearly. I never met anyone like him again. It's appropriate he's been buried here at the foot of Ben Kenneth. He told me once that he fell in love here. We watched a burning boat going out to sea.'

Sir Ichibod spoke only to read a poem written by his son.

'The Immaculate Heart'

Farewell, then, love, I barely knew you.
Let me not fight this solitude, this desolation,
give me her arms, give me words to catch them.
In my dreams, that's when I miss her most.
Her tender breast, it was my pillow,
and not even God can
lift this devil from me:
it is my nightmare.
My dream: a wish I had: to love and be loved.
All I ever wanted was to dance
through the corridors of your delicious heart.
This rusty heart of mine,
that immaculate heart of yours,
I was so scared I'd never find.

Acknowledgements

I'd like to thank my publisher Mark Buckland more than my meagre lexicon can communicate. When no one else believed, and all that ... My editor Cameron Steel, for teaching me the reality of a novel: that it's a team effort in the final stretch (the book is so much better for your input, Cam). Also to Gill Tasker (world's foremost Trocchi scholar), David Flood for always lightening my bloody awful mood, Craig Lamont, and all the other 'believers' at Cargo.

To all the friends I left behind for the writing and editing of this novel. Like an absent father, I know I can never really get back the lost time or pay back the alimony. Sorry. It's in the mail.

I'd also like to sincerely thank Kirsty Neary for reading me in draft form, her smart notes, and her companionship; Anikó Szilágyi for her academic work (partly) on me, but mostly for her friendship; Ewan Morrison, Christopher Brookmyre, Doug Johnstone, Suhayl Saadi, Alex Gray and Alan Bissett for support of the professional variety.

And Valley Girl: the most beautiful, intelligent brain-grenade I've ever met. Thank you for everything. I couldn't have understood what I was writing about in this book without having met you. My heart is so full up I have no words left.

Finally: anyone who has supported me; attended readings; bought Cancer Party or given Cancer Party to a friend; told me I was a useless, untalented waste of paper and ink; given me a pat on the back; given me a light; bought me a drink, or taken a drink away from me.

And you, yes YOU the humble reader, filler of my – very slight – coffers. Thank you for buying this.

If you want more personalised thanks or just want to talk you can email me at andrewdrennan@hotmail.com or through www.cargopublishing.com.

Also by Andrew Raymond Drennan:

Cancer Party

Andrew Raymond Drennan is the author of the novels "Cancer Party" and "The Immaculate Heart." His third novel will be released in 2012. He lives in Paisley, Scotland.